Eat Your Heart Out

CHERRY
WHISKIN

Published by Goldcrest Books International Ltd
www.goldcrestbooks.com
publish@goldcrestbooks.com

ISBN: 978-1-911505-44-0

PROLOGUE

*I*t is some time in the twenty first century. We are in the UK, but it's not as we know it.

We are in the middle of an epidemic! An Obesity epidemic.

The Government decides to act and brings in a raft of new laws associated with food. Restaurants, hotels, pubs, cafe's, in fact anywhere that sells food has become subject to inspection and they have to be very careful that they only sell healthy meals.

All employers have to take out Health Insurance on behalf of their employees and premiums rise if the Annual medical isn't satisfactory.

For some people this isn't a problem but for others, it is a nightmare.

On the plus side, Britain being what it is, Underground Foodie Bars start to emerge. Dark, secret places where serious, illicit eating takes place.

Imagine the scene. You know you shouldn't be there. You know it's dangerous. The menu says, Steak and kidney pudding, Sausage roll, Sticky toffee pudding, Treacle tart and many more tempting dishes. You can smell the food, your mouth starts to water. You should leave, but then, a handsome man smiles at you as he puts the plate down; a beautiful woman is waiting expectantly for your order.

What's a body to do? EAT.

CHAPTER 1

"You had the keys, because you drove to the airport."
Hilary was insistent.

"Yes, I know I drove to the airport, but I gave the keys to you. I always do."

"If you'd given them to me, Jack, I'd know where they were. You had them; now where did you put them?"

It was pouring with rain and Jack was frantically searching through suitcases and in pockets whilst Hilary looked on, her face set in a grim expression.

Once they and their clothes were thoroughly soaked, the keys appeared as if by magic in the pocket of Jack's trousers, a pair he'd already searched, of course.

They drove away from East Midlands airport in stony silence, which gave Jack the chance to escape the rain and the humiliation and drift back to their holiday.

It had been a blissful week, thought Jack, just the two of them for the first time for years, as they'd decided Simon and Anna were old enough to leave with his parents for just a week. So he and Hilary had enjoyed a second honeymoon of sorts, except it wasn't quite as passionate as the first one. For a start, Hilary had got up early each morning to jog on the beach. She really did take this fitness thing a bit too far at times, being a

P.E. teacher didn't mean to say you had to be Superwoman. But Hilary thought so!

Jack had stayed in bed, dozing and feeling randy and had been grumpy when Hilary refused to join him on her return from the beach. She preferred to have her muesli and then drag him out of bed so as not to 'waste the day'. Still, all things considered, it had been good. They had explored the steep streets of Valetta together and had long lazy lunches in pavement cafés. They'd swum in the sea, sunbathed on the beach. Had romantic candlelit meals by the harbour, walked hand in hand back to the apartment and made love in a much more leisurely and carefree manner than they ever did at home these days.

"Shall we do the shopping first or pick the kids up?" The question roused him from his thoughts with an unreasonable sense of irritation; he wasn't ready for mundane matters just yet.

"Oh, I don't care, whatever you want," he snapped. Hilary gave him a sideways glance; *he's always been the same*, she thought, *if he's in the wrong, he somehow manages to blame me*. She bit back a retort and instead just said, "I think we'll do the shopping first, it's easier without the kids."

So they pulled into the supermarket and battled their way around the shelves, stocking up on essentials, while Jack dreamed of delicious pizzas and sizzling seafood drenched in garlic. He hated supermarkets anyway, because they were work to him. He did allow himself one glance in the dairy section just to be sure that Holme Farm Dairy products were represented .Yes, they were. It was good to check up on return from holiday that the firm one worked for was still trading! His mind wandered back to spaghetti carbonara.

"Will you snap out of it, Jack. We're back now, you know!" Hilary was getting irritated now, as they'd reached the checkout, and he was standing uselessly by the trolley and leaving her to unload the shopping.

"I'm sorry but it was just so laid back, wasn't it? The Maltese are just so relaxed about everything."

"Yeah, well we are back to reality now. The cash out computer is telling us we've reached our credit limit." Hilary hissed at him, "I told you to go easy while we were away!" The cashier, who was used to this situation, waited patiently while they decided that baked beans and toilet rolls were more important than pesto sauce and frozen Indian takeaways, both of which Jack had put into the trolley.

When they were safely back in the car, Jack exploded, "God, it gets on my bloody nerves! Why aren't we allowed to get into debt? What's wrong with a healthy bit of debt anyway?"

"It's not that, and you know it," Hilary calmly replied." We are allowed to go into debt if we want, as long as it's pre-negotiated and we stay within the limits. We've had all this out before, Jack. It was a joint decision and it is for our own good. You know what you're like! I told you we were spending too much on your card. That lace tablecloth you bought your mother was ridiculously expensive!" she tutted.

Jack didn't bother to reply. He could have asked Hilary where her card was when they got to the checkout and then the credit check would have been okay, but she had done this before, it was her way of punishing him. This was an old argument; Hilary was for self-control in all things and part of him knew she was right, but rules and regulations had always been like a red rag to a bull for Jack. As soon as someone told him he couldn't do something he immediately wanted to do it. He slumped down in the seat and brooded. Work tomorrow, back in gloomy old England with its discipline and rules and regulations. They had just seen the plus side of Europe in the 21st century, relaxed, sensuous, warm and fun, but now they were back to the downside; control in all things.

The British government had made the decision a few years ago to actively promote healthy and responsible living. The Nanny State gone mad!

They had brought in new laws banning 'unhealthy' foods and had employed inspectors to take over the licensing of restaurants and cafe's to ensure they only sold the right things.

Don't eat too much, don't drink too much, don't drive too much, don't spend too much; the list went on and on, and there were government laws for all of them.

The government loved the fact that they'd managed to offload a lot of healthcare onto the individual because British companies had been forced to take out health insurance for their employees. This meant that the NHS could concentrate on people who were really ill, as opposed to being lazy and weak-willed. It also meant that becoming overweight could affect your job prospects as companies weren't keen on higher insurance premiums.

The banks were encouraged to monitor excess spending and loved the added surcharges for debt of any kind; a complete turnaround from their previous behaviour. It had taken a lot of arm twisting from government to achieve that one.

The government had been meddling in the food industry for years but could never make its mind up.

Finally, however, the obesity epidemic had forced it's hand and the new, 'Food Laws' were draconian. Luckily for the dairy industry, the jury was still out on the question of fat.

This brought his thoughts back to work again and it was too early to think about that, so he went back to his grievance with Hilary.

The banks' latest idea, instant credit recognition or I.C.R, was a good thing, Hilary had said. "We don't have to have it but it will help me to budget and it will mean we always know where we are."

Always know where we are! Sometimes Jack didn't want to know where he was.

Luckily they were at his parents' house otherwise Jack could have worked himself up into a really bad mood.

The kids ran out to meet them and Jack realised how much he'd missed them. Simon, now eleven, was becoming more like a friend every day and he and Jack could have quite serious conversations at times. Anna, at nine, was still preoccupied with the latest music, fashion and TV, *but she was good at hugging*, thought Jack as she clung to him.

Charlotte, Jack's mum, or Charlie as everyone called her, was in the hall, dusting away cobwebs from around the front door with her hands.

Charlie and Alec lived about forty minutes' drive away from their son and daughter-in-law, in a sleepy Warwickshire village. They had bought a brick-built cottage there when they retired and had spent a lot of time and money altering it to their liking.

"I'll have some serious housework to do next week," she commented, "but it's been a pleasure to have them. They've been as good as gold." She smiled and ruffled their hair as she spoke. "How was the holiday?"

"Great," Jack murmured as he bent to kiss her on the cheek.

"How about you, Hilary?" Charlie asked, "Did you have a good rest?"

"Oh yes. It was brilliant. Just sorry it's over really. This next term is always a busy one."

"Ah, don't mention school, Mum," Simon moaned, "I don't want to think about it."

"Have you finished your project?" Hilary asked.

"Yeah, most of it, Grandpa's been helping me."

"Oh that's OK then. So, what have you all been up to while we've been away?"

The family all settled down at the kitchen table while Simon and Anna described their various activities with their grandparents.

As the kids talked, Charlie busied herself making mugs of tea and coffee and 'magicked' some cake out of the cupboard. She stood back and listened while her grandchildren chatted on about trips to the Black Country museum and Ironbridge, not to mention the big new Entertainment Centre in Coventry. That was one good thing about living in the Midlands; there were always plenty of places to go. She'd been worried that the kids might have been bored by the choices of venue. Alec, as a retired engineer, had never lost his love of machinery but not everybody shared that enthusiasm for moving pieces of greasy iron and steel. It seemed though that the children had thoroughly enjoyed themselves.

She pushed a wispy piece of grey hair back into her ponytail and sighed. Her son and daughter-in-law looked relaxed and tanned, sitting there at the table cradling mugs of coffee in their hands. She hoped they'd been able to regain some closeness while they'd been away. She had been worried recently that they were drifting apart – their jobs keeping them so busy and Jack's in particular, keeping him away so much. The children, too, had let the odd comment slip about arguments.

She watched her son listening attentively to his children. His dark hair was receding now and he wasn't as lean as he used to be. He must be forty-one now, she realised with a shock. So how old did that make Hilary? Thirty-nine? She turned her attention to her daughter-in-law; there was no flab on her. She was fit and muscular, as you would expect a P.E. teacher to be. The only sign of age was weathered skin from being outside so much. Her short hairstyle didn't help that though. *She should have something more feminine*, thought Charlie. She shook herself away from her thoughts and walked over to the table. "You've certainly brought a change of weather back with you," she interrupted, "it's been lovely here all week, crisp and fresh in the mornings, and sunny in the days. Your dad's been out in the garden, most of the time."

"Talking of which, where is the old devil?" said Jack as he got up from the table and stretched his legs.

"He's in his shed of course." Charlie smiled indulgently, "You can take that coffee out to him if you like."

"I'll come too, Dad. I want to see how his latest invention is getting on," Simon said eagerly.

"What invention?" Jack asked as they made their way out of the house.

"Oh, it's something to do with saving water, I think, but Grandpa will explain it."

Simon hopscotched ahead of Jack along the soaking path. *God, he's growing fast,* thought Jack. *Just one week away and he seems to have shot up!*

They reached the shed and Jack shouted, "Hi, Pop. We've got coffee here for you!"

Long years of training meant Jack never went into the shed without announcing his presence first. His father had taught him long ago that it was dangerous to enter unannounced. Alec might be working with welding equipment or chemicals or any such thing, and Jack and his brother and sister soon learned to treat the shed with extreme caution.

"OK, come on in. I've nearly finished for today."

Jack and Simon stepped through the narrow door and Jack was struck by the familiar and comforting smell inside the shed. It was impossible to analyse but it was most definitely masculine and it always made Jack feel secure.

Alec looked up and ran his fingers through his thick grey hair. He was a fit man for someone in his late sixties, tall and muscular, with crinkly blue eyes and grey stubble on his chin. He hated shaving and never did, until as late in the day as possible. He stood up straight from where he had been bending over his workbench and rubbed his back, tucking in his T-shirt where it had parted from his oily jeans at the back.

"Well then, good to see you. How was the holiday?" Alec wiped his hands on an oily rag and patted his son on the shoulder.

"Brilliant! I really liked the Maltese, they are so relaxed and friendly, and they seem to like the British!"

"Oh, yes. They forged a very special relationship with us during the Second World War. Got the George Cross for bravery you know – the whole island! Marvellous people."

"Yes," Jack replied, "We went to an exhibition about it, still, they seem to be alright with the Germans now; there were loads of them there on holiday and most other European nationalities as well."

"Yes well, times are different now. Got to move on, you know."

"Yes, you have. I really enjoyed the food though, Dad. You could get anything there. No restrictions at all."

"Yes, but they eat a Mediterranean diet, don't they. You don't see many fat Maltese."

"Only if they eat nothing but Maltesers," Simon quipped.

"Ha, ha," Jack laughed and ruffled his hair.

"Seriously though, they did all look good. I don't understand it."

"Well if you don't and you work in the industry what hope is there for the rest of us?" Alec looked round with a twinkle in his eye but Jack looked serious.

"It's getting worse, Dad. The Government are bringing in new legislation all the time and we can't keep up with it. How do they get away with it all?"

"Disillusionment! I blame the British disease – disillusionment and resulting apathy. A few years back, politics and government became an object of derision. We all just got fed up with the whole thing and lost interest and look where we are now! Did you vote at the last election?"

"No, I had a late meeting and – "

"There you are then," Alec said with disgust.

"Yes, but that doesn't excuse what they're doing now – look at this bloomin' I.C.R. business. Do you know, we couldn't even pay for all the food we bought."

"You always did hate rules, Jack, and that I.C.R. is nothing to do with the government really, it's the banks, and what's more you don't have to have it if you don't want to, son." Alec looked at his son in a meaningful way and Jack knew exactly what he meant. Alec did not always approve of Hilary's way of going about things.

"I know, I know," he said resignedly, "anyhow, what's this new invention of yours?"

Alec sighed and turned away to his workbench to show Jack the plans. He knew the score, Jack did not want to discuss his wife's character and neither did Alec really, but Jack's marriage was a source of worry.

"I'm working on a scheme to recycle our household supply of water so that I can use some of it to irrigate the garden."

"That's a good idea," Jack said enthusiastically, "How will it work then?"

"Well that's what I'm working on at the moment. Probably a system of syphons and pumps but it's still in the early stages. Come on, let's go in, or young Simon over there will need a bath!"

Jack looked up to see Simon squatting on the floor in a corner of the shed. He was completely absorbed in oiling the pieces of an old bike and he'd been so quiet that Jack had forgotten he was there.

"Are you having a good time over there?" Jack asked.

"Yeah, it's great. I've been working on it all week, haven't I, Grandpa?"

"He's been enjoying himself," Alec said with an indulgent smile.

"I wonder who he reminds me of?" laughed Jack.

The three males made their way back to the house and, as Simon ran inside, Jack said, "Thanks for having the kids, Dad. We do appreciate it."

"That's no problem, son. It's been a pleasure. There is one thing though; young Simon seems very worried about school at the moment. Your mum and I tried to find out what it was but he didn't want to talk about it."

"I'll have a word with him." Jack frowned.

As Jack and Alec stepped into the warm kitchen, Jack heard Hilary shouting," Come on, you two. Get your things together. We've got to go."

"Aren't you going to stay for something to eat?" Charlie asked.

"No. Sorry, Charlie, but we've got to get back. There's a lot to do before tomorrow."

Thanks for consulting me, thought Jack. He walked forward and hugged his mum. "Thanks for the offer, Mum. I'll phone you in the week."

"OK, love. Take care of yourself," Charlie replied.

Everyone piled into the car and waved goodbye. This time, Jack was driving. He was concentrating on the road and also musing about his parents, and how well they seemed to have coped with the kids, when he heard Hilary say, "Grandma says you've been worrying about school, Simon. Are you having problems with your project?"

"No," Simon muttered in an accusing tone.

Jack cringed inwardly. *For God's sake*, Hilary, he thought, *couldn't you have waited until we got home*?

"Well what are you worried about then?" Hilary was relentless once she got on to something.

"Nothing. I'm not worried about anything," Simon said in the same tone.

"He's worried about his French," Anna said impatiently.

"What about his French?" Hilary snapped.

"He's got an exam this week, that's all."

There then ensued a fierce hissed argument between Anna and Simon, punctuated by various thuds and gasps and finally an indignant, "Ow!" from Anna.

For once, Jack's voice was there before Hilary's. "Pack it in, you two!" he shouted in such a way that even Hilary decided to shut up.

"Now, Simon, what is the problem with your French" Jack asked in a quiet but no-nonsense tone.

"I hate it, that's all and I'm no good at it, all that accent stuff. I feel like a complete prat."

Jack smiled to himself and remembered his own embarrassment when it came to speaking French. He was just about to say so when he heard Hilary say, "Well perhaps I ought to have a word with Mr Bowden tomorrow if it's worrying you so much."

"Ah, Mum, don't do that. I'll be OK," and then to Anna, Simon hissed, "This is all your fault!" and the back seat erupted again, to such an extent that by the time the Baker family reached home, all thoughts of sun, sand and relaxation were well and truly banished from Jack's mind.

Their own home was also in a village, but it was modern, just as Hilary had wanted.

Everything in the house was in order, the computer having done its job efficiently, as always. The finance programme had listed all the bills and payments; Jack winced as he saw the bank balance and quickly switched to the next week's appointments. He printed off a list for each member of the family, carefully avoiding his own work page; he wasn't ready for that yet.

Both Simon and Anna sought the sanctuary of their own rooms and settled in; Simon preferred his action games where he could escape into his virtual world. Anna preferred, on this occasion, to listen to music, although she could give Simon a run for his money when she felt so inclined, but at the moment she felt like being soothed after her fight with her brother. She was already up to date with all her messages.

Taking advantage of the peace, Hilary and Jack went about their own business. Jack unpacked the shopping, still stinging with annoyance that his beloved delicacies were not there. He was surprised that Hilary didn't choose to do online shopping because she knew Jack would always add treats to the basket! She was obviously still in relaxed holiday mode. It wouldn't last long.

Hilary, meanwhile, sorted out the laundry. She still remembered how long it used to take before the new machines came in. It gave her organised mind particular pleasure now, to watch how quickly crumpled, dirty clothes, emerged, pressed and clean as new.

The family finally came together at 7 o'clock for a meal that Jack had prepared – a task he found enjoyable and relaxing. Since Hilary had very little interest in food, it suited them both. He was still annoyed that Hilary had refused a meal at his parents' without even consulting him. Charlie was an excellent cook and he knew she would have been hurt by the curt refusal. It was some consolation to him, however, that she had loved the lace tablecloth he had given her.

Later, that evening, in a quiet moment, Jack went up to sit with Simon for a while.

"Are you OK?" Jack asked his son, who was now lying on his bed, reading a book.

"Yes, I'm fine. Everything is ready for tomorrow and I've done some French revision."

"I didn't like French either, you know. In fact I didn't like any languages."

"Oh, that's where I get it from is it?" Simon grinned at him and Jack ruffled his hair and said goodnight. He stumped wearily back down the stairs to where Hilary was sitting at the kitchen table, surrounded by papers.

"Do you want a coffee?" Jack asked her.

"Uhhhmmm. Yes please," she replied distractedly.

"I've spoken to Simon," Jack said, as he put coffee into mugs.

"So have I."

"You have! When?" snapped Jack.

Hilary's head snapped up. "About ten minutes ago, while you were fiddling with your precious computer."

"I wasn't fiddling, I was catching up," Jack corrected her.

"OK then, catching up," Hilary sneered, "You just can't believe that I could have had a valuable conversation with Simon. You think you are the only one who can do that!"

"That's not true and you know it. I'm just fed up with you running me down all the time. You don't think I'm capable of anything do you? You were the same on holiday – can't you swim further than that? – You're not hungry again are you? – Surely you don't want a starter and a sweet! – Nag, nag, nag."

"Yes, well, I was only thinking of you. Have you seen yourself lately? You're putting on weight, Jack – if you're not careful, you're going to fail your next medical."

"Oh, yes, you'd love that wouldn't you, so you could put me on one of your famous diets and nag me even more." He instinctively reached for the biscuit tin.

"Oh don't let's start. I've got too much to do tonight," Hilary replied dismissively, and returned to her papers.

Jack was only too happy to leave her to it. He was tired of the same old argument. He picked up his coffee and pile of biscuits and went back into the den. He picked up his laptop and felt himself relax; *she* never nagged him or belittled him, she was always pleasant when she spoke and only gave him the information he asked for and nothing else. He logged on to his work programme and noted that tomorrow he was due to travel to headquarters for a meeting. That was good. He'd have to stay overnight as they always went on late. He suddenly realised that he was looking forward to a night away from his wife.

CHAPTER 2

Jack was not in the best of moods as he got into his car the next morning yet, as always, once he got onto the open road, his spirits lifted. En-route to the motorway, he passed through the English countryside at its best. The morning was crisp, clear and sunny. He passed ploughed fields in uniform patterns of brown stripes flanked by hedgerows hung with lacy webs and plump, juicy blackberries. The sun turned the inside of his car into a kaleidoscope as it shone through branches still full of leaves brushed with autumn colours, and the tarmac glistened ahead of him beckoning him towards the blue sky on the horizon. He loved driving on his own, and this particular morning, as the sun's warmth penetrated his taut muscles, he felt his face break into a smile and he reached forward for the CD button, to complete his mood.

Hence, by the time Jack reached Holme Farm at 11a.m., he felt like a different person. Anyone watching his rapid and confident progress up the motorway system would have been sure that this was a man at ease with his car, the road, and the world in general.

He drew into the car park, grabbed his suit jacket and briefcase from the back seat, and made his way towards the double glass doors, set into the grey stone building that was his headquarters.

Holme Farm Dairy products had begun as a small concern. It was just as organic food became popular. Everything was a rebellion against mass production at that time and real ale, real bread and real cheese became very desirable.

Robert Holmes decided to use his precious Friesians' surplus milk to make 'real butter, cream and cheese' and sell it in a small farm shop. The idea worked well because families en-route to and from the Lakes stopped and bought 'real farm goodness' by the basketful. Then he opened the café and never looked back. Hence, by the time 'Bobby' retired he was able to hand over a thriving business to his son Bernard.

Holme Farm Products expanded and became the company they were today.

Bernard was not only a good businessman, he also fancied himself as something of a philanthropist. He had no children of his own and so he looked upon his workforce as his family. The monthly gatherings for his sales team were certainly not necessary for communication purposes; that was no problem in this day and age. No, Bernard believed these gatherings were good for morale. He thought selling was a lonely job and he liked his workforce to work as a team but he also liked to keep a fatherly eye on them. The group of men and women represented a large investment and Bernard Holmes kept a close eye on any investment he made.

This particular October morning, Bernard had invited a well-known doctor to talk to the group about their own lifestyles and what they should be doing to stay fit; he didn't just want a happy workforce, he wanted a healthy one! The company health insurance premiums were hefty and he didn't want them going up any more.

"We can have someone with you within the next half hour, dear," the woman from the breakdown service had told her.

Angela checked her watch – twenty-five minutes ago! What could you do? Stuck in your car by the side of the road at eight o'clock on a wet Monday morning. Phone your boss and grovel – which she'd already done. Bernie was the perfect gentleman as always.

"Do you want me to come and fetch you?" he'd asked, but she'd had to say no, it was only a flat tyre and she'd be in as soon as the breakdown man had changed it.

At least he hadn't suggested she change it herself as her husband Peter would have done. She'd lost count of the number of times he'd told her to enrol on a car maintenance course.

"You should do it, Angie. I don't like to think of you being stuck on the side of the road in the middle of the night."

If he were here with her instead of being halfway across the world most of the time, then she wouldn't need to do any bloody car maintenance! She tossed her head in exasperation. There was so much to be done this week – she just couldn't afford the time to be stuck here. She drummed her fingers on the steering wheel and mentally ticked off her list of jobs.

Bernard Holmes, her boss, and Managing Director of Holme Farm Products, was on a health kick. He had decided that all his employees must be fit and well, not only to comply with the latest legislation, but also to help promote the premise that dairy produce was good for you. So he had arranged for Simon Fletcher, the TV doctor, to come to the monthly sales meeting and give a talk. As Bernie's PA, Angela had been given the task of setting everything up and this included meeting Simon as he arrived and checking all that his 'people' had instructed her to provide met with his satisfaction. Talking of satisfaction! Simon Fletcher was gorgeous and Angela couldn't wait to meet him, instead of which here she was, stuck by the side of the road! She groaned out loud in frustration and banged her fists on the steering wheel.

"Morning, love." She swung round to see a cheerful face peering in at her through the steamy window. She'd never felt more like kissing a stranger. He soon sorted her wheel out and she was back in business.

An hour later, calm, composed and looking highly efficient in her best suit, Angela handed Simon Fletcher his cup of coffee.

'Thanks. I'm ready for this."

He was just as gorgeous in reality as he was on the TV. Tall and dark-haired with crinkly blue eyes and a boyish smile – she could have stood and gazed at him all day, but Bernie kept giving her jobs to do.

"Is everything ready in the hall now, Angie?" he was asking her.

"I think so," she said as she turned to Simon. "Have you got everything you need?"

"Yes, I checked it earlier – everything's there. Very efficient, Mrs Carter."

"Oh please call me Angie. Everyone else does."

"OK then, Angie – thanks for everything."

"OK then. Let's get this show on the road." Bernie was rubbing his hands, ready for the fray. Angela just wished he'd take his time for once.

As Jack walked into the lecture hall, he heard his name being called. He looked around and spotted his mate Don standing by the coffee machine at the back. He walked over.

"Well! Where have you been then? Down the local solarium?" Don asked.

"You know I've been to Malta for a week," Jack told him, "I told you last time I saw you that we were going."

"Oh yeah, I'd forgotten. Good was it?"

"Yes, very good actually – we had a brilliant week – very peaceful without the kids."

"Ah second honeymoon job, eh!" Don nudged Jack just as he had filled his coffee cup, and hot coffee slopped onto his hand.

"Ow! Watch it!" Jack yelled, sucking his hand. "No, I wouldn't say that – but not bad!"

Don laughed and walked ahead of Jack to some seats on the back row.

Jack had known Don White a long time. They had joined the company about the same time about ten years ago, both of them having had a succession of jobs before that. They had been in the same group during Bernard's initial recruitment drive and training course and they had become friends of a sort. Jack could only tolerate Don in small doses because he was one of those blokes who you could have a good time with, but if you wanted to discuss anything serious, it was a waste of breath. For one thing, he never appeared to listen to a word you said, unless it was to do with work or the latest social scene. There was one thing though, when Jack was with Don, he never had to make conversation because Don did the talking, and he never had to worry about where to go because Don was one of those people who always knew somewhere to go.

They had been out in a foursome together in the early days with Hilary and Tricia, Don's wife. Hilary, however, had hated and despised Tricia almost on sight, describing her to her mates as 'a mindless bimbo with too much make-up, too short skirts and too high heels'. Jack, on the other hand remembered her as being pleasant enough, but he admitted to himself that she had left very little impression on him other than the fact that she had an irritating giggle whenever Don made a joke.

After the second attempt at a night out, Hilary had announced that if she ever saw that woman again she would 'wring her bloody neck' and that had been that! Jack didn't really care one way or another as long as he could keep on seeing Don at these work do's because they always had a good time.

At this precise moment, as they sat drinking their coffee and waiting for the meeting to start, Don was talking about how he and Trish had installed a circular whirlpool spa into their guest suite and Jack and Hilary must come and stay with them so they could try it. Don seemed to have forgotten that he hadn't seen Hilary for about eight years. He was talking as if the four of them were bosom pals. Jack let his voice wash over him while he thought back to breakfast and the row that had ensued because he had announced he would be staying away.

"You know we always have a long staff meeting on the first day back and you know that Anna has a dental appointment because you gave us all the appointment sheets yourself!" Hilary had raged.

In the end, Jack had simply slammed out of the house, and he knew it was wrong. Normally he would have tried to find a solution, normally he would have told Hilary the night before or even a week before that he'd be away, but recently he'd begun to feel more and more rebellious about family responsibilities. Hilary took him for granted. She could sort this one out for herself!

He came to, as Don nudged him, in time to see Bernard Holmes stand up to face his workforce.

Bernard was a short, plump man with a ruddy face, a grey moustache and grey hair that skirted his shiny, bald, head. For someone so concerned with the health of his workforce, Bernard was not a good advert. Within his own four walls, he enjoyed the good things that his good fortune could buy him. He had been brought up on full fat farm food and he continued to eat it whenever he could. He also liked good red wine and cigars in full measure and fortunately or unfortunately for him, as the case may be, Mrs Holmes was not the sort to deprive her husband of anything he wanted. Added to this, Bernard did not have to worry about a favourable health report, as did so many of his workforce. He owned his own company and had the means to pay his premiums no matter what the state of his health.

"My purpose in asking Dr Fletcher here today is twofold," he was saying, "first of all, I want to be sure that all of you are aware of what constitutes good health in your own lifestyles, and secondly, I want you to become aware of the latest government guidelines as far as food products are concerned. There is a lot of pressure, as always, to ensure that our products meet the guidelines, and I want you to sell to distributors with this in mind. Finally, I shall be reminding you all to have your annual medical as soon as possible. Some of you are scheduled for this afternoon and others will receive appointments in the near future. Now I'll hand you over to Dr Simon Fletcher."

Bernard sat down, mopping his brow. *It's warm in here, but not that warm,* thought Jack; old Bernie was looking distinctly podgy, he'd better listen to Dr Fletcher.

Simon Fletcher was popular with viewers of breakfast television. He was young, good-looking and clean-cut and really could have been an actor, or presenter, if he'd wanted, but he had chosen medicine instead.

He made his talk interesting and Jack found that he was thinking to himself, *Hilary does that. Yes. Hilary eats that. No that's right, she won't touch that* and so on, so that by the end of the talk, Jack had managed to superimpose himself onto Hilary in his mind, and he was feeling extremely self-righteous. Don soon put an end to that as they sat down to lunch, by saying,

"Bet you're dreading that medical this afternoon aren't you?"

"No. Why should I?" Jack asked him.

"Well you've definitely put weight on since I last saw you."

"I don't think so," said Jack defensively, "don't forget I've just been on holiday for a week."

"Yeah, I know, but how much exercise do you do?"

"I walk a lot and I garden and I'm always active you know." Jack was desperate to change the subject but Don was going on.

"Nah, that's not exercise! I mean proper exercise. I play squash every week. I work out every day and I still play golf twice a week and that's not enough. I'm thinking of starting to run every day. You want to be careful, Jack. I'm sure your medical will show you're not fit."

Jack said nothing and carried on munching his salad. "What have you got lined up for me tonight then?" Jack asked, relieved he'd finally thought of a diversion. Don looked quite secretive and patted the side of his nose.

"I've got something quite unique lined up for you," he said and winked.

"Ah come on," Jack moaned, "You can't do that. Where are we going?"

"You'll see," laughed Don, "but I guarantee you'll love it."

The rest of the day was taken up with the medicals and health seminars including a questionnaire, which Jack found extremely depressing. They were all told that they would be sent their test results and health and fitness advice in due course, but the works doctor had told Jack there and then that he must lose weight and get fitter, very much as Don had predicted.

"I'll meet you in the bar for a drink," Don shouted across at Jack as they went to get into their cars at the end of the day.

"Okay. See you there," Jack shouted back.

Jack and Don always stayed at the same place when they came to the meetings. Don lived just outside Preston and covered the North West as his patch, so he could have easily gone home but he never did. The Holme Farm headquarters was just north of Lancaster and despite the fact that it was so near home, Tricia understood that this was 'Don's night with the boys', and she didn't mind.

Jack and Don always booked into The Fellside Inn, a medium-sized pub that served good beer and a good English breakfast. The English breakfast had remained sacrosanct amidst all the new dietary advice and government directives, due to public pressure. No doubt the debate over it would continue to rage, but for now it was still widely available and Jack always took advantage of this fact when he was away from Hilary's health-conscious eye. Unfortunately, as far as Jack was concerned, the same could not be said for the good old pub grub he remembered from his childhood.

The government's new laws had resulted in inspectors being appointed and they certainly did their job.

Their search results into obesity and food production in general had given them the perfect excuse to crack down on establishments that sold unhealthy food. They made it so difficult for any place that served lunches and dinners to get a licence that the majority of pubs had stopped serving food altogether. This left the bistros and organic restaurants which tended to be mostly vegetarian. Expensive restaurants and hotels managed to employ highly trained chefs who knew all the ways to create a delicious meal using a scrap of fish and a flower made out of a carrot, but you paid through the nose for it and neither your average British landlord nor your average British beer drinker could afford it. So, good old British food had all but died out. You could still cook it in your own home of course, but who had time to cook nowadays? Most ready meals sold in the supermarkets were very strictly controlled as Jack and Bernie knew from experience.

Was it all working? Nobody seemed to know.

Ironically though, as Jack had noted, you could still buy all the foreign foods that the Brits had come to love over the years. It had been decided at the very top level of government that ethnic food must be left alone, the powers that be deciding that it would have been far too politically incorrect to ban foreign food. Ironically, this meant that a lot of the food the Brits bought from takeaways, such as curry, pizzas and Chinese had been left alone and only the good old stodgy British food had been banned. Of course fish and chips and the iconic British fry up had been left alone too. No government would dare touch them!

Jack thought the whole thing was madness, but then he thought most things the government did were madness.

The Fellside, because it was in a holiday area, had managed to retain its B&B label and so served breakfast, but it didn't do an evening meal.

"So where are we going then?" Jack asked again as they both supped their pints.

"We're going to a foodie bar," Don told him.

"A foodie bar!" Jack exclaimed, "What the hell's a foodie bar?"

"Ssshhh. Keep your voice down. It's a place where you can get all the food that we're not allowed to eat any more," hissed Don.

"What sort of food?" Jack whispered

"You know, puddings and pastries and dumplings and pasties, plus all the meats that are supposed to be so bad for us these days. Mince and chops and ribs and kidney and faggots and anything that's been banned, basically."

Jack's mouth was already watering. He was fed up to the back teeth with all the legislation and the gradual demise of what he considered to be perfectly good British grub.

"How did you find out about it?"

"Never you mind. A friend of a friend. Come on, drink up. We haven't got all night."

They downed their pints and set off in Don's car through the country lanes. It was a beautiful crisp evening with that particular autumnal scent of rotting leaves and wood smoke in the air. The two men drove in companionable silence for a while and Jack took particular note of the route.

"I'm surprised at you coming here when you're so health conscious," Jack remarked.

"Oh, I don't come here often. That wouldn't do me any good at all. I've just brought you because you need cheering up and I know how you love your food." Don was smirking.

Yeah and you know I've just been told to lose weight, thought Jack, but he didn't say anything.

They drew up in the market-square of a large village and parked the car. Don led the way down a couple of streets until they came to a plain, two-storey, stone building. Jack could see through the steamy window that it was a restaurant, and as they walked inside, the smell of garlic and cheese made him hiss at Don, "This doesn't look very secret, it's an Italian restaurant."

"Just be patient. We're not there yet," Don responded. He marched to a bar at the back of the room with Jack on his heels and said to the barman, "I booked a special table for this evening. Name of White."

"Yes, sir. Follow me please," the barman said, and led the way through a door at the back of the room. They went along a corridor and through another door and then down some steps where the barman opened yet another door and then left them.

As soon as the door opened, Jack's nostrils went into overdrive. There was such a combination of different smells that he actually stood still just to try to define them all. They were standing in a square, underground room with a plain stone-flagged floor and pillars at intervals. The lighting was dim and as far as Jack could make out, it was coming from candles in wine bottles, placed in the centre of each table. There wasn't much noise, just a low hum of conversation and the sounds of people eating, no, not just eating, but shovelling down food as if their lives depended on it. By the time he'd taken this all in, Jack realised that Don was already sitting at a table against the far wall and grinning at him. As Jack sat down, he said, "I knew you'd like it. Take a look at the menu."

The menu was written out by hand and consisted of four main courses and four puddings.

Steak and kidney pudding
Minced beef and dumplings
Sausages and mash
Belly pork and crackling with all the trimmings.
Followed by:
Jam roly-poly,
Syrup sponge
Spotted Dick
Apple pie, all with custard.

Jack couldn't believe it. No salads, no sorbets, no fresh fruits; and the only vegetables were carrots, peas, and chips or mash. His mouth was watering as his eyes roamed over the menu in gastronomic foreplay and he could feel Don's eyes on him as he broke out into a sweat of indecision.

"Oh God!" moaned Jack, "I want it all."

He finally decided on Steak and kidney pudding and Spotted Dick, just as the waitress appeared to take their order. She turned to Don first and as Jack looked up, it was all he could to stop himself gasping out loud. She was gorgeous! She was about five foot seven, with long dark hair that curled round her face and a figure that could only be described as voluptuous; big boobs, small waist and long, shapely legs. She turned towards him, and Jack saw her big brown eyes and full mouth for the first time. He felt like a drowning man as he managed with some difficulty to place his order. She scribbled on her pad and walked away.

Jack's eyes followed every undulation of her beautiful bottom bulging beneath her tight, short skirt. He knew Don was shaking with laughter across the table but he didn't care.

"Wow," he breathed, "What a place! If I lived up here I'd come here every night."

"Well, it wouldn't do you much good if you did," Don told him, still laughing and pointing to Jack's stomach.

"Why haven't you told me about this place before?" Jack snorted indignantly.

"For that very reason. You'd be up here all the time and die of a heart attack in no time. Besides a man's got to have some secrets. Anyhow I've brought you now, so stop moaning and enjoy yourself."

"Oh, I'll do that alright," Jack assured him. "What about that waitress. She is something!"

"Oh yes, the luscious Louisa. She's Italian and a cousin of the owner."

"Who is the owner?" Jack asked.

"I don't really know, but my 'source' tells me that they are a local family, the wife's from round here and the husband's Italian. He runs upstairs and she runs down here. There is a rumour that a local businessman put up the dosh, but nobody seems to know who that is."

"It's a brilliant idea. Do they ask for a joining fee?"

"No. It's all word of mouth. You phone up the Italian upstairs and ask for a 'special' table and then you say, 'Do you do English food?' and they know you mean down here."

"Well it seems simple enough, but how the hell have they managed not to get caught by the food inspectors?" Jack asked incredulously.

"Aw, come on, Jack. Don't be so naive! They charge the earth down here and it's only cash. They must be raking it in, so there's plenty left to grease someone's palm. Somebody's on the make."

The food, when it arrived, lived up to every promise that the smell of it made. It was piping hot, perfectly cooked and absolutely delicious. Every mouthful deserved to be savoured and Jack did just that, murmuring every now and again at the sheer ecstasy his taste buds were experiencing. He was not too distracted, however, to miss the movements made by the luscious Louisa, and between mouthfuls he watched her undulating progress, either coming or going – each one was equally pleasurable for him. He could have stayed there all night but Don wanted his bed and he was driving, so reluctantly he dragged himself away.

Later on, alone in his bed, Jack couldn't sleep. For one thing he had chronic indigestion, and for another thing, he couldn't get the whole experience out of his mind. It had seemed so illicit and so exciting and all his senses seemed aroused. He tossed and turned, but sleep eluded him. All he could see when he closed his eyes, was Louisa passing to and fro in front of him with a playful smile on her lips. *I'm sure she's related to the Mona Lisa*, thought Jack. *Well. I've just got to get up here again on my own and get to know her a bit better.*

CHAPTER 3

*H*ilary sat at her desk in the relative quiet of a lunchtime classroom, munching an apple and marking maths books. She was still cross from the morning and had vowed to sit down with Jack when he got home and have it out with him.

Why is he being such a selfish shit recently? she asked herself. *Maybe it's the male menopause or something. It's just typical of him to go through it before me*, she thought. Her whole morning had been spent thinking how to get around the problem of Anna's dental appointment. If Jack had only told her in time, she could have sorted something out – but it was such short notice! In the end she had phoned Alec and Charlie during break, praying they would be in. The conversation had been very short because she couldn't hear due to the din in the staff room, but she had gathered that they'd be delighted to help. Then she just had to phone Anna's school to leave a message that Anna would be picked up by her grandparents, but by then, break was over and she should have been on duty. She was reminded by the Deputy Head on his way up the corridor. "Still in holiday mode eh, Mrs Baker!" he said cheerily, but she knew it had been noted. *God, I'll kill Jack*, she thought as she made her way back to the classroom.

Now, munching on her apple, she realised that she hated having to ask Alec and Charlie because it meant she was in their debt so much. Hilary had always been independent, her own mother was never around very much when she was young but now she was divorced from Hilary's father and living it up with some bloke in Spain, Hilary never saw her at all. As for her father, she hadn't seen him in years. Her only sister was living up in Scotland and although they spoke on the phone occasionally, they rarely saw each other. This meant that Alec and Charlie played a much greater part in her life than any of her own family and although she was very fond of them, she still resented the closeness.

The bell rang and she remembered, with a start, that she should be out on the field for a games lesson. She grabbed her whistle and ran out of the classroom, muttering, "Shit, shit, shit," to herself.

Later on that evening, driving home after the staff meeting, Hilary realised that she was very hungry. *Oh, it would be nice if Charlie has put some food on*, she thought. Then she got cross with herself and planned a healthy salad and baked potatoes.

She opened the front door to the sound of the children screaming with laughter and she walked into the kitchen just in time to see them chasing Alec round the kitchen table with a celery stick.

"Oh hello, dear," Charlie said quickly, "We all thought we'd start the tea for you, salad and baked potatoes. Is that alright?"

Hilary slumped heavily into a kitchen chair and said, "Oh yes, Charlie. That's fine. I was thinking of having that anyway. You are both so good. Thanks for today! It was just such short notice."

"Oh don't worry about that. We are always glad to help."

I wish I could just say your son is a selfish so and so, Hilary thought, but instead she said to Anna,

"How did your dental appointment go, love?"

"He said my teeth are fine at the moment and he'll see me again in six months," Anna replied with great precision; then she continued to chase her grandfather out of the room.

Just then the phone rang, and Anna shouted, "It's for you, Mum, it's Karen."

Karen was Hilary's mate from school – they both taught P.E. but although Karen was only a few years younger than Hilary, she'd only just got married.

"Hi, Karen. What's up?"

"Oh I'm glad you're there, Hils," Karen answered. "I've got some hot gossip for you and it won't wait until tomorrow. Guess what? Dai's getting divorced!"

Dai Evans was the Head of P.E. at Carrisbrook Middle School where Hilary and Karen worked.

"No. I don't believe it!" Hilary shrieked, "When did you hear that?"

"After you left, Doris told me – I looked for you but you'd gone!"

"Yes. I had to get back for the kids," Hilary explained. "God. What a turn up for the books, eh! Poor little Harry, he's only a little mite. I wonder who'll have him."

Harry was Dai and Lynda Evans' five-year-old. He had just started at their lower school and Dai adored him. "Did Doris say why they were getting divorced?" Hilary went on.

"She didn't know," Karen replied, "But she was going to say more when the Head came back in and then everyone drifted off. Hopefully we'll find out more tomorrow."

They went on to talk about a few arrangements for matches and so on but neither of them felt much enthusiasm. They were both fond of their head of department and upset for him.

Hilary put the phone down in a daze. She'd always liked Dai; he was a good bloke. She wondered how this might affect him at work. You needed to be on top form, both physically and mentally, to be Head of P.E.

Later that evening, when Alec and Charlie had left and the children were in bed, Hilary poured herself a gin and tonic and sat quietly thinking about Jack. Why had her easy-going and happy-go lucky-husband suddenly turned moody and unapproachable? Since they got back from holiday, he seemed to be in a permanently bad mood. Was it something she'd done or hadn't done? He needed to go on a diet, that was his problem – his system was overloaded with all those toxins. She thought about Dai and his divorce and for the first time in her married life, she felt insecure and a little afraid, but she dismissed the thought immediately because it was a weakness and she couldn't afford a weakness.

On the Tuesday evening, when Jack got home, he was surprised to be met by the smell of cooking. He walked into the kitchen, already tugging at his tie, and gave Hilary a peck on the cheek as she stood, stirring pasta.

"Hello. How are you? Did you get home early today?" he said in a surprised tone.

"Yes. No meetings, matches or crises," she replied. "How was your meeting?"

"It was OK really, I suppose. The famous Dr Simon Fletcher came to talk to us."

"Ooh I wish I'd been there. He's really fanciable," Hilary smirked as she joined Jack at the kitchen table.

"Well I didn't fancy him!" Jack laughed, and then he pulled a face. "Nor did I fancy what he told us."

"Why? Did he give you all individual medicals?" Hilary asked.

"No, but the company doctor did, and he told me I've got to lose weight and exercise more," Jack moaned.

"Well, it's only what I've been telling you for a while now," Hilary said, frowning." You know what you should do, but you're too lazy to do it. I'm fed up with telling you, Jack – that's it now – you've got to make an effort!" She stalked back to the stove and jabbed at the food aggressively.

"Alright, alright! Keep your hair on." He suddenly felt incredibly tired and depressed. "I'm going for a shower."

Jack showered, changed, and thought that life was not going to be particularly pleasant for a while. He sighed to himself; ah well, at least he had Louisa to think about.

He popped in to see Simon on his way back downstairs. "How did the French exam go?" he asked his son.

"Not too bad, but I never know how I've done until I get the results."

"Yeah. I know what you mean," Jack said. "I used to be the same. Anyway finish what you're doing 'cos dinner's nearly ready."

Later on Jack and Hilary sat in the lounge drinking coffee. The TV was on but the sound was down. Jack reached for the remote and Hilary said, "Just a minute, before you start watching something, I want to talk for a while."

Here we go, thought Jack, *she's going to have a go at me on two counts now.* He slumped down in the chair and assumed a bored expression, then he realised Hilary was looking at him expectantly.

"What did you say?" he asked.

"You see, that's what I'm talking about. You are distracted all the time," Hilary snapped and then more slowly she said, "I asked you if anything was the matter, you have been acting very strangely recently."

"No, nothing is the matter. I'm fine." Jack felt like a worm on the end of a fishing line, he wanted to wriggle free but there was nowhere to go.

"Well you're not acting fine, Jack, ever since we got back from holiday, you've been acting as if something was irritating you."

"The only thing that's irritating me, is you asking me all these questions," Jack retorted.

Hilary gasped for a moment, almost as if he had hit her, and then her face went red and she shouted, "ME irritating YOU. Well let me tell you, you selfish PIG. YOU are irritating ME. Slamming out of the house like a bloody prima donna yesterday while I'm left with the problem of the dentist."

37

That's right, Hils, thought Jack, *don't mince your words.* She was going on,

"And who do you think I had to call? YOUR PARENTS – there was nobody else to take Anna while you went off to your precious meeting without a care in the world."

Jack was stunned. It had never occurred to him that Hilary would ask Alec and Charlie. In fact, it had never occurred to him that she would ask anyone at all. She was right. He hadn't thought about it. He instantly felt about twelve again and he could see his mother's sad, reproving look whenever he had disappointed her in any way.

"What did you have to drag them into it for?" he asked in a wounded voice.

"I didn't have any choice," Hilary retorted through gritted teeth, "And I didn't DRAG them, they were only too happy to help."

Jack closed his eyes and let his head drop back against the chair.

"Let's just say I'd had a bad day, shall we. We'd just got back from holiday and I didn't want to get back to the old routine. I know I should have given you more notice. I usually do, and I will in future. OK?"

He sat back up and looked at Hilary, who looked slightly mollified.

"OK. Thank you," she said as she stood up with her empty mug, and she walked out of the room, as if to stay would have meant she'd given away too much ground.

Jack sat back again in the chair and flicked the remote to the CD listings. He selected one of his favourites and hoped it would soothe his jangled nerves. He was not at all sure what Hilary might have said to Alec and Charlie and he felt quite unsettled by the thought. He was really angry with her for using them to make him feel guilty in this way. *Well, I bloody well won't feel guilty,* he thought, *I've done nothing wrong! It's so typical of her to make a mountain out of a molehill. She should be supporting me in my hour of need instead of which, she's making out everything is my fault.* And he sat back in a cloud of righteous indignation.

In the kitchen, Hilary started the dishwasher and thought, *that wasn't the way I wanted that to turn out at all. Somewhere along the line I lost my temper.* She frowned to herself as she went over the conversation again in her head. She had wanted to have a rational discussion and point out to Jack that he had been selfish, but instead it had turned into a row. That always seemed to be happening these days. She sighed in exasperation – ah well, Jack had promised to give her more notice in the future and that must suffice. Now she had the added problem of getting him fit as well. Life was certainly not easy at times.

As if to underline the fact, Simon shouted down, "Mum! Where are my football shorts?" Hilary sighed and made her way upstairs, glad of the distraction.

The next night was Halloween, and Hilary, Jack and the kids had a great time, scooping out pumpkins and telling creepy stories. Anna and Simon joined their friends, trick or treating round the village, and everyone joined up in the village hall for a part, organised by the local scout group. Simon was a member and he took his responsibilities seriously, handing round red punch, supposedly blood for the vampires, and chicken legs which, he told Anna, were frogs' legs.

As they all walked home, Hilary thought that at least last night's row had cleared the air and as she watched Jack chasing the kids down the road with a big rubber spider, she smiled to herself and thought everything seemed back to normal.

For the rest of the week, the Baker household returned to its usual routine, and by Saturday morning the Maltese holiday seemed a lifetime away instead of just a week.

Jack woke up feeling randy again and reached out for Hilary but she'd already gone – he groaned out loud as he remembered she'd got a netball match to referee. He had been detailed off to chauffeur the kids around and do the shopping. He rolled over and squinted at the clock, 8.45a.m, early yet, he'd just close his eyes a bit longer and dream of Louisa. He imagined her walking towards him as she undid her blouse to reveal a low-cut bra supporting her ample breasts and then she reached behind her back, and suddenly they were bouncing free and she was smiling at him.

He was just picturing himself burying his face in the soft, warm flesh and realising that he had an enormous hard-on, when he heard Simon's voice shout, "Dad, are you awake?"

"Yes. What do you want?" Jack managed to croak.

"I'm supposed to meet Peter at the E. Centre at nine-thirty and it's almost nine now."

"OK. OK. I'm coming," Jack shouted back and then he thought ruefully, *I wish I was.*

Monday night was November 5th, and Jack was looking forward to it. It was one of his favourite nights of the year and he always made sure he didn't travel very far that day so he could be back in time to cook a huge chilli and baked potatoes.

There had been rumours that only organised bonfires were going to be allowed this year and also that fireworks were to be banned altogether but, as was the case every year, none of this came to fruition and Jack had built their usual bonfire from garden rubbish and carefully prepared the ground for their personal fireworks. They always had their own display and ate early so they could go on to the Scout bonfire later.

Alec and Charlie always came to join them and Charlie always brought flapjack, parkin and treacle toffee as her contribution, all of which Jack adored; he always pigged out on Bonfire Night.

Over breakfast, the kids were very excited. "Have you bought those screamers again, Dad? The ones you had last year?" Simon asked.

"Just you wait and see. I'm not telling you." Jack smiled at his son.

"Awww, Dad .Say you've got them," Simon moaned. "They're great, they are." And he proceeded to leap around the kitchen screeching like a tomcat in a fight, whirling his arms around his head.

"Alright, alright. I've got them, pipe down," Jack shouted above the din, but he was smiling, because he loved the screamers too.

Anna and Hilary smiled indulgently and carried on eating their breakfast and Jack started opening his mail.

"Oh no!" he moaned, looking at one of the letters. Hilary looked up.

"What is it?"

"It's my medical results. They say I've got to lose a stone and get fitter and they've sent me a diet and exercise programme," Jack told her in an affronted tone.

"Well, what did you expect, Jack? A pat on the back? That's it. We're starting tomorrow. Let me see what they say!" She made a grab for the paper, but he was too quick for her and held it out of her grasp.

"*We* aren't starting anything!' Jack shouted back, "I'm quite capable of doing this on my, own thank you."

"Well, you just make sure you do, Jack Baker. I don't want to be a widow before my time, thank you very much!" With that she stalked out of the room, leaving Jack to put his tongue out behind her retreating back.

The children got up quietly and cleared their empty dishes while Jack sat down at the table and held his head in his hands. He picked up the paper again and studied it in more detail.

"God! It's worse than I thought!" he said out loud. The letter told him that he had to report back to the medical centre in two months for another check- up. *Oh I hate this*, he thought and he groaned out loud as he realized how much Hilary would love it.

When he'd showered and dressed, Jack gathered up the offending papers to store them safely in his briefcase. As he tried to get them back inside the envelope, he realised there was another slip of paper in there.

WEEKEND HEALTH & FITNESS SEMINARS
If you need help in your efforts, come and join us at Holme Farm for the weekend and we'll give you all the encouragement you'll need!

It went on to list various dates when the seminars would be held.

Jack's face broke into a grin and he kissed the little slip of paper. *Thanks, Bernie*, he whispered to himself. This was just the opportunity he'd been looking for to go and visit the foodie bar again. He'd been wracking his brains trying to think of a way of getting up there without Hilary getting suspicious and old Bernie had handed it to him on a plate! He went downstairs, whistling to himself.

That evening, the family had their usual great time. The fireworks were even better than usual and Charlie had excelled herself with her baking. As Jack helped himself to his third piece of flapjack, Hilary said, "Take it easy, Jack! Have you forgotten already?" Jack groaned and pulled a face, and Anna pulled the plate away from him, shielding it with her body.

"Dad's got to lose weight, Grandma, the doctor said so," she told Charlie with great solemnity.

"What's all this about then?" Charlie asked Jack, the concern showing in her eyes. Jack sighed. "I had to go for my yearly medical and they told me I'm not fit enough and I've got to lose a stone," he said in a resigned voice.

"Oh dear, if I'd known that, I wouldn't have brought all my usual goodies," Charlie told him.

"Ahh, Grandma! We can still eat them," Anna protested, still shielding the flapjack from her father.

"Yes, of course you can, love – well, eat them up quickly before your dad can get them."

Jack turned away in disgust. He felt as if they were all ganging up on him, but when he caught a glimpse of his mother's face, he could see she was really worried. He went and put his arm round her. "It's OK, Mum. I'm going to do as I'm told. I'm perfectly fit apart from that, so don't worry!"

"Well mind you do, Jack Baker," Charlie smiled at him, "I don't want a roly-poly for a son, you know!"

Jack walked over to where Alec was poking at the bonfire and he smiled to himself. He thought about the weekend seminar he'd booked himself in for in two weeks' time. He couldn't wait to visit the foodie bar again. Praps he'd have jam roly-poly next time; it was one of his favourites!

CHAPTER 4

Jack decided that since he only had two weeks before he saw Louisa again, it would be a good idea to take the diet and exercise seriously and try to make himself more presentable. Unfortunately for him, however, Sod's Law chose that particular week to put in an appearance.

Hilary was particularly busy at work so she asked Jack to do the shopping. This was always fatal because Jack threw everything in the trolley that took his fancy and then he was forced to cook it and eat it so it wouldn't go to waste.

Then, two of his distributors chose that week to take him out for a working lunch and on the Friday night Hilary reminded him that they had been invited out to dinner. Hence, by the time Saturday morning came, Jack had actually *gained* two pounds!

Hilary's week was not much better. It had been the sort of week that P.E. teachers dread; it had bucketed with rain all week, so all outdoor lessons had to be held in the gym. The kids were as high as kites, the noise in the changing rooms was deafening, and it took every ounce of energy just to keep order and discipline.

After a particularly gruelling session with Year 7, Hilary made her way to the staff room for a welcome cup of tea. There weren't many people in, because during wet breaks all staff were expected to stay with their own classes.

Dai Evans was slumped in a chair, head back, eyes closed, as Hilary walked in. She didn't say anything in case he didn't want to be disturbed.

"How were the hooligans today then?" Dai asked her.

"Same as usual!" Hilary replied as she brought her cup of tea over and sat down. "I'm worried about Sean Abbot though; I kept expecting him to be his usual cheeky self but he's gone all moody and aggressive."

"Yeah well, his mum finally walked out last week apparently."

"Did he tell you that?"

"No, Doris did; the fount of all knowledge."

Doris Bates was the school secretary and there was very little that escaped her. Doris was in her mid-forties, short and plump, but always smartly dressed in blouses and skirts. Her hair and make-up were always immaculate and she only had two weaknesses; high-heeled shoes and the Head. Not necessarily together, you understand! Her love of the former earned her the nickname of Imelda on some occasions and her love of the latter earned her the nickname of 'The Dragon' on others. She was extremely efficient and business-like in everything she did and *nobody* got past her command post in front of the Head's office unless she wanted them to. She had this habit of looking at people over the top of her spectacles, which could stop an army in its tracks.

Although Doris had never been a teacher, she had no difficulty in disciplining pupils, parents and staff alike. Quite a few pupils were more afraid of Mrs Bates than they were of their teachers!

On the other hand, if anyone had a real problem or was ill, she could be an angel of mercy and very, very kind. It was this last trait that enabled her to gain the majority of her 'info' as Doris called it.

There were some staff and parents who believed that it was really Doris, and not the Head, who ran the school, but they would never dare say that in front of Doris as she was fiercely protective of her boss and fussed over him like a mother hen. It didn't pay to upset Doris because if you wanted to see the Head and Doris didn't want you to, you might as well try crossing the Alps with a herd of elephants. On the other hand if Doris liked you, then it made your life at Carrisbrook Middle School a whole lot easier.

"Oh dear, poor lad," Hilary was saying, "He and his mum are very close. I'm really surprised she didn't take him with her."

"I've heard she was pretty beaten up. She'll come back for him when she's feeling stronger, I'm sure."

"Well at the moment he must be feeling very hurt and abandoned, poor thing."

"I know how he feels," Dai said quietly as he stood up.

Hilary could have bitten her tongue off.

"If you need anything, you'll let me know won't you," she said.

"Thanks, Hils, but I'll survive," he said with a wry smile.

As Hilary made her way back to her classroom, the grey, wet day seemed to match her mood. She had been told that Lynda Evans had left Dai for another man and taken Harry with her. Everyone seemed to think that Dai was coping very well and doing all the right things but Hilary wasn't sure; she knew that he was fiercely proud and independent and he wouldn't ask for help unless he was desperate. She pushed open her classroom door in time to see two of her naughtiest boys leaping across desks. "OUT HERE. NOW!" she bellowed, and was glad of the release.

Jack looked down at the scales in dismay. He groaned in frustration and stumped downstairs to the kitchen where he promptly cooked himself bacon and egg in defiance.

Hilary, of course, wasn't there, so it was her fault. She was covering yet another match for that Evans bloke because he was getting a divorce. Jack had never liked Dai Evans – probably because he was tall, athletic-looking and had a boyish look about him that Jack resented. People of his age shouldn't look that young, it wasn't right! However, if Jack was honest with himself, the bloke had never done him any harm and from what Hilary had told him, he'd had some bad luck recently.

Anna, rushing into the kitchen, interrupted Jack's thoughts.

"Daaaad! Will you take me out on my new bike today? You promised you would."

Jack had no recollection of any such promise and was just about to say so, when he remembered the two pounds *and* the bacon and egg.

"OK then. Where do you want to go?"

"Just round the park will do. I want to practise."

"Give me a chance to get showered and dressed then and I'll be with you," Jack told her.

As he was getting ready, he felt better, at least this would give him a chance for some exercise – the only time he'd managed to put an exercise DVD on last week, he'd fallen asleep watching it!

Simon opted to stay at home so Jack and Anna made their way to the park. Anna could already ride a bike but this was a new super-duper thingy that Hilary had insisted she have for her birthday last month. Jack wasn't sure that she was ready for it yet but Hilary was very competitive where her children were concerned and if Anna showed signs of being interested in biking at a higher level then Hilary would ensure she got the chance to do it.

It was a sunny day, cold but clear, and there was a biting wind that could find any gaps in your clothing. Jack watched Anna's progress as she rode up and down the path; she was doing OK.

"Can we go over to the rough ground, Dad?" Anna shouted, "I want to try it on the slopes."

"OK. I'll follow you," Jack shouted back. He wandered in the direction of the rough ground. This was land which had been left to nature, as it were, and all the local kids enjoyed it better than the landscaped part. Some of the lads used it for scrambling and others practised on their mountain bikes. It was always cut up and muddy, as it was today. Anna could be seen taking a run at the hills and then disappearing down the other side, manoeuvring her bike backwards, forwards and sideways and obviously thoroughly enjoying herself. *Just like her mother*, he thought, *bloody determined*! And he smiled to himself. The fresh air was clearing his brain, and he was just deciding to renew his dieting efforts when he heard barking. Jack turned round, just in time to see two dogs come running towards him, barking furiously. The first dog kept turning round to see if the other was gaining ground and in an instant, they were past Jack and racing up the hill. Next thing he knew, Jack was running, as he heard a scream and saw Anna come hurtling through the air towards him, followed by her bike. He was there and lifting the bike off her, before she'd realised what had happened. He picked her up and tried to set her on her feet. "Are you alright?" he asked anxiously.

"I've hurt my leg," she said, wincing in pain.

Jack looked down to see a deep gash just below her knee; it was bleeding badly.

"Alright, poppet, we'll just get you home and see to that, shall we?"

He picked her up in his arms and manoeuvred her so that he could keep a hand free to push the bike. Luckily they weren't too far from home, but all the same, he was gasping for breath by the time they got into the house.

Simon took one look and announced that Anna would need stitches and at that point, Anna started bawling her eyes out and Jack could have killed him. Eventually they managed to find a clean cloth to hold on the wound and Jack packed them into the car.

The health clinic that they attended was only fifteen minutes' drive away, luckily, and Jack felt a great sense of relief as a competent nurse took over, asking Anna questions and looking at her leg.

"She'll need a few stitches and a tetanus jab, but she'll be fine," the nurse announced. Just then, Hilary appeared. "How is she? What's happening?" she asked breathlessly. Jack had only had time to write the briefest details when he'd texted.

"She's cut her leg, Mum. She fell off her bike," Simon reported very succinctly.

"She needs a few stitches and a tetanus jab," Jack added, but he could tell by the way Hilary was looking at him that she was blaming him. "Two dogs ran across her path, she was doing fine until then." But she just set her mouth into a tight line and followed Anna and the nurse into the treatment room.

Jack and Simon waited in silence, expecting to have to listen to screams of pain, but none came, and eventually Hilary came out carrying Anna, who wasn't exactly smiling but certainly didn't seem too traumatised.

"Come on, let's get you home, little one, and see what we can find to cheer you up," she was saying, and didn't appear to be at all breathless as she carried Anna back to the car.

Jack drove home in silence brooding on his lack of fitness and the fact that he knew Hilary was going to have a go at him once they got home.

Once they all got back home and Anna had been propped up in bed, fed painkillers, and given her favourite DVD to watch, everyone started to relax. Jack waited for Hilary to blame him but she didn't; this left Jack restless and irritable as if he was on remand and he snapped at Hilary and Simon all day.

On Sunday they went over to Alec and Charlie's for lunch and they were all grateful, for once, for Charlie's pampering.

"How's the diet going, dear?" Charlie asked Jack as he helped himself to another slice of apple pie. .He looked up guiltily but was relieved to find she was smiling at him.

"Not very well really, Mum, I'm determined to start tomorrow." And he went on to explain how the week had proved difficult.

"Never mind," Charlie told him, "tomorrow is another day!"

"Yeah. Another day to eat too much," Simon piped up and everyone laughed.

I'll show you all, thought Jack, and he changed the subject by talking to Alec about his project.

"Come and see what I'm doing," Alec invited him, so the two men wandered out into the garden.

Alec showed Jack a rather large hole in the ground.

"Have you done all this yourself?" Jack asked incredulously.

"No, Jack Briggs has been giving me a hand now and then, but I've done most of it. It's got to be finished before the frost really sets in."

"Who's Jack Briggs?"

"He's a bloke I have a pint with now and again – self-employed – Jack of all trades, you might say," and Alec smiled at his own joke, "he's done a fair bit of building in his time and he knows his stuff."

"You could have asked me to help, you know, Dad." Jack sounded hurt.

Alec smiled, "Yes I know but you've got your own life to lead and you're busy, besides as I say, I've done most of it myself."

"So what's the hole for anyway?" Jack asked, slightly mollified.

"My holding tank for the water I syphon off. I'll take water from the washing machine, bath and shower and feed it through that filtering system over there and then it's stored in here, ready for irrigation," Alex explained.

"It's very clever, Dad, next time there's a drought you'll still have fat, juicy vegetables!"

"That's the theory! Talking of which, you will try and do as the doctor says won't you, 'cos you know if you don't, old Bernard will be perfectly within his rights to withdraw your health insurance subsidy and worse still, you could lose your job!"

"I know, Dad." Jack kept his head down and kicked the earth around with his feet. The problem was he was only too aware of the consequences and he felt like he used to when he was a kid again and he'd done something stupid. "I'll start properly again tomorrow," he assured Alec.

"Well, we'd better have a beer now, then." Alec patted his son on the back as they headed for the house.

"Well come on. What's he like then?"

"Who?"

"You know very well who – Simon Fletcher – is he as gorgeous as he looks on the telly?"

Carla sat forward in anticipation as Angela busied herself around the kitchen. At least once a week Angela cooked an evening meal for Carla. They had been friends since their schooldays despite the fact that their lives had taken very different paths. Carla had left school at sixteen and now worked in the packing department at Holme Farm and Angela had stayed on at school, attended a local college and worked her way up to being Bernie's personal assistant.

Angela was married with her own house and Carla was single and lived in a tiny flat above a shop in Carnforth.

"Yes, he is just as gorgeous as he looks on TV, in fact, even more so. He's got those crinkly eyes that melt you when he smiles and a really sexy voice."

Carla adopted a dreamy expression. "Oh, I wish I could have met him. You never know, he might have fallen madly in love with me and then I could have had his babies."

"Just two things wrong with that," Angela reminded her," One – he's already married, and two – you don't want children."

"That's true. You're the one who loves children, but it's a minor detail." Carla laughed. "Anyhow, did you get to hear his talk?"

"Bits of it – enough to know that I'm totally unfit and overweight and I must do something about it."

"Yeah. I know what you mean." Carla was staring into space when the tea towel wrapped itself round her head.

"You cheeky cow!" Angela yelled, "What do you mean – I know what you mean? My lack of fitness and rolls of fat are that obvious, are they?"

Carla gulped. "No. I didn't mean that. I meant that I must do something too."

"You!" Angela squawked, "There isn't an ounce of fat on you!"

"I know, but I'm totally unfit and the doctor asked me last year if I was eating healthily."

Angela smiled. "I see, so you'd like to come on one of these weekend courses with me, would you?"

Carla tried to look innocent. "What weekend course is that then?"

"You know very well. I was talking about it last week. Bernie is paying for some experts to give advice on diet and exercise and so on. Don't pretend you don't know what I'm talking about."

Carla laughed, "Ok, Ok. Yes. I'd like to come – it could be fun and you never know, I might just meet someone." Angela just tutted and shook her head.

"You're incorrigible. Now then, set the table and I'll start the process of fattening you up."

All the next week, Jack tried really hard to stick to his eating programme and by Thursday he really felt he was getting somewhere. He decided to go and get his hair cut at lunchtime to spur him on. When he came out of the hairdressers, the sun was shining, the air was crisp and his spirits lifted, so he walked into Marks and Spencer's and bought himself some new boxer shorts and socks. The woman on the cash desk gave him a big smile; things were looking up. He whistled all the way back to his car. Tomorrow he'd be off to freedom! He must remind Hilary that he was driving straight up after work tomorrow. He'd got a last call booked in Birmingham, so there was no point in driving back home first but he wanted to be sure this time that there would be no recriminations. He and Hilary had hardly seen each other this week, and what with chauffeuring the kids around and parents' evenings at Hilary's school, there hadn't been much time to talk.

"I'll be driving straight up tomorrow night, after work," Jack said as he and Hilary were clearing away the remains of the meal.

"Driving where?" Jack's stomach lurched. *Oh God! Don't tell me she's going to make a fuss*, he thought.

"To my weekend health and fitness course." He tried to keep his voice as normal as possible.

"Oh no, I'd forgotten all about it." Hilary looked genuinely mortified and so Jack just held his breath because he just didn't know what to say. He must have looked horrified though, because Hilary smiled and said, "Don't worry. I'll sort something out. Karen can handle the matches tomorrow and I think I'll invite her and Geoff over tomorrow night for a meal."

Jack allowed himself to breathe again – he had to turn away so Hilary wouldn't hear the rush of air as his lungs relaxed. He still didn't trust himself to say anything so he busied himself with the dishwasher. Hilary came up behind him and put her arms round him. "I'll miss you, you know – don't go overdoing it. I don't want you coming back with a hernia!" Jack couldn't help chuckling. He turned round to have a full-blown hug.

"Don't worry. Have you ever known me to overexert myself?"

"No, not overexert," Hilary smiled and looked at him in a very meaningful way, "but you've come close to it a few times." She laughed and he chased her out of the kitchen and up the stairs. The kids were quietly occupied and even if they noticed their parents going into their bedroom and closing the door, they didn't think anything of it, it had happened before.

Jack watched Hilary undress and he admired her trim figure, as he always did. As far as his own body was concerned, he gave it very little thought; all he was usually interested in, was getting his clothes off as quickly as possible and getting on with things, but he was feeling the benefit of a few days of careful eating and, for once, he felt quite good about himself.

They made love as they always did, almost automatically. They knew what turned each other on and they didn't waste time on too much foreplay; it wasn't necessary anymore. Jack thought it could be described as competent lovemaking, not passionate, not exciting, but adequate, and when it was over, they were both satisfied.

As Jack was getting dressed again and Hilary was still lying there, she said, "I hope you enjoy the weekend, because if you do, it will encourage you to carry on."

Jack stood sideways and looked at himself in the mirror. "I think I look alright. I've done very well this week."

Hilary propped herself up on one elbow and smiled, "Yes, you've done very well, but that's just one week, Jack – you've got a long way to go yet!"

"That's just so typical of you," he snapped, "Knock me back before I've even started. You've got to criticise, haven't you!" He stumped out of the bedroom and slammed the door, leaving Hilary to flop back against the pillows and groan out loud.

CHAPTER 5

That Friday was one of the longest days Jack had ever experienced. He kept looking at his watch and felt sure time was literally standing still. He had a strange sensation in his stomach and chest area, which he knew he'd experienced some time before, but he couldn't remember when; then it occurred to him that it must have been when he first went out with girls, nervousness mixed with excitement.

Eventually, all his calls were over and he headed north. It was already dark and it had started to rain and as the car ate up the miles, that rain turned to sleet and finally to snow. Jack wasn't too worried because it didn't seem to be settling and he hadn't got far to go in any case, but by the time he pulled into Holme Farm, the car park looked as if it had been dusted with icing sugar.

The reception area was all lit up and full of people milling about, when Jack checked in at the desk. No one paid any particular attention to him, which suited him fine, all he wanted to do was get to the Fellside and then out to the foodie bar as soon as possible.

"Jack Baker," he said to the receptionist. She scanned her list and said, "Ah yes, Mr Baker. Here is your schedule and name-tag. Have you got somewhere to stay?"

"Yes, thanks." Jack grabbed the piece of paper and tag and turned away, anxious to escape; then he realised that she was still speaking in that cheerful, but automatic way that people talk when they've said the same thing numerous times.

"Over there and then you are to go into the lecture hall for 7 o'clock."

"Pardon?" Jack swung round in alarm.

"There's coffee and tea over there, Mr Baker, and then you are due in the lecture room at 7 o'clock," she repeated patiently.

"What, tonight!" Jack heard himself almost screeching with impatience.

"If you'll just refer to your schedule, sir." The receptionist gave him a cold look and turned to the next person.

Jack stood to one side and stared at his sheet.

HOLME FARM HEALTH & FITNESS SEMINAR

FRIDAY NOVEMBER 16TH

Registration	6.00 – 7.00 p.m.
Introduction in Lecture Hall	7.00 p.m.

SATURDAY NOVEMBER 17TH

Dietary Advice	9.00 a.m.
Fitness assessment	10.00 a.m.
Gym	11.00 a.m.
Lunch	12.00 – 1.00 p.m.
Fell-Walking	1.00 p.m.
Swimming Pool	4.00 p.m.
Evaluation	5.00 – 6.00 p.m.

SUNDAY NOVEMBER 18TH

Aerobics	9.00 a.m.
Coffee	10.00 – 10.30 a.m.
Optional Session	10.30 a.m.
Lunch	12.00 noon.
Optional Session	2.00 p.m.
Evaluation	4.00 p.m.

Jack was stunned. He couldn't believe that the weekend was so organised. He just hadn't thought about it, but when he made himself, he realised he must have had some vague idea of a few talks and a few sessions of demonstrations of gym equipment maybe. This was such a tight schedule that he'd be lucky to have any time to breathe, let alone get to know luscious Louisa.

He felt like turning round and getting straight back into his car, but how could he? What would Hilary say? And not just Hilary, but Simon and Anna and Alec and Charlie as well! No, he'd have to stay and get on with it, he realised with a sigh.

He looked up and saw that everyone was filing into the lecture hall. He recognised a couple of faces and one or two people nodded to him, as his legs moved stiffly to follow them. He was glad of the opportunity to sit down and take stock of the predicament he found himself in. Jack Baker, whose whole life revolved around methods of avoiding exercise at all costs, was actually faced with a weekend dedicated to very little else. Jack shook his head in disbelief. What had he come to!

He turned his attention to the group of people at the front of the room. There was a mixture of men and women, but they all looked fit and they all looked young. They were all dressed alike, in polo shirts and jeans. One of the men stood up and moved forward.

"Good evening, everybody, and welcome to the first of our Holme Farm health and fitness weekends. I hope you all had reasonable journeys, considering the weather. My name is John Fielding. I'm the co-ordinator for the weekend and this is my team."

He went on to introduce the young men and women, who each bobbed up and smiled. John went on, "I've seen one or two unhappy faces as you've been looking at your schedules, but I want to assure you, first and foremost, that the idea of this weekend is to encourage and help you in your efforts,

57

not beat you into submission! You will not be asked to do anything that you do not want to do."

Thank God for that, thought Jack and he began to relax, and pay more attention to what John was saying.

"Now I know you are all tired and hungry tonight so I don't intend to keep you long. All we really want to do is introduce ourselves and organise your groups for the weekend. If you look in the top right-hand corner of your sheet, you'll see a number and that is your group number." John continued by telling each group where to assemble in the room.

In a couple of minutes, Jack found himself in the back, right-hand corner of the room with a group of six other people. He didn't know any of them, which was a relief, although he thought a couple of the faces were familiar. They all stood, looking expectantly towards the front of the room for their anonymous leader, occasionally giving each other little sympathetic glances, which said, *I know how you're feeling. I'm feeling the same.*

Jack decided it was just like being back at college. *What am I doing here?* he asked himself, but then he remembered, and checked his watch – *7.30* – *Oh come on!*

Then, a voice said, "Sorry, ladies and gentlemen," and everybody swung round to see John Fielding approaching them from the other direction.

"I had to make sure that everyone was where they were supposed to be, and it seems they were, so I won't keep you long. I just want us all to introduce ourselves and say what we do for Holme Farm Products and then I'll go over our schedule and we'll be finished. Shall we start with you, sir? Bill, isn't it?"

Jack hurriedly fished his name-tag out of his pocket and pinned it on. He looked up to find one of the women, a plump and pretty brunette, smiling at him. He smiled back sheepishly and just had time to grasp that Bill was a bio-chemist, working in the labs. Next came Jean, a stern-looking blonde who definitely gave the impression she was not to be messed with. She worked on the production line. There was a driver, Danny, who had only just joined the company; he certainly looked a prime candidate for a health and fitness weekend as he was very overweight, but he had a cheeky grin, which Jack liked. The next one was Ken, who worked in accounts – Jack had him pegged as a wimp, he was small and indiscriminate looking, with old-fashioned spectacles and he seemed very shy. John had to repeat what he'd said because his voice was so quiet. Then came Angela, a secretary, the woman who'd smiled at him and finally, it was his turn. "Jack Baker from the sales department." His own voice sounded clear and confident.

"Thank you, Jack, and finally we have – Carla, isn't it?" John looked enquiringly at the last member of the group. A tiny young woman with short-cropped hair and a boyish figure. *She only looks about fifteen*, Jack decided. *Anna's got more flesh on her*! It turned out that Carla worked in the packaging department.

John was speaking again and Jack weighed him up. He was balding but he looked incredibly fit, although Jack couldn't have said why. He had very hairy forearms but that didn't necessarily mean anything. No, it was just an impression!

"OK," John was saying, "now let's have a quick look at your schedules, you'll see we start with dietary advice in the morning, that session will be taken by Debbie, our dietician and then at ten I'll be taking you into the gym for your fitness assessment. Hopefully we can design an individual programme for each of you. Then we've got lunch and in the afternoon, our fell walk. I know it's straight after lunch, so we'll be taking it easy to begin with. Anyone forget their walking boots?" Silence. "Good."

Jack looked round the other faces at this point; nobody looked in a panic, they were all listening attentively to John, and had calm, interested expressions. Jack's face wore the same calm expression but inside him, panic was rising. After he and Hilary had made love, he'd been very cool towards her and although she'd asked about boots, he'd muttered something from his position by the computer, and she'd gone away again. He remembered finding a load of stuff in the hall and throwing it in the boot of the car, but he really didn't know if it was boots or not. He wasn't going to admit it though – if he didn't have any, then tough, he couldn't do it could he? John was talking again. "You will be bussed to the swimming pool in Lancaster and then back here for evaluations. Any questions?"

Carla asked, "What happens if you just can't do any of these activities? For instance I can't swim!"

"Don't worry about that, Carla. If at any time you don't want to do an activity, or can't do an activity, then you don't do it. It's as simple as that. This weekend, as I've said, is about helping you do what *you* want to do. It's not an endurance test."

Everyone nodded and smiled in relief and John finished off by describing what would happen on Sunday. He listed the options they would be able to choose from and even Jack felt that there might be *some* aspects of the weekend he could enjoy. He'd always enjoyed bopping about on the dance floor so disco dancing could be fun, and from what he'd seen of yoga, a lot of that could be done lying down! Hence, by the time the session broke up, he was feeling more optimistic about the weekend ahead.

The journey to the Fellside was uneventful luckily. The snow had stopped and the gritters were out, the moonlight making the roads glisten. Jack allowed himself to think of the evening ahead and he realised that the first thing he must do was book himself a table. He'd have to use a pay-phone because he didn't want the number to appear on his mobile bill. He was slightly surprised at his own deviousness, but then he decided he was being overcautious. He was always phoning clients and one more unfamiliar number didn't matter. He pulled into the Fellside car park and retrieved the precious number from his wallet.

"Good evening, Giovanni's. Can I help you?" a voice answered.

Jack looked at his watch. Good God! 8.30 already! "I'd like a special table for this evening please, the name's—".

"I'm sorry, sir. We have no more special tables available for this evening. We could find you an ordinary table, if that's any good."

The disappointment welled up in Jack's chest and seemed to stick in his throat.

"Oh – no tables at all," he heard himself saying just to give himself time to think.

"Yes, sir. We have some tables, ordinary ones, but no specials." There was a pause. "I could offer you a special table for tomorrow night, sir." It was like a lifeline, and drowning, Jack grabbed it.

"Yes. Yes that's a good idea – tomorrow night – er do you do English food?"

"Yes, sir."

"Oh good, well I'd like a special table for tomorrow night – the name's Baker, Jack Baker."

"That's fine, Mr Baker, it's booked for you for tomorrow."

"Um, just a moment." Jack had just realised how hungry he was and his brain had recovered enough from the shock to realise that an ordinary table meant the Italian upstairs. It would do for tonight – besides he liked Italian food.

"I'll take that ordinary table for tonight if I may?"

"Of course, sir. What time?"

"I should be able to get there by 9.30."

"That's confirmed then, sir, for 9.30 this evening."

Jack made his way up to his room, showered and changed in a daze; it had never occurred to him that he wouldn't be able to get a table. He was lucky he could get one for tomorrow night!

The back roads to Underbarrow were un-gritted and extremely icy, so all his concentration had to go into his driving and by the time he'd parked the car, Jack realised he felt calmer.

The restaurant was warm and welcoming as he walked inside and he was shown to a table near the back. He ordered minestrone soup followed by lasagne without much enthusiasm but when the soup came, it was thick, hot and spicy and very, very good. Just the thing for a cold night; it also made him realise just how hungry he was. The lasagne was just as good, obviously home-made and delicious, with one or two flavours Jack couldn't recognise – partly because he'd burnt his tongue on the minestrone. He was just enjoying the last couple of mouthfuls when he saw her. The luscious Louisa! She'd marched through the door at the back and was obviously less than happy with the barman, pointing her finger at him and jabbering away in Italian, pushing him in the chest every now and then as if to underline a point. He was saying very little, and what he did say, appeared to be ignored by Louisa, who simply carried on unabated. Finally, she flung a tea towel she'd been carrying at the barman's face and flounced off in the direction she'd come, slamming the door behind her.

Jack watched in amazement, taking every detail of her tight, stretchy top, her short, tight skirt and her high-heeled, strappy shoes. She'd tossed her head as she was arguing and her gorgeous bust wobbled up and down as she'd waved her arms about. Then she was gone!

Jack realised he was dribbling, whether over the last of the gorgeous food or the sight of Louisa, he couldn't be sure, but as he wiped his mouth on his napkin, he felt as if he'd just enjoyed something particularly satisfying, whichever it was.

The barman appeared to be completely unmoved by the encounter and was polishing glasses as if nothing had happened and he didn't have a care in the world, he was even smiling. Jack couldn't understand how he could have been that close to Louisa without grabbing her in a passionate embrace.

The waiter came to clear away his plate so Jack took the plunge. "That lady who was talking to the barman just now," he ventured, "She didn't look very happy. Is there a problem?" The waiter smiled, "No problem, sir. That's Louisa. She's Italian, you know. She and Luigi are always fighting."

"Luigi?"

"Yes Luigi, the barman. He's her husband."

"Oh, I see," Jack replied automatically as his brain did a double flip; *but of course she's married, you bloody fool,* it was telling him. *Nobody could walk around looking like her and not be married!*

God, I've been fantasising about her for weeks and there's no way I can ever have her. Why didn't Don tell me she was married? I bet he knew! He probably thinks it's a huge joke. God, I'll kill him when I see him! This whole weekend, all for nothing! No wonder that barman was so oblivious to her charms. He can have her any time he wants.

Jack ran his hands through his hair and downed his beer. He suddenly felt incredibly tired and incredibly depressed. All he really wanted to do was go home but he couldn't. The hotel room and his bed would have to do for now.

Back at the Fellside, he decided he deserved a whisky after that shock. It would make him sleep. The bar sounded quite lively as he walked in and he recognised the group of people over by the fire as his group from earlier. They seemed to be having a good time, laughing and joking but Jack wasn't in the mood. He just wanted a whisky and his bed. A voice at his elbow said, "Come over and join us. Jack, isn't it? Here let me get that." Before he knew what was happening, the man had bought his drink and propelled him across the room to where the others were sitting.

Everyone moved up to make room for him and he found himself squashed between Angela's ample curves and Carla's bony thigh.

"We were just discussing how we felt about tomorrow," Angela told him, "Are you looking forward to it?"

"No, not really." Jack pulled a face. "I'm only here because I've been told to lose weight and get fitter."

"Join the club!" moaned Angela, "I think we're all here for that."

"I'm here to put it on," Carla announced and everyone groaned.

Jack realised that it was Bill who had kidnapped him at the bar, as he came back with everyone's drinks. He sat down on the other side of Angela, who told him, "Jack is here to lose weight and get fit too."

"Ah! Fell foul of the old medical eh? Never mind, I reckon we can have a good time while we're here. Isn't that right, old girl?" and he patted Angela's thigh.

"You two know each other already then?" Jack asked.

"Only through work," Angela was quick to reply.

"She does my typing for me," Bill explained, "and a bloody good job she does too."

"He has to say that," Angela confided to Jack, "I'm the only one who can read his scruffy handwriting."

"Why don't you dictate everything straight onto computer, like the rest of us?" Jack was amazed.

"Can't be bothered, old boy. I'm just old-fashioned I suppose. Old Bernie has tried to bring me up to date over the years but I've resisted, and he needs me more than I need him."

"How come you haven't managed to find a way out of this lot then?" Jack challenged him, as he indicated the rest of the group.

"Ah! I have my reasons," and Bill took a swig of his beer and just smiled.

Don't we all, thought Jack wryly. *Don't we all*!

CHAPTER 6

*H*ilary slept late on Saturday morning and when she did wake, she luxuriated in turning over and snuggling down again. She could hear the kids' voices, not far away, chattering on, and she felt cosy and relaxed. It was very rare for her to have a Saturday lie-in, with absolutely nothing she *had* to do. *It's a pity Jack's not here*, she thought, *we could have just had a cuddle and a chat like we used to do.* She remembered what it was like when they were both students; Jack at the catering college and her at teachers' training. They were young, innocent (although they didn't think so at the time!) and carefree. They used to share her single bed and sleep together like two spoons, hardly moving all night except to make passionate love, because it *was* passionate back then. One Sunday, she remembered, they didn't move from her bed all day, except to make tea and toast and visit the loo. Then they got dressed about 5 o'clock and went out, meeting their friends later in the pub.

They were teased mercilessly and told that it was surprising they could still walk. They hadn't cared though; they were too much in love.

Hilary sighed; she seemed to be doing that a lot lately. Jack had been so slim and handsome then, he'd had so much energy. Nowadays, he always seemed to be too tired or too busy to indulge in sex for very long. Sometimes she wished she could turn the clock back.

Time for a cup of tea! She pulled on her fleecy, full-length dressing gown and felt for her slippers. It was certainly cold.

She looked out of the window – just a sprinkling of snow. *I hope Jack got up there all right*, she thought, but she had very few doubts about his abilities as a driver. Funny how she missed him now she had a bit of time to think! Marriage was a funny institution – your partner got on your nerves so much sometimes that all you wanted to do was to get away from them, and yet the minute you were apart – you missed them!

This train of thought brought her back to Dai Evans. She'd been thinking about him a lot recently. Then she had an idea and she shuffled off downstairs to make tea and toast.

Later on that day, Hilary was feeling more relaxed than she had in ages. She had prepared a meal for everyone and it was simmering away in the oven; she had spent time with her children, fun time, which was rare for her these days. They'd been out for a walk round the village and come back all rosy-cheeked and then made popcorn. They'd talked about plans for Christmas and what to get for Jack, Alec and Charlie. They had all suddenly realised that there was only just over a month to go and the kids had started to get quite excited.

Now Hilary was sitting with her feet up, hugging a mug of coffee in her hands and listening to some of her favourite music. This was sheer bliss! She'd even had time to have a bath, wash her hair and wax her legs. A rare treat indeed – she really must take more Saturdays off. Just then the phone rang – it was Karen.

"I just wanted to check the time and see if you want me to bring anything," she said.

"Sevenish and no," Hilary replied, "I thought we'd all eat together, you know how the kids love your company."

"I expected that anyway. I enjoy theirs and we're bringing booze!"

"OK. Oh and er, Dai's coming."

"Wow, that's a coup," Karen exclaimed, "Are you sure he'll come?"

"Well he said he would but you never know. I just thought it must be lonely for him on his own all the time, so ..." she finished lamely.

"Oh I think it's a great idea. See you later then!"

Hilary looked thoughtfully at the phone. What did Karen really think? she wondered. Ah well it was done now, and she went back to her music.

As it turned out, Dai and Karen and Geoff arrived at the same time and everyone piled in, chatting away. Simon and Anna knew all three really well and were always spoiled rotten. They had discovered, long ago, that off-duty teachers could be great fun; almost as if they had to prove they were human!

Everybody devoured the chicken casserole with great relish and Dai even had second helpings of the fruit crumble and custard – a rare treat, he said. Hilary felt a warm glow of satisfaction, it wasn't often she was complimented on her cooking, mostly because she rarely did any, she acknowledged. Maybe she was turning into a Charlie in her old age; God forbid! And she reached for her wine glass.

Karen and Geoff offered to clear up and Simon and Anna said they'd help. Hilary raised her eyebrows. "I can't believe you two! Whenever Dad and I ask for your help, you've always got a million things to do!"

"Yeah but you and Dad aren't as much fun as Karen and Geoff," Simon told her, "Geoff walks like a gorilla with a mugs in one hand and scratches." At this point Geoff grabbed hold of him from behind and clapped a hand over his mouth; frog-marching him into the utility room, he shouted, "That's it! Open the dishwasher – he's going in, for giving away state secrets."

Screams and shouts, followed by howls of laughter emanated from the utility room.

"Just take care with that leg of yours and don't go mad," Hilary shouted to Anna.

"OK, Mum."

Hilary and Dai escaped into the lounge, closing the door on the ensuing chaos.

They collapsed into companionable silence, sipping their wine.

"Where did you say Jack had gone this weekend?"

"To a health and fitness seminar up at Holme Farm. He's been told he's got to lose a stone and get fitter!"

Dai sipped his wine and smiled, "I can't imagine Jack enjoying that."

"No, neither can I." Hilary jumped, as high-pitched shrieks came from the kitchen, "especially as it's so cold," she went on and she giggled. "Do you remember that time he came with us on the camping weekend in the Dales and he sprained his ankle half way up Jacob's Ladder?"

"Oh yeah," Dai smiled with recognition, "and one of the governors – what was his name? His son's name is Stuart."

"Councillor Payne," Hilary reminded him.

"Yeah, Councillor Payne, he had to help him all the way down the other side and back to the campsite, they were both knackered!"

"Yeah and then we had to wait on him hand and foot for the rest of the weekend." They both laughed.

The four hooligans invaded their memories at this point and they all played quiz games until it was time for Anna and Simon to go to bed.

Dai decided it was his turn on duty and he'd tell them just *one* creepy story.

Hilary made coffee for everyone and came back in to find Karen and Geoff snuggled up on the settee. They sat up guiltily. "Don't mind me, lovebirds." Hilary smiled.

"It's been a great night, Hils, thanks for inviting us."

"I've enjoyed it! Very relaxed."

"How does he seem to you?" Karen jerked her head in the direction of the ceiling.

"He seems fine, but we haven't talked about – you know who."

"If it was me, I wouldn't want to talk about – you know who," Geoff retorted, as he took his coffee, "the poor bloke probably just wants to relax and forget about it!"

"Yeah but men never want to talk about things, they just bottle everything up – come to that, some women do too!" Karen looked meaningfully at Hilary, who protested,

"I don't bottle things up!"

"Oh yeah!"

"Come on, you two!" Geoff put his hands up. "Time out. Let's watch a DVD !"

The rest of the evening passed in the same easy-going manner and when she got to bed, relaxed, after a few more glasses of wine, Hilary slept like a log.

The alarm went off at 7.30a.m. and Jack surfaced from a very deep sleep.

It took a few moments to remember where he was and when he did, he got that sinking feeling in the pit of his stomach that you get when the day promises something unpleasant. He stumbled out of bed, because it was always better to be active on these occasions. He looked at his face in the mirror above the basin and stuck out his tongue – that nightcap had turned into a few more but he didn't feel too bad and the gang had been good company; particularly Danny, who was a good joke-teller, he'd had them all in stitches.

Once he was dressed, the next job was to check his equipment. He went down to the car and checked the boot. Yes, those bags Hilary had left in the hall contained his walking boots, some thick socks and his parka. Good old Hils! He smiled to himself; she probably wanted to make sure he didn't miss the torture!

He decided to have the full cooked breakfast; he'd need the energy. So he sat down to bacon, egg, sausage, tomato, fried bread and hash browns followed by toast and marmalade and two mugs of tea.

Hence it was a little after 9a.m. when he pushed his breathless way into one of the offices at Holme Farm.

The others were all ensconced and listening to Debbie, the dietician. She was perched up on the desk, looking all bright-eyed and bushy tailed, which is more than could be said for some of the others.

Jack made for the only vacant chair, which unfortunately, was right at the front.

"Ah, good morning, Jack, good to see you! We were just discussing Brassicas and how good they are for you!"

Jack's head shot up in surprise and Angela and Carla burst out laughing. Only Ken managed to keep a straight face.

Jack picked up his printed diet sheet and pretended to study it. He sneaked a look at Debbie, who had gone very pink and was trying to carry on talking and ignore the heaving shoulders and streaming eyes of Angela and Carla. He felt sorry for Debbie and so he tried to take his mind off things by reading his diet sheet. It didn't tell him anything he didn't know, he hadn't lived with Hilary all these years without learning about a healthy diet; but it didn't mean he had to like it.

The session ended and the group made their way to the gym.

"I'm not looking forward to this," Jack muttered. He was really talking to himself but Bill heard him.

"No, neither am I, the awful truth is about to be told!"

In actual fact, it wasn't as bad as they'd all thought. They were all given assessments, consisting of readings for stamina, endurance, flexibility and muscle strength. They were given their printouts to study in more detail later; then John showed them around the gym, demonstrating how the machines could be programmed for their individual needs. He used Angela to demonstrate, punching in her details on the main console.

As she moved around the gym, each machine spoke her name and described how to use the piece of equipment. It amused Jack that when Angela was on the rowing machine, the female voice said, "Please lean all the way back, Angela, you are not utilising the routine to its fullest extent." Angela put her tongue out and pulled a face, as she attempted to put more energy into her rowing and he could have sworn he heard her mutter "cow" under her breath. She finished her round, puffing and panting and sweating profusely, but at least she got her chance to rest as the others took their turn.

Ken didn't even appear to be sweating; far from being the wimp that Jack had predicted, he turned out to be as fit or even fitter than John.

Over lunch, there was much discussion about the fitness assessments.

"How about Ken then?" Carla whispered. "He's as fit as a fiddle, isn't he?"

"Yeah, he's a dark horse alright," Angela was saying as Jack joined them at their table,

"Who's a dark horse?" Jack asked.

"Ken; he's as fit as John, I heard him telling him. Why has he come?" Carla was just asking as Ken came over so they changed the subject.

"Poor Danny's got a lot of work to do," Angela said.

"Yeah but he's the sort who'll cope, one way or another," Jack mumbled through a mouthful of salad.

"He'll have to take it easy though," Ken joined in, "because he'll overdo it if he's not careful."

"What about you then, Jack?" Angela asked, "It sounded to me as if you weren't as unfit as you thought."

"Oh, I don't know! My stamina and endurance leave a lot to be desired but apparently my muscle strength is quite good. John reckons I could do alright if I do some aerobics or cycling, which I think I could manage!" Jack was secretly very pleased with his assessment and it had inspired him to make an effort when he got back home.

"Well mine was awful," Carla moaned, "I'm weak in all areas! Still, John seems to think he can help me."

"I'll carry you round if you like." Danny had joined them, carrying a tray laden with food. He was grinning broadly as he put it down. "I bet you're lighter than this tray!"

"Ah go on with you. That won't help me, will it – you carrying me," Carla scolded him, but she was smiling.

"No, but it will help me." Danny grinned at her.

They all laughed. "Bill and Jean haven't said much about their assessments have they?" Ken remarked. They all looked over to the table where the older couple were sitting, deep in conversation. "I don't think they're particularly interested," Angela replied.

After lunch, they all piled on the minibus and made the relatively short journey to the drop-off point. They were all kitted out in walking gear, except Danny, who seemed to think that walking in trainers and wearing a big baggy jumper and jeans was perfectly adequate. He had also brought 'supplies' from a local shop to 'keep him going'.

By the time they set off, the sun was shining out of a blue sky and the snow had melted, except for a few pockets here and there in shady dips and hedgerows. John led them along country lanes to begin with and then over a stile and across a couple of fields before they came out of a wooded area and started to climb gently up an escarpment.

Jack seemed to have been adopted by Carla and Angela, who flanked him, rather like bodyguards, talking across him most of the time. He didn't mind; he enjoyed their cheerful chatter. They were still giggling about the dietician's session and how 'Brassicas 'were good for you, both of them hitching up their boobs to demonstrate. Jack couldn't help noticing that Angela had a lot more to hitch up than Carla!

"You're cruel, you two," he scolded them, "Poor Debbie."

"Poor Debbie my foot! You fancied her that's all," Carla teased him.

"No, I didn't," Jack lied, "and I love broccoli, it's good for you."

"Oh, that's what she was talking about!" Angela said and the giggling started again.

Ken was walking out in front with John and Danny bringing up the rear, sweating profusely by the time they started to climb. That left Bill and Jean in front of Jack and his bodyguard. They seemed oblivious of everyone else, heads close together, talking seriously. Then they would stop now and then to look at the view.

Jack thought the scenery was beautiful and he was wondering if he and his family lived up here, would they love it? He thought they would, and he could imagine them all coming for walks together. As if she could read his mind, Angela said, "Have you got children, Jack?"

"Yes, two, Simon's eleven and Anna is nine."

"Quite a handful then! But then I suppose if your wife is a teacher, she can handle them alright!"

"Yes she can, but sometimes she expects too much of them I think. They're great kids," Jack said with pride. "Have you got a family?" he asked.

"No children, but I've got a husband, when he's at home!"

"Oh, does he travel then?"

"Yes. He's a civil engineer. He's working on a project in China at the moment."

"Doesn't that get lonely for you?"

"Yes, it does, very lonely. You can see my house down there actually." Angela pointed and Jack could see a small hamlet, nestling in a dip in the coastal plain between the escarpment and the sea.

Carla came back to them. "Danny's knackered," she announced bluntly. The others stopped and looked back to where Danny was sitting on a rock, panting.

Angela called out, "John. I think we need a rest. Danny is tired." John stopped immediately and walked back to talk to Danny. The others all gathered together and looked out at the view.

"I never knew it was so close to the sea here. It's beautiful," Jack observed.

"Not the most inspiring coastline in the world." Jean screwed up her face. "It's very muddy!"

"Yes, but that means we get a bit of peace and quiet, 'cos all the tourists pass us by and go on up to the Lakes!" Bill said triumphantly.

John re-joined them. "He's OK now but we'll keep an eye on him." He looked back to where Danny was tucking into a pasty which he was holding, wrapped in a brown paper bag.

"God, Danny. That's no good for you. When are you going to start taking this seriously?" Jean snapped impatiently. Danny just smiled and carried on munching. So Jean turned away and marched off after Bill, shaking her head.

Jack's trio joined up with Danny. "Don't you worry, Danny boy," Carla said, linking her arm through his, "We'll look after you!"

"Thanks," Danny spluttered, spraying pasty crumbs everywhere as they walked on.

"What are you planning to do tonight?" Angela asked Jack. He thought a moment before answering and then he said, "I was going to that Italian place in Underbarrow." Angela looked round, Carla and Danny had fallen behind. "Not a 'special table' by any chance?" she said, giving him a sideways look. Jack's head jerked round. "Yes, do you know it?"

"I know all about it! I'm local, don't forget!"

Jack smiled. "Of course. Well, I'll let you into a secret. I fell for the luscious Louisa and I had fancied my chances," he shrugged, "but then I found out last night that she was married."

Angela laughed out loud, "God. You and how many others! She certainly brings the customers in!"

Jack looked sheepish. "I know. Bloody stupid! Still, that's where I'm going. How about you?"

"I'm going there too, with Carla. She's never been and I thought it would do her good. Put a little flesh on her bones! You can join us if you like?"

"Thanks, I'd like to." Jack felt quite relaxed in Angela's company and he had no objection to spending a night with 'the girls' as he had christened them in his mind. Now he wasn't intending to pursue Louisa anymore, it would be good to have some company. Just then Carla shouted, "Hey. Danny's not well!"

They all stopped and John ran back to where Danny was bent forward, hands on his knees, looking distressed. Everyone gathered round and John shouted, "Please give him some air, he's having an asthma attack. Danny, where's your inhaler?"

"Can't find it." Danny spoke with great difficulty.

Jack felt that panicky feeling again. He knew that an asthma attack, without the proper medication, could be extremely dangerous. John was on his mobile phone, calmly issuing instructions and Ken had grabbed the brown paper bag from Danny's hand and was emptying the pasty crumbs into the wind. He guided Danny to a rock and sat him down, talking quietly and calmly all the time.

"You'll be fine, Danny. You're panicking, that's all – it's not a bad attack. Now breathe slowly and deeply – into this bag – come on, now, John's getting help. You'll be fine, s-l-o-w-l-y, that's it."

Danny did as he was told and, as the others watched, he seemed to visibly relax, he was still wheezing but his breathing had slowed. John came over and took Ken to one side. "They're sending an ambulance, but the nearest place it can get to is that lane down there." He pointed.

"Could you get down and show them the quickest way back up, do you think, Ken?"

"No problem," Ken nodded and he was already on his way.

Carla was squatting down next to Danny, and John walked over to them, leaving the other four to their own devices.

"He should never have come!" Jean announced, "He's just not up to it!"

"Well John had everyone's medical records, so he must have been aware of the asthma," Angela told her.

"Well I can't understand it." Jean shook her head.

"He could die up here! It's just not right!" She stuck her hands in her pockets and marched up and down. Bill and Jack were both quiet, each with their own thoughts. They watched Ken as he made his way down the edge of the escarpment, nimbly hopping from rock to rock like a mountain goat. Jack felt totally inadequate and realised this was the second time recently that he hadn't known what to do in a medical emergency.

They all watched the ambulance arrive and the medics jump out, carrying equipment. Ken reached them and took some things and then they started back up again. Jack couldn't believe how quickly they made progress. He turned round to look at Danny and he certainly seemed calmer. Carla was holding his hand and John was talking to him quietly just like Ken had done.

When the medics arrived, they gave Danny an injection and an oxygen mask and everyone waited to see if he needed to be stretchered down. Jack was secretly hoping he would and then he could make himself useful and show his superior muscular strength. As it was, Danny was able to make it with help, without the stretcher, and they all made slow progress back down the route that Ken had taken. Jack noticed, to his disgust, that he didn't even seem to be breathing heavily.

Once Danny was in the ambulance and on his way to Lancaster to be checked over, the others all breathed a sigh of relief. Nobody felt like going to the swimming pool, so John suggested that they all make their way back to the minibus and get back to the centre.

Everyone felt subdued.

"Will he be alright?" Jack asked John, as they were driving back.

"Yes. He'll be fine. I'm sure. He was already starting to recover and the hospital check will just be a formality. Carla's gone with him to hold his hand and I'm sure he'll be back with us tomorrow."

Jean wasn't convinced. "How could he be allowed to come on something like this; he obviously wasn't fit enough for it!"

John kept his eyes on the road but he answered her very patiently. "He was capable of it, Jean. He's asthmatic, but he has medication and if his inhaler hadn't fallen through a hole in his trouser pocket – then he would have just had a squirt and carried on. As it was, he panicked because he couldn't find it and he hyperventilated; that's why Ken used the brown paper bag so successfully."

Jean still didn't look happy but she didn't say anything, just turned and looked out of the window.

It wasn't until they got off the bus and were walking towards their cars that Jack and Angela thought about their plans for that night. They both started speaking together.

"What about the—" they both laughed.

"Carla's gone with Danny," Angela said quickly, "so I don't know." She hesitated. "I tell you what – we'll meet you at the foodie bar – what time are you booked for?"

Jack looked puzzled. "I can't remember," he told her, "I wasn't thinking very clearly at the time."

Angela laughed, "Typical! Louisa seems to have that effect on men! Well, we're booked for 8 o'clock so we'll see you there then, OK?"

"OK, see you later," Jack called out as he got into his car. *Ah well,* he thought, *I'm not going out with the luscious Louisa, but I'm going out with two women instead – can't be bad!* And he wondered what would be on the menu tonight.

CHAPTER 7

*A*ngela was nervous as she scurried about the house, getting ready. She'd spent a lot of time preparing herself – washing her hair, exfoliating, bathing in scented oils and rubbing in loads of moisturiser – to such an extent, that, as she walked around in her robe, all her body parts were sliding against one another provocatively, giving her some very pleasant sensations!

She wasn't quite sure *why* she was taking so much trouble, as she picked out her best black, lacy underwear; she wasn't sure why she was doing that either – she just was!

Carla had phoned earlier, to say that Danny had been checked out at the hospital, given two new inhalers, and discharged, so she'd invited him back to her place for a meal.

This meant that Angela knew that she would be going out with Jack on her own; something he didn't know yet.

She liked Jack very much, even though she'd only just met him. She'd known of him for much longer, typing up memos and reports for him and sending messages via email, just as she did for all employees, but now she could put a face to the name and she liked what she saw.

He was good company, easy-going and relaxing to be with, and she fancied him. There was something about his brown eyes and the way they twinkled when he looked at her. His lashes were very long and she'd always had a weakness for that. Also he smiled a lot. Pete didn't smile much at all – he always seemed to look serious and he talked very little, always putting the onus on her to make conversation. She'd lost count of the number of times she'd felt more bored in his company than on her own. Jack, on the other hand was a good talker and good fun. He was also married, a voice reminded her. Oh dear! This was ridiculous. She sat down on the bed and looked around her. How many nights had she slept here alone? How many times had she tossed and turned, wondering if Pete was faithful to her? She really didn't know, but she knew she was terribly lonely and life was not a dress rehearsal, besides, she wasn't going to sleep with Jack – she was going out to have some fun and there was nothing wrong with that.

She stood up and started looking for something to wear.

The perennial question. *Well, come on, Angie girl – use some logic! It can't be white because you're wearing black underwear and it can't be too flimsy because it's bloomin' freezing outside!*

In the end she settled on black trousers and a low-cut velveteen top, which was slimming and seductive as it showed off her cleavage. She added dangly earrings and then went to town on her face and hair. She did a final twirl in front of the mirror; definitely on the plump side, but she'd made the best of herself – you never know, he might go for voluptuous women, Louisa certainly wasn't a bean-pole! By the time she got into her car, she was already ten minutes late.

Jack sat at the table in the foodie bar, sipping his beer and surveying the menu. God! What a decision! Should he have game pie or stew and dumplings? Followed by sherry trifle or sticky toffee pudding? His mouth was watering; he looked at his watch. *Come on, girls, I'm starving!*

He looked up and watched Louisa strutting around the room in a short, red dress, which seemed to cross over at the front and push her boobs up. It also had the effect of pulling the back tight across her bottom, which wobbled as she walked. Ah well, at least he could dream – he sighed and then he spotted Angela hurrying across the room towards him, looking flushed and quite flustered, he thought, which gave him a strange sensation. He wasn't used to flustered women, Hilary remained cool at all times; he suddenly realised that he liked it; it made him feel protective.

"I'm sorry, I'm late, Jack – Carla didn't phone until just before I left," she panted as she sat down.

"That's alright, don't worry," he smiled at her. "Is she coming?"

"No, she's invited Danny over for the evening."

"Aha! He's obviously recovered then!"

Angela giggled, "It seems like it. Have you ordered?"

"No, I've waited for you – here's the menu – I can't decide between game pie and stew and dumplings!"

Angela slipped her arms out of her jacket and studied the menu.

Jack noted that she was looking very bright-eyed and had obviously taken great care with her hair and make-up. He liked the way her shiny, black hair fell over her face when she looked down and she hooked it back behind her ears. Her fingers were long and delicate and she was wearing nail varnish; *she looks so feminine*, Jack thought. He couldn't help noticing how her boobs seemed to be straining against the fabric of her top, almost as if they were fighting for freedom! He'd like to free them, he thought. He managed to drag his eyes away and up to her face just in time as she looked up.

"I'm going to have the steak and kidney and then, the sticky toffee," she announced.

"Good choice. What would you like to drink?"

"White wine please."

"Shall we get a bottle?"

"Oh, I don't know, do you drink white?"

"No, red. I'll tell you what, I'll order a carafe of each." Jack surprised himself; he wasn't usually so decisive.

They chatted on until the meal came and then they were silent as they tucked in. Jack was pleased that the food was just as good as the last time and he took great pleasure in watching Angela eating. They tasted each other's food, exchanging forkfuls across the table, which Jack found extremely erotic, especially as Angela had to lean forward to meet his fork, enabling him to look down her cleavage.

Once they'd finished eating, they settled down to just enjoying each other's company.

"This really isn't what we should be doing on a health and fitness weekend!" Angela giggled.

"No, I suppose not," moaned Jack, "But what the hell, it's bloody good fun anyway! Tell me about the others in the group, you all seem to be locals, and you know them fairly well."

"Danny isn't local, he's from Carlisle. But yes, the rest of us are."

"Did Danny and Carla know each other before this weekend then?"

"Only for a short time. Danny's just joined the company, he's a driver, and Carla works in the packing and distribution department, so they've met a few times. Carla has been after him for a while, that's really why she wanted to come on this weekend."

"What about Bill and Jean, that seems an odd combination!"

"Yes, well they're just old friends, they've known each other for years. Jean is divorced and Bill's wife is terminally ill so I suppose they would support one another, but I think that's all there is to it. Bill is devoted to his wife, but I expect he just needs a break occasionally."

"What about Ken then? He's a dark horse. I had him down for a wimp, but he's far from it. He's as fit as a fiddle, I can't see why he needs to come on this weekend at all."

Angela smiled. "Ah well. I know Ken and I know his wife, she's a high-flying accountant, hardly ever at home! They've got a baby daughter and Ken spends a lot of time looking after her. I suspect that he just wanted a bit of time to himself!"

"Seems to me that the majority of people on this weekend had an ulterior motive for coming," Jack pronounced, taking a slug of red wine.

"Quite, Mr Baker," Angela said with mock severity, looking pointedly in Louisa's direction.

Jack had the grace to look sheepish.

"Yes. Well. And what about you – Mrs Carter?" He looked at her sternly. "What about your motive then?"

She smiled mysteriously, "You'll never know. I'm far too devious."

"You must get lonely with your husband being away so much," Jack probed.

"Yes. It's very lonely," she said, turning serious, "he's away for months at a time. The money's good but that isn't everything. We've been married three years and I've hardly seen him."

"Can't you go with him?"

"Some wives do, but I don't want to – I love my home, my job and my family – I have a mother and two married sisters who live nearby. My mum's a widow and she's getting on and depends on me quite a bit. Besides, Pete has never exactly forced the issue – I think he enjoys his freedom too much." She took a sip of her wine, lost in thought for a moment, Jack felt admiration for her. She was strong and yet vulnerable. She looked up and smiled. "What about you? I know you're a married man with two kids," she grinned mischievously, "who fantasises about sexy Italian women."

"Watch it!" warned Jack but he was smiling too.

"Are you happily married, Jack?" she asked suddenly, taking him by surprise. He shifted uncomfortably in his chair, took another drink, and looked at her.

"Yes and no. I was happy when we first got married, and in fact, until not very long ago, but lately, I've felt taken for granted. Hilary is very controlling, and sometimes I just get this urge to get away." He was surprised at his own honesty.

They ordered more wine and as the night went on, they discovered a love of cooking in common, several films they'd both loved, several books they'd both enjoyed reading and several artists whose music they both admired. By the time they stood up to leave, they were both bathed in that warm glow that comes from discovering a soul mate.

Jack stopped on the way out to go to the loo, and as she waited for him, Angela realised just how much she fancied him. She'd watched him as he walked to the Gents and she liked his tall, strong frame and easy walk. She liked the way his trousers were tight across his buttocks. He certainly wasn't a slim man, but he wasn't fat either, and although his waist didn't exactly go in, his shirt fitted well across his chest; she just found him attractive, she couldn't help it.

They walked hand in hand back to the market square and as they got nearer, Angela said, "Would you like to come back to my place for a nightcap?" Jack hesitated and looked down at her. She was looking at him tentatively, almost expecting him to say no, he realised.

"Yes. I'd love to." He said it softly and slowly, and surprised himself because he didn't want to hurt her, and it was a new sensation for him.

He followed her car along country lanes in a kind of trance, not really seeing where he was going.

She pulled into a gravel yard in front of a detached, stone house. It looked newly renovated; the front door was central to the house, with large, small-paned windows on either side.

Upstairs there were three similar windows; it was a very symmetrical house. Inside, everything smelt new and fresh, a mixture of paint, new carpets and plaster.

Angela showed him into the lounge, putting on lamps and music, and then she busied herself in the kitchen. Jack stood by the window which looked out onto a large back garden, lit by the moonlight. He could make out the outline of the hills in the distance. It was peaceful and new and strange, yet he felt at home.

"Sugar?" Angela called out from the kitchen.

"Yes, two please." There was a change between them, Jack thought, a formality that hadn't been there in the restaurant.

Angela brought in a tray with a cafetiere and mugs and cream. She'd kicked off her shoes somewhere and she looked smaller and more vulnerable somehow. He took off his jacket and sat down on the settee.

"Would you like a brandy?" Angela asked.

"Just a small one please – I shouldn't be driving as it is!" He frowned, thinking he would never have done this at home – he and Hilary were always scrupulous about taking it in turns, one to drink and one to drive. He shook his head to dispel the thought.

Angela sat down at the other end of the settee; one leg hooked under her, and sipped her coffee.

"Thanks for a lovely evening, Jack – I haven't enjoyed myself so much for ages."

"Neither have I. Can I fix *you* a brandy?"

She smiled apologetically. "Oh, Yes. I'm sorry. Bottle and glasses are in that pull-down unit over there," she pointed across the room.

He stood up and set about pouring brandies. The atmosphere was suddenly charged with something neither of them could control and as he handed her the glass, he bent to kiss her very gently on the mouth and that was it – that was the trigger! The next thing they knew, they were lying full-length on the settee, puffing, panting, kissing, nibbling, moaning and grappling with each other.

They giggled a lot, partly in embarrassment and partly because they had cold hands! Eventually, they decided, without saying a word, to find somewhere more comfortable. Angela led him by the hand up the stairs and into her bedroom, where they stripped off what was left of their clothes.

The sight of Angela's body delighted Jack. She was so voluptuous; curves everywhere, and flesh that wobbled – not in an unpleasant way, it just wobbled. He was used to Hilary who was taut all over, with small breasts and muscly arms and legs. He watched in fascination as she came towards him, her breasts bouncing gently as she walked. He couldn't wait to bury his face between them and he did so at the earliest opportunity, nibbling her nipples until the intensity became too much for her and she moaned and grabbed him by the ears. They made love passionately, as if they were starving and hadn't eaten for a week, and when it was over, they lay there, panting and sweating for some time, before they turned on their sides and looked each other in the eyes.

"WOW!" Jack breathed.

Angela giggled, "Yes, wow! Would you like your brandy now – only for some reason, you abandoned it downstairs."

"That seems like a good idea," he told her as he stretched out like a cat.

She hopped out of bed and grabbed her robe, toddling off downstairs. Jack put his arms under his head and grinned – he felt, quite literally like a new man!

Angela came back with their brandies and sat cross-legged on the bed. She waited until he had propped himself up on his elbow and then she handed him his glass.

"Next decision! Are you going back to the Fellside or staying here?" She looked quizzically at him.

He looked away. "I should go back, I'll need my stuff for tomorrow – it will look really strange if I turn up in my suit and tie for aerobics won't it?"

"Yes I suppose so."

He reached out and tilted her chin up so she had to look at him. "I'm sorry, Angela."

"Why are you sorry?" Her eyes flashed and she jumped off the bed. "What is there to be sorry about? We're both consenting adults."

"I'm sorry to have put you – put us – in this position – that's all."

"Well *I'm* not sorry," she said defiantly, and then she looked at him and smirked, "And I definitely liked a couple of the positions we were in."

"You're cheeky," he laughed and grabbed for her robe, pulling her towards him and managing to pull the robe off at the same time.

This time, he took time to give her pleasure, revelling in the soft plumpness of her flesh and of her appreciative moans at his efforts; they both climaxed together, in traditional missionary position, looking into each other's eyes, and lay in each other's arms for a long time.

Finally Jack said gently, "I suppose I'd better go." She looked up and stroked his face and he was filled with so many different emotions at once that he felt quite lost. He kissed her gently and got out of bed and by the time he'd finished in the bathroom and got dressed, Angela was back downstairs, dressed in a big, baggy t-shirt and shorts. She was busying herself in the kitchen and he stood in the doorway, looking at her.

"I'd better be off then," he said awkwardly.

"OK, take it easy won't you, although you never did drink your brandy," she smiled at him.

"I'll see you in the morning."

"Yes, bright and early for aerobics," she said brightly, lifting her knees and flinging out her arms, so they both laughed. He walked over and kissed her on the cheek.

"I won't see you out, Jack, but I *will* see you in the morning," she told him gently.

He didn't say any more, just turned around and let himself out of the front door.

As he drove back to the Fellside, Jack felt that one way or another, he'd never be the same again – he'd stepped into another world somehow, rather like *Alice Through the Looking Glass*, and he wasn't sure he'd ever be able to get back again.

Angela woke up feeling deeply depressed on the Sunday morning. She lay, curled up in bed, thinking, *why did I have to fall for a married man? – if it comes to that – why am I married?*

She'd been over this so many times before. It wasn't working, her marriage, they spent most of their lives apart and she really wondered if they loved each other anymore or even, for that matter, if they ever had!

They'd met when Pete was working locally on a road project. It had been a whirlwind romance really, but once they'd settled down to everyday life, Angela had discovered that was just what Pete couldn't tolerate – everyday life! He'd been living the ex-pat life too long and he was used to exotic locations and variety, whereas she had no desire to travel. Pete wasn't prepared to change his lifestyle and neither was she – so stalemate.

Stalemate, she thought it ironic, because that's just how she felt – her life was stale, her relationship was stale, she was stale. Now she'd met someone who made her feel good about herself and he was married. What was worse, she'd committed adultery! It had all seemed so right last night and she had certainly enjoyed it, but it was wrong, it was disloyal, and disloyalty was not something that Angela approved of. She sighed and sat on the edge of the bed – now what? She had to spend the rest of the day in his company – how should she handle it? How would he handle it?

She put her head in her hands and muttered out loud, "What a mess!"

Jack too woke up feeling depressed. He'd had a one-night stand, he told himself, people did it all the time! It was no big deal, you just put it behind you and carried on.

In reality though, he knew this wasn't like that – not that he'd ever had one before anyway – but this was different, he couldn't get Angela out of his mind. He hadn't made love to anyone else but Hilary since he'd been married and he was really sorry to admit it to himself, but he'd enjoyed it. A lot!

Angela was a good lover and in many ways she'd awakened him to aspects of his love life which were sadly lacking. He got dressed with a heavy heart because he didn't like the way his thoughts were going.

Later at Holme Farm, the whole group including Danny entered their aerobics session with a certain amount of trepidation, but John led them into it gently and gave many warnings about stopping if it got too much. In the event, they all enjoyed it – the music was good and the activity did wonders for their morale.

Everyone went for coffee, but it was very crowded in the dining room, as all the other groups were gathering at the same time. Jack got separated from the others and was just getting up to go to yoga, when he spotted Angela over the other side. He hurried over and tapped her on the shoulder.

"Hello."

"Oh hi, Jack," she said it with a kind of false casualness.

"How are you this morning?" He smiled at her.

She looked away from him and then said, more seriously, "I'm alright. How are you?"

"Fine," he answered her, "What are you doing now?"

"Badminton."

"I'm doing yoga," he grimaced, "I think we can go the same way."

They walked along together and when they got to a quieter part of the building, they both stopped for a while and leant against the wall.

"What happens now?" Jack asked.

"I don't know, Jack. What do you want to happen?"

"I don't know either," he said miserably, "but I want to see you again, "he blurted out.

Angela thought for a moment. "Are you coming up for the December meeting?"

Jack's face brightened. "Yes, I am."

"Well, let's leave it until then and see how we feel, shall we?"

"That's a good idea," he said with relief. "Have a good day, I'll see you before I leave," and he rushed off quickly, not seeing the look she gave him as he walked away.

He got through the yoga and disco-dancing somehow and didn't see her at lunch, but he knew they'd meet up again for the evaluation, so he steeled himself for that.

Everyone gathered in the hall at the end of the day to listen to John's closing comments, and then they were split into their small groups to be given their targets and contact numbers for the next month. John was making sure they had all the back-up they needed to achieve their goals – he was only too aware that Christmas was coming.

Jack made his way to the back of the hall where he could see his group. There was no sign of Angela. He took Carla aside and said, "Have you seen Angela?"

Carla gave him an old-fashioned look. "Yes. I've seen her."

"Where is she?" He didn't feel like making small talk.

"She's gone home, she's got a headache!"

"Oh."

That was all he could think of to say. He didn't know how much Carla knew and he didn't want to discuss anything with her in any case. He turned away and half-listened to John whittling on about encouragement and achievement, and as soon as possible he grabbed his papers and ran out to his car. He looked at his watch, 4.45p.m. He had time to go and see her – but what would it achieve? They'd made their plan and he would stick to it! He got into his car and made for home, playing his music loud and driving as fast as he dared. That way he had to concentrate and he couldn't think about anything else. Thinking just confused him.

CHAPTER 8

*H*ilary felt distinctly harassed; it had been one of those days again. Two staff were absent, so she was covering lessons instead of getting on with marking or preparation. The gym was set up for rehearsals for the Christmas concert, so she'd had to take the Year 8 girls outside in the cold and drizzle, and they had moaned incessantly – thirteen-year-old girls could be so bolshie!

Now she had a lunchtime meeting with the Educational Welfare Officer about Sean Abbot. She shouldn't have been going to the meeting, it should have been his class teacher, but he was away, so Doris, in her wisdom, had given Hilary's name because she knew Hilary cared about him – he'd been in her class last year. She downed her coffee and made her way to the interview room with a heavy heart. Sean had been missing school on and off for the best part of three weeks now; Hilary knew why – it was because he was worried about his mother, she'd come back home again and Sean was frightened that his dad would beat her up again.

She opened the door of the poky little room and there was Sean, head down, studying the floor, while Carole Duncan, the EWO, was talking quietly to Mrs Abbot.

They all looked up as she walked in. "Sorry I'm late," she apologised as she sat down, and looking at Carole, who she'd known for a long time, "You know how it is."

"That's okay. Mrs Abbot and I were just chatting about a few things. Now we'll make a start," Carole announced in a business-like manner. "First of all, Sean, we've got to find out why you haven't been coming to school." She looked at Sean expectantly.

"Don't like it."

"Why don't you like it?"

"They're always getting at me!"

"Who is always getting at you, Sean?"

"Me mates and teachers and everybody," the boy muttered.

Carole looked at Hilary, and Mrs Abbot patted Sean's hand in sympathy.

"Well if you tell us what people are saying to you, Sean, then maybe we can help you."

Hilary sighed; she'd heard it all before, and it was partly true but not the whole truth by any means.

"They're always saying me mam's a slag," he looked up at his mother and then at Hilary, "things like that," he finished lamely.

"Teachers wouldn't say those things, Sean," Hilary was quick to assure him.

"No, they don't say that, but they're always nagging me."

Carole interrupted him, "How do they nag you, Sean?"

"They say, have you done your homework? Why haven't you got your P.E. kit? Where's your tie? – things like that." Sean was warming to his theme. He looked down at the floor again and fiddled with the frayed edge of his sleeve. The three women exchanged knowing glances and Carole said, "OK, Sean, you've told us why you haven't been coming to school, but if Mrs Baker talks to the teachers and asks them to give you a bit of space and if your class teacher talks to your mates, do you think you could start coming back to school?"

He looked at his mother and so did Hilary. She'd met her last year and she had deteriorated since then; she looked tired and defeated, dressed in tight jeans and a bomber jacket, with her blonde hair tied back in a ponytail. She had

91

made some effort for the appointment, putting on lipstick and eye-shadow, but it didn't disguise the lines etched round her eyes and mouth. Her nicotine-stained fingers played incessantly with the strap of her cheap plastic bag. Hilary felt both admiration and respect for this woman; she knew that life was a daily struggle for survival and she managed to just hang on somehow, for no other reason than that she loved her son. She looked at him now and smiled encouragement, as she nodded her head at him. He, in turn, looked back at Carole and said,

"S'pose so."

"Good. Well I'll come round to your house tomorrow and we'll talk about it – maybe we can get a system running where we can reward you for each full week you do?" She looked expectantly at Hilary and her heart sank. *Not again*, she thought, *we did all this last year and it came to nothing*!

Some teachers said, why should we reward that little so and so for doing something the law says he should do anyway, and others said, he was such a b-nuisance that they didn't want him in school anyway. So it had come to nothing! But she smiled, and said, "I'll talk to Mr Clarke, Sean, and we'll put something in place – pr'aps you can come and spend some time with me each week and help me with the Year 5s."

Sean gave her a knowing look – *he knows the score*, she thought, but he nodded and they all stood up.

"You'll be staying for the rest of the day then, Sean," Carole announced – it wasn't a question!

He looked at his mum and she whispered something in his ear – he nodded his head and walked reluctantly to the door. Hilary's heart went out to him. When he'd gone, Hilary and Carole exchanged glances. "I'm just going to talk to Mrs Abbot a while longer, Hilary, and then I'll come and have a chat," Carole said.

"Well, I'm outside all afternoon, it's Games with Year 7, so just come and find me," Hilary told her, knowing she wouldn't come.

"Oh, dear, and I've got a meeting after school, how about early tomorrow morning?"

"OK. I'll see you then." Hilary closed the door and made her way back to her classroom just as the bell rang. "No peace for the wicked," she muttered.

Jack was in the loft, rooting around for Christmas decorations, getting cold, dusty and bad-tempered.

God, what a lot of rubbish we've got, he thought, but he didn't dare say that to Hilary, or else she'd have him clearing it out! He passed boxes down through the gap to Simon, who was balancing on the ladder, pretending to be a trapeze artist. As Jack's head appeared, he swung round, one foot on the rung and one hand on the frame of the steps. "Stop messing about!" Jack snapped, "and take this."

Simon took the box and jumped down, nimbly, onto the landing – he and Anna had it open immediately and had started rooting about.

"Leave that alone and come and get this!" Jack shouted; he knew he was getting irritable, this should be a happy occasion. Hilary had taken a rare Saturday off and gone Christmas shopping, leaving strict instructions that the Christmas decorations should be brought down by the time she got back. She wanted to sort them out and see if anything wanted replacing before they started the Christmas decorating.

Jack loved Christmas. He knew he was still a kid at heart and he'd always enjoyed it; but since they'd had kids, it gave him even more pleasure – but he just wasn't in the mood today. Since he'd got back from the fitness weekend, he'd been very busy at work, fitting in a lot more calls, ready for the pre-Christmas food rush and Hilary had been busy at school and harassed. They hadn't had much time together at all, which suited him in one way, because he was still in a confused state.

He closed the loft and dusted the cobwebs off himself as he stood on the landing, surrounded by boxes. Simon and Anna

93

could be heard downstairs, arguing over some hand-made decorations from last year.

"I made that! It's mine," Anna was wailing.

"No you didn't, it's too good for you, you were only eight, you couldn't have made anything that good."

"Oh, yes I could, I'm not rubbish at art like you are, I'm very good at making things, Mummy said so."

At this point there was loud squealing and Simon belted up the stairs triumphantly waving a cardboard and cotton-wool snowman aloft. He cannoned into the last box, which Jack had brought down and placed at the top of the stairs, and went sprawling into the pile of boxes, scattering Christmas paraphernalia in all directions.

"THAT'S IT!" Jack roared. "Into your rooms, the pair of you, and don't come out until I tell you. You don't deserve Christmas!"

The two children looked at him with frightened eyes and gingerly stepped over tinsel, glass balls and scattered ornaments, quietly closing their bedroom doors.

Jack ran his fingers through his hair and set to, sorting out the debris.

By the time Hilary got home, laden with bags, the house was very quiet – Jack was dozing in front of the TV and her two errant children were still in solitary confinement.

She came in all bright-eyed. "I've got most of it done today – I can't believe it – you should see what I've got for Anna," she babbled, but then she stopped. "What's the matter?"

"Oh nothing, except those two hooligans scattered the contents of the loft all over the landing," he muttered.

"Oh, I see. I thought it was quiet!" and ever practical, she said, "Ah well, I'll hide all this lot while they're out of the way then," and she went out.

Jack felt miserable; why couldn't he just have let her have her moment of enjoyment? Why did he have to burst her bubble? He should apply for rat of the year award! He got up to go and make a cup of tea.

This was no good at all. Since he'd been back from the fitness weekend, all he'd felt was incredible guilt. Every time he looked at Hilary, every time he looked at the kids, he just felt like a criminal. He simply wasn't cut out for adultery. Monday was the monthly meeting – he would be seeing Angela again – it was also the pre-Christmas, company 'do' in the evening and he had to go. He hadn't heard from Angela since the fitness weekend and he hadn't made any contact, so he wasn't sure what kind of reception he would get. He might have made a complete idiot of himself and she might ignore him, or she might greet him with open arms. Whichever it was, he had to tell her he couldn't see her again because he couldn't go on living with this guilt.

Hilary wandered into the kitchen and started squirrelling Christmas goodies into various hiding places. Jack watched her; it was the same every year, she bought all these gorgeous things to eat, threatened the whole household with death, or worse, if they touched them – only to find, that at Christmas, everyone was too full to eat them, so they were wasted. He sighed and went back to the TV.

Angela stared at the pile of cards on the table; she spread them out and snow scenes, angels, holly, robins and Nativity scenes swam before her eyes. She was *not* in the mood! You had to be in the right mood to wish people merry Christmas, season's greetings, joyous celebrations – bullshit!

She stood up and went into the kitchen. She needed a drink. Having raided the bottle of white wine in the fridge, she walked back into the lounge and looked out of the window. It was pitch dark – Saturday night and nowhere to go. She drew the curtains and switched on the TV, at least it was company, of sorts. She knew she was just going through a phase, she felt lonely, abandoned and miserable – in fact, thoroughly sorry for herself. She wasn't looking forward to Monday night at all. She'd talked to Carla at length about Jack, and Carla had told her how shocked he'd been when she hadn't turned up for the evaluation.

"He hardly said a word, Angie, just went really white and then he rushed off! I was sure he'd come round to see you."

Angela's headache had been genuine and she couldn't face seeing Jack again, feeling as she did.

She hadn't heard from him since, but they'd agreed to wait until the meeting, he had said he wanted to see her again. She sighed and sipped her wine, staring into the fire. How was it going to feel on Monday night? What would he do? Ignore her or be friendly but coldly polite, or whisk her back here for a night of passionate love, she had no idea. She really didn't know how she was going to react either – all she knew was, she had to go!

The phone rang and she jumped, spilling wine in her lap. "Hello, Mum. What, tomorrow? Yes OK, if you want – no, I'm not doing anything, I'll take you."

Taking her mum to a Christmas Fair would at least take her mind off things.

Jack and Don were downing pints in the bar at the Fellside. Jack was listening with half an ear as Don was telling him all about the holiday he and Trish were planning to Vienna, just before Christmas.

"It's a really good deal, all inclusive, and you get a night at the opera thrown in."

"I didn't know you liked opera." Jack was surprised.

Don looked sheepish. "Well we don't as a rule, but you've got to do it, haven't you? I mean Trish has bought this bloody expensive long dress and everything."

Jack almost laughed out loud but he managed to choke into his beer instead.

"Well, are we off to the bash then?" Don drained his glass. "I s'pose so."

"You sound as enthusiastic as I am," Don told him, "They're always the same aren't they? A few drinks, a few gropes on the dance-floor – and then you step over the drunks on your way out." Don was not filled with enthusiasm. "Do you want to drive or shall I?" he asked.

"Um. I think we should go separately." Jack gulped.

Don gave him a hard stare – he was too bloody astute by far, Jack thought.

"What have you got in mind then, Jack me lad?"

"Nothing at all – but I'm not sure I'll stay that long, I might just press on home tonight. I've got a busy day tomorrow," he lied.

Don stood up and gathered up the glasses. "Whatever you want – no problem."

The room was hot, dark, noisy and crowded – just what you'd expect really. The dining room at Holme Farm had been transformed into a disco for the night. Subdued lighting, a disco and Christmas decorations disguised its usual corporate coldness. The tables had been pushed back to the sides, and the centre of the room was a heaving mass of gyrating bodies. Some were moving smoothly in time to the music but others were making spasmodic and jerky gestures like puppets out of control.

Jack walked to the bar, allowing his eyes to adjust to the light, he scanned the room for Angela, but he couldn't see her, so he stood back, sipped his pint, and observed his fellow workers at play. People were always hard to recognise in these circumstances; ordinary, everyday folk were transformed into 'night people', the men in jeans and casual shirts, or shirt-sleeves, with ties askew and sweat running down their faces. The women, made up to the nines, hair done, tottering on high heels and restricted in tight skirts – none of them looked the same!

Then he spotted her, draped over some bloke he didn't recognise, eyes closed, arms hanging down his back like a rag doll. It was her hair he recognised first, it was flopping over her face as her head lolled on the bloke's shoulder. *She's drunk!* he thought with some distaste. He felt disappointed and angry, followed very closely by a protectiveness, which surprised him – someone might take advantage of her. He made his way across the room, sidestepping dancers with difficulty, especially as he still held his pint. He put that down on a table and carried on – it did occur to him that the man might be her husband, so he approached with caution, but as he got closer he realised it was Ken. To his relief, Ken looked pleased to see him, and immediately began untangling Angela's arms from around his neck, supporting her with one arm, and moving towards Jack. "She's a little the worse for wear," he shouted over the music, "Started early, I'm afraid!"

Angela pivoted round and flung back her head, focusing with difficulty on Jack's face, then she grinned. "It's Jack!" she said in the same tone women use for babies and puppies – he expected her to say 'coochy coo' and tickle him under the chin at any moment!

"I thought you weren't coming," she pouted, and immediately launched herself in his direction, almost as if he was a lifeboat and she was on a sinking ship. He caught her with difficulty, the impact knocking him backwards a few feet, and when he'd regained his balance and managed to look around the curtain of her hair, Ken was nowhere to be seen.

They made slow, staggering progress towards an empty table and he managed to deposit her on a chair. She cupped her chin in her hands, elbows on the table and smirked at him. He sat down opposite and couldn't help himself from reaching over and taking a strand of hair away from his mouth.

"I'm here now," he said.

"Yes. I can see that." She was still smirking. "I've missed you."

"I've missed you too."

"I missed you so much, I got drunk!"

Now it was his turn to say, "I can see that." They both laughed.

"Take me home, Jack," she said, with longing in her voice.

"Is your car here?" This was not turning out at all as he'd expected.

"No – I got a taxi – I think – Yes, I got a taxi!" She nodded her head up and down and then stood up, holding on to the table; she put her chin up and looking very determined, she pointed to the door and said, "Home, Jack!" in a very forceful manner. It didn't seem he had any choice, because she headed for the door, at least, the top half of her body did, but her feet stayed planted very firmly on the floor. He only just caught her in time, and they staggered together towards the reception area.

"Did you have anything with you – coat – handbag?" he asked.

"Err – Yes – now where did I leave them? I know – the cloakroom." And she pointed to a door on the right, but didn't show any inclination to move.

"OK, in you go and find them then, I'll wait here." He said it very patiently and patted her on the bottom, pushing her in the right direction.

She managed to propel herself towards the door and disappeared inside. Jack wished he smoked because it seemed the right thing to do just then, so he walked over to a notice board instead and pretended to study it. Just then, he heard a voice he recognised. "Hello, old son – getting interested in the works football team, are we?" It was Don. Jack groaned inwardly and glanced nervously over his shoulder towards the cloakroom.

"Oh, you know – just passing the time," he said, as casually as he could.

"I thought you were off home at the earliest opportunity?"

"Yes, well, I'll be off in a minute." *And sooner than you bloody well think if you'll just piss off*, he thought.

If the power of thought could move people, Don White would have found himself out in the cold night air two miles away, but unfortunately, this was an art Jack had not yet perfected.

Right on cue, the cloakroom door swung open and Angela appeared, obviously having trouble, because her coat and handbag were hopelessly tangled and the cloakroom door had increased in weight by about two tons. She was in grave danger of being either strangled or crushed. Jack rushed over. "Can I help you?" he enquired with a certain formality, holding the door open so that she fell through, regaining her balance a few feet away.

"Yes. You certainly can, my man," she said in a mock aristocratic accent and then burst into a fit of the giggles. "Stop messing about, Jack, and take me home." She put her arm round his waist and nestled her head into his shoulder. Don's eyebrows went up – he grinned and then let out a low whistle. "Better do as the lady says, Jack – you don't want to keep her waiting!"

It was at moments like this that something inside Jack just said, what the hell, and he turned round and almost carried Angela to the door, not even looking back over his shoulder.

On the short journey back to her house, Angela fell into a deep sleep, head back, mouth open, snoring loudly. Jack felt irritated with her. How could he talk to her seriously when she was in this state? Then again, it was probably partly his fault – he should have contacted her, he should have arrived earlier, he should never have slept with her in the first place!

Once they got inside, Angela kicked off her shoes and with a slightly unsteady gait, made her way towards the kitchen "Do you want coffee?" she asked him.

"I'll make it," he said gently," You go and sit down."

She didn't need telling twice, and staggered off into the lounge.

When he brought the coffee in, she was propped against the cushions on the settee and she pulled herself up into a sitting position with difficulty. He put the coffee down beside her. "Here drink that – it will do you good."

She picked it up immediately and slopped some down the front of her dress. "Oh shit – this cost me a fortune." He took the cup from her and put it down, saying, "Angela, I've got something –" at which point she lunged towards him and kissed him, almost knocking his own coffee everywhere, until he had the presence of mind to put it down.

"You're such a nice person, Jack – I think I've fallen in love with you."

"If I was such a nice person, I'd have arrived earlier and then you wouldn't have got drunk."

"No, it wasn't your fault – I just couldn't bear the thought that you might not come."

This was getting harder and harder. He took her hand and looked at her, not knowing how to begin, but she snuggled up against him and closed her eyes. He rehearsed what he was going to say; 'I love my wife too much' – no, not a good idea, 'it was a mistake to sleep with you' – even worse. He looked down and realised that she had fallen into a deep sleep. So now what? He could just leave her and drive home, maybe phone her? No, that was a cowardly way out, so he gently extricated himself and stood up, thinking he had better find a duvet. Angela suddenly sat bolt upright and then ran; she just made the toilet in time before being violently sick.

"Ooh, Jack, I don't feel very well," she groaned as she came back and sat down again.

He'd fetched water from the kitchen. "I know, here, drink this." One sip was enough and she was off again.

About an hour later, Jack decided it was safe to leave her asleep on the settee and he went in search of a bed, finally crawling into a single one in a spare bedroom and falling into a deep sleep.

Angela woke up with a stiff neck and a sore head. She remembered snatches of the night before and groaned out loud – she needed the loo and she needed a drink of water. She stumbled about, feeling very sober and very stupid. Had Jack stayed? She peeped out of the window and saw his car with relief – at least she'd get a chance to apologise.

She tiptoed upstairs with two mugs of tea. Jack was asleep in the spare bedroom, and she looked at him lovingly and decided against waking him just yet. She showered and changed and cleaned her teeth three times before remaking the tea and going back upstairs. She woke him gently, he looked all tousled and sexy, with dark stubble beginning to form on his face, and her stomach turned over. She climbed in beside him and started kissing him.

"No, stop! Please!" He sat up quickly.

"What's the matter?"

"I wanted to tell you last night." He ran his fingers through his tousled hair. "Only it was rather difficult. You see, I find you so attractive, but ..." He got out of bed, dressed only in his boxer shorts, looking so vulnerable as he paced up and down.

"When I got home, after that weekend, I just felt so incredibly guilty, I'm just not cut out for being unfaithful, I'm afraid. Please don't think it's anything to do with you. I think you're wonderful, it's just me, that's all." He finished lamely and looked at her, as if waiting for the axe to fall.

She looked at him very carefully for what seemed like an eternity, and then said, "It's alright. I know how you feel. I feel just the same. We're just not the adulterous type, are we?"

"I'm sorry."

"Now that will annoy me, if you start saying that, I told you before, I'm not, I have no regrets at all." She got off the bed. "You'd better go and spruce yourself up a bit and I'll make us some breakfast. Bacon and eggs do you?"

He smiled. "That will do me fine." He walked over, kissed her on the cheek and made his way to the bathroom feeling as if the world had been taken from his shoulders.

Later on they sat in the kitchen together, eating bacon and eggs and drinking brewed coffee. The radio was on and there was a warm and cosy atmosphere in the room; they were enjoying each other's company, as they had all along.

This was the scene that Peter Carter walked in on when he returned home from an early-morning flight.

He opened the kitchen door to find a strange man sitting at *his* kitchen table, opposite *his* wife, and looking very much at home!

"Pete!" Angela shrieked, as he walked in. "What are you doing here?"

"I thought I'd surprise you," he said dryly and then looking at Jack, "and it looks as if I've succeeded."

"This isn't what it looks like," Angela said quickly.

"Really?" Peter was still looking at Jack.

Jack had stood up and now he was weighing up this other man. He was tall but slimly built, more wiry than muscly but he had a mean look about him – he had sandy coloured hair and wore glasses, which magnified a pair of cold blue eyes.

A million thoughts were going through Jack's mind in what must have been milliseconds – *is he going to hit me? – what a good job we're both dressed – doubly good job he didn't come half an hour ago. Concentrate – concentrate!*

"Please enlighten me!" Peter Carter was saying.

"Well, I got very drunk last night at the works do and Jack very kindly brought me home." Angela was babbling.

All Jack wanted to do was run away as fast as he could but he mustn't act guilty – *you've done nothing wrong*, he told himself, *listen to what she's saying.* They were both looking at him now,

"Yes," he said. "I'm afraid Angela was the worse for wear so I thought I'd better bring her home."

Angela was recovering her composure. "This is Jack Baker, he's one of our salesmen – Jack, this is my husband, Peter."

The two men looked at each other and Jack knew the situation was in the balance.

"I'm sorry," he said, as genuinely as he could, "I know what it looks like, but Angela was rather ill and, to be honest I didn't like to leave – she might have choked or something."

The other man obviously had enough doubt in his mind to stop him doing anything too drastic; instead he grunted and walked over to the kettle.

"I've got to be going anyway – I'll just get my jacket," and he made his escape upstairs, walking as slowly as he could make himself.

As he came downstairs, he could hear Angela saying, "I spent the night comatose on the settee – go and look if you don't believe me."

Husband and wife walked into the hall. "Thank you for taking care of Angela," Peter said in a slow, calculating sort of way.

"Oh, that's alright – no problem –thanks for breakfast." He said it all as casually as he could while Angela opened the front door for him. As he backed his car out of the drive, he looked back and saw her wave briefly, and shut the door.

His heart was beating like the clappers and his hands were clammy on the wheel. He hardly remembered getting back to the Fellside and checking out. As soon as he got to the first services, he stopped for a coffee and took several deep breaths.

God, you've really done it now, he told himself, *he'll probably file for divorce, and then Hilary will find out – there'll be hell to pay! How could you be so stupid!*

He had another coffee and reappraised his situation. No it was still bad, and what about Angela? Was he the sort of bloke to take it out on her? Would she be sporting a black eye when he saw her again? Saw her again! *Are you completely out of your mind, Jack Baker?*

Once back in the security of his car, he calmed down a little, and thought about the plusses – the double bed wasn't slept in, the duvet was on the settee, the single bed was slept in – there was a chance he'd believe her! *Would I believe Hilary? She wouldn't give me any choice!* That thought cheered him. Angela was strong – she'd be alright.

All the rest of the day, the horror of that moment in the kitchen kept coming back to haunt him – he could see it in every detail, and every time it did, he broke out in a cold sweat. That's just what he did over the next few days as well – sweated! He didn't want to contact Angela in case it made matters worse for her, but by Friday, he couldn't stand the suspense anymore, so he phoned her at the office.

"Mrs Carter is taking a few days annual leave," a young girl informed him, "Her husband's come back unexpectedly from abroad." *Tell me something I don't know*! Jack thought.

"Can I take a message?"

"No, it's not important, thank you." Jack pressed the off switch. Now he was going to have to suffer until after Christmas.

CHAPTER 9

Christmas in the Baker household carried on pretty much as usual, despite the turmoil that was churning away in Jack's head. He worked up until the last minute on Christmas Eve and only just arrived home in time for the annual village carol service.

Simon and Anna were very excited and didn't get to sleep until late, so, it was gone midnight before Hilary and Jack finished the stockings and the distribution of presents.

Jack had allowed his guilt to affect his pocket, and he'd splashed out on Hilary, buying her new ski gear and a very expensive gold chain and pendant. She liked plain things and the design was simple but the diamond-shaped pendant was set with amethysts, her favourite stone. He put the small box into her stocking, praying she'd like it.

Hilary had been her usual, practical self and bought Jack low-fat recipe books and a rowing machine, as well as a few of his favourite treats, whisky-flavoured liqueurs among them.

The children had done very well, as always, Simon gaining yet more virtual reality games, some ski-gear and a French language disc that Hilary had insisted on.

Anna had the new music and video station that she'd wanted; it included a mixing facility, and Jack wasn't sure this was a good idea. He had visions of cracks appearing in the plasterwork as the vibrations from her creations shook the house. Hilary assured him that the headphones would take care of that problem and that only Anna would be deafened by her efforts.

Despite their late night, the children woke early, and Jack felt Hilary heave herself out of bed at some ungodly hour. He turned over and slept again, finally coming to, as a cup of tea was put next to him.

"What time is it?" he asked sleepily.

"It's eight-thirty, no self-respecting parent should be asleep at this hour! Come on, open your presents."

Jack groaned and sat up, groping around in his stocking. He pulled out the customary boxer shorts, socks, chocolates and tangerine, and when he turned to look at Hilary, he was touched to find her wearing the pendant and smiling at him.

"I love it, Jack – thank you!" and she kissed him gently on the cheek – he felt immensely relieved.

"I'm glad you like it," he said truthfully.

Just then, they were both nearly knocked out of bed by a cacophony of sound coming from Anna's bedroom.

"HEADPHONES," bellowed Hilary, but it took her two shouts and a hammering on the door before peace was restored. She climbed back into bed to find Jack giving her his 'told you so' look, so she attacked him with her pillow.

Angela stretched like a cat, in pure, wanton luxuriousness. The sun was warm on her body as she turned over onto her stomach – it was time to brown her back. She sneaked a look at Pete, who he was deeply absorbed in a novel he'd bought at the airport.

All had been explained after Jack had left. Pete had come home early to surprise her with a pre-Christmas week in Marrakesh. She was, of course, delighted, and was thoroughly enjoying herself. The 'Jack' incident hadn't been mentioned since their initial row. Pete had accused her of having an affair and she had defended herself magnificently.

The row had gone on for the whole day, back and forth with accusations and counter accusations – finally ending up with Angela saying it would have served him right if she was having an affair as he left her on her own so much. She had taken herself off to her mother's and gone to work the next day without contacting him.

The next day a huge bouquet of flowers had arrived for her at work and when she got home in the evening, Pete had apologised and they'd made love very passionately. Since then, he'd been extremely attentive and loving towards her. She chuckled to herself – it was amazing what a bit of competition could do to a man, she should have thought of it before. Life with Pete might not be perfect, but it wasn't bad either; most of her problems, she realised, came from loneliness and that was something they must discuss at some point, but not just now.

The holiday was near perfect – a luxurious hotel in Marrakesh, gorgeous food, sunshine and exotic sights. The Medina enthralled her, and she'd already overspent on rugs, brass lamps and leather goods. Pete didn't seem to mind, he was relaxed and happy – he still didn't say a lot, but that would never change. She thought of Jack; she must contact him as soon as she got back. She was sure he'd be worried and it wasn't fair to leave him suffering, it hadn't been his fault and he'd been really sweet to her the night she'd got drunk. She smiled to herself, stretched, and turned again, this heat was making her feel extremely sexy.

So it was that Jack got his best present when he logged on to the computer just after breakfast to find an email from Angela. It was a straightforward memo, reminding him that the monthly meeting would be in the middle of January and not at the end, as was usual. It also said that his medical check-up would take place that day, which made him pull a face, but all his troubles were forgotten as he read the words at the bottom – 'Everything is fine up here – no problems – Merry Christmas – Angela'.

He deleted it immediately, but he could remember the words quite clearly – no problems, thank God! He told himself he'd been extremely lucky to get away with it, there was no way he was going to tempt fate again.

So it was that Jack was able to enjoy Christmas day with his family. He even managed to compose what he thought was a reasonable piece of music on Anna's equipment, and he felt extremely pleased with himself.

It was just the four of them for Christmas Day – Alec and Charlie had been invited for Boxing Day.

Usually they had all their family to them, a tradition on Boxing Day, but not this year. Jack's younger sister, Susan, and her husband were going to the States, skiing, they had no kids, and had only been married a couple of years, so it was the right time to do it. His older brother, Jim, and his wife, Bethany, and their three kids were staying at home in London. Bethany's mother was very ill and she didn't want to go far, so they'd invited Alec and Charlie to them for Christmas lunch.

Hilary had suggested that they invite his parents over to them for Boxing Day. She said it 'would do Charlie good', not to have to cook, and it would be a pleasant change to be at home on that day.

The four of them thoroughly enjoyed their Christmas Day, eating, drinking, playing and sleeping, finally falling asleep watching yet another space movie at 10 o'clock!

The next morning Hilary woke up feeling particularly active, so she dragged the kids out for a walk, and Jack enjoyed himself, pottering in the kitchen. Turkey pie was one of his favourites and he made it with a great deal of loving attention – nurturing the stock and setting some aside for soup; stripping the carcase and using only the best meat, which he had to sample, of course and finally, making the sauce, with the greatest of care. He was so inspired that he even decided to make a starter with smoked salmon and cream cheese. The dessert was no problem – Charlie always brought one of her delicious Christmas puddings.

When Hilary and the kids came bursting in, full of energy, Jack was sitting in front of the TV, feet up, glass of red wine in his hand, enjoying some football. There were some delicious smells emanating from the kitchen.

"What time are Grandma and Granddad coming?" Anna asked.

"About one o'clock, they said," Hilary told her.

"Well I'm going to compose something specially for them!" she announced.

Simon groaned and ran upstairs shouting, "Earplugs, where are you?"

"This should be interesting!" Jack mused.

Alec and Charlie drew up promptly at one o'clock. They'd dispensed with presents long ago and only gave money now to children and grandchildren alike but they never came empty-handed and Charlie loved delving in her bags for wine, chocolates (even Hilary couldn't object at Christmas!) mince pies, whisky and, of course, her Christmas pudding.

Everyone was very relaxed; the grandparents loved Anna's composition and Charlie proceeded to have a go herself, composing a lovely compilation of Christmas music; she'd always been musical, singing in choirs and playing the piano, and she was perfectly at home, sitting cross-legged on Anna's bedroom floor, surrounded by equipment.

Later on, as they all sat over the remains of the meal, Charlie asked, "So, how is the diet going then, Jack?"

"To be honest, Mum, I've been too busy to think about it, I haven't even weighed myself."

"Wasn't that health and fitness weekend any good then?" she persisted.

"Yes, it was very helpful but I suppose it was badly timed really, what with Christmas and everything," he finished lamely.

For once, Hilary rescued him, as she brought in the coffee. "He's got another check-up in the middle of January, so there's time before then to cut down, and I've bought him the rowing machine!" She smiled at him and Charlie wisely changed the subject.

"What did you get for Christmas, Hilary?"

Hilary's hand went up to her neck and she proudly held up the pendant.

"Ooh, it's beautiful – Jack, you've excelled yourself."

"Yes, he's spoilt me this year," Hilary smiled as she went on , "I've got new ski-gear as well!"

"Oh yes, the school ski trip, when's that?"

"End of January, a week in Aviemore and Simon's coming too this year, aren't you?" Hilary ruffled her son's hair.

"I'm really looking forward to it, Gran. I'm the same age as Mum's group now and Mr Evans said I could go."

"That's brilliant!" Alec said, "You can teach me some of the moves when you get back. I've always wanted to learn to ski, but never got round to it somehow."

Charlie laughed, "That's all I need! Next thing I know, I'll have a ski-lift in the back-garden."

Jack thought how relaxed his parents were looking; that was what you call a good marriage, fifty odd years and still as devoted as ever.

If there was one thing Jack hated, it was going to work and leaving Hilary and the kids in bed. There was nothing more miserable than creeping around an empty house, trying to be quiet, while everyone else slept on.

Christmas was a busy time for the food industry, though, most supermarkets only really closed on Christmas Day; and on the days between the 27th and 31st of December, the wiser food companies reminded their distributors that they were around. The other factor was that health-food products were in demand after the Christmas binges and Holme Farm made sure that all potential dieters were well provided for.

Jack made himself tea and toast and wandered into the lounge to watch ten minutes of breakfast TV There was a strange stillness about the morning and a soft light coming through the curtains; Jack drew them back and gasped. The world had been transformed into a winter wonderland! Thick, deep snow blanketed everything. It muffled all sound and covered all imperfections, coating the landscape, like an alpine film-set. Soft, fluffy flakes were still falling gently, and a robin sat precariously on a pyracantha branch, next to the window, pecking at the berries.

If Jack hadn't been going to work, he'd have been delighted. He loved to play in the snow with the kids, building snowmen and going sledging, but not today. Today he had to get to work. He groaned and switched on the TV According to the weather station, the whole of the Midlands was covered in snow, and, as always nobody was prepared, nobody knew it was coming and consequently chaos reigned. People had been caught by surprise on the MI and the M6 and were stranded in their cars. Roads were blocked, power lines were down, airports were closed and rail services disrupted. The advice was, don't go out unless you have to.

Jack sighed and went upstairs to the computer and logged on. Holme Farm itself was fine – there was no snow north of Manchester. The advice from Head Office was to do all you could from home via phone, and email but not to venture on the roads until the weather situation improved. Good old Bernie. He wasn't going to risk expensive vehicles unless he had to.

Jack felt his mood lightening – maybe life wasn't so bad after all. He could spend a couple of hours on the computer and then take the kids out. He made Hilary a cup of tea and woke her gently.

"Guess what?" he whispered.

"What?" she murmured sleepily.

"It's snowing."

"Really!"

"Yes, really – proper deep, thick snow!"

"Oh, how lovely! The kids will be happy." She was awake now, and her face went serious. "What about work?"

"Advice is, do what you can but stay at home. So, I'll do a couple of hours on the computer and then the day is mine."

"Well, aren't you the lucky one?" she murmured, lifting the duvet and patting the space next to her.

Once Simon and Anna woke up and saw the snow, all peace was gone. Hilary managed to contain them with difficulty until Jack had finished his business calls and then, once everyone was ready, they set out on foot, pulling the sledge. The kids were like two greyhounds out of the traps, bounding about in the snow, covering twice as much ground as Jack and Hilary; *they* were left like two sherpas carrying the loads! Jack pulled the sledge, and Hilary carried the ski-gear, as she'd decided it was the ideal opportunity for Simon to practise. Eventually, they put the gear on the sledge and ordered their offspring into hard labour; this plan, of course, only lasted so long, as arguments ensued and valuable gear was in danger of being lost. They headed for a slope just outside the village, but it was already full of gleeful children, sliding about on anything from the latest hi-tech sledge to a plastic tray. Eventually they found a relatively quiet slope farther away. Jack and Anna took the sledge, whooping and squealing with delight as they descended the slope.

It wasn't long before Jack was puffing and panting – coming down was great, it was going back up that was the problem. By the third climb, his muscles ached and he was short of breath and knackered. He plonked the sledge down at the top of the hill and sank down onto it with relief.

Anna studied him for a moment and said, "Come on, Dad! Let's go again."

"You go down on your own this time, while I have a rest," he panted.

"You're not going to die are you, Daddy?"

Jack smiled, "Well, I might feel like it at times, but I'm not intending to do it just yet, poppet." He gave her a hug. "What makes you say that anyway?"

"Well Janet's daddy died, just before Christmas, of a heart attack."

Jack looked at his daughter's innocent little face, studying him so intently, and his own heart went to jelly. "I'm sorry about Janet's daddy, you haven't mentioned it before."

"I talked about it to Simon, he knows her brother, they were both off school, and missed the Christmas party and concert and everything."

"How old was her daddy?"

"I don't know, old like you I suppose."

Jack smiled and hugged her again. "Don't worry, darling, I'm not going to die, not yet anyway. I'm going to lose weight and get fit. I've got my rowing machine, remember?"

Anna looked at him very earnestly for a couple of seconds and then she said, "OK," and picked up the rope of the sledge, waiting patiently for him to struggle to his feet. He watched her slide down the slope and vowed there and then to lose weight and get fitter.

Hilary and Simon had made some progress but not a lot. Simon had learned how to get the skis on and off and he was now learning how to fall, or that's what it felt like. He seemed to be getting rather good at it. Hilary was trying to teach him how to do the snowplough, that most basic of movements; she said it was simple and absolutely vital to lots of other manoeuvres like turning, traversing and so on. All you had to do was point your skis at the front and come to a stop. Simon tried, but every time, his skis crossed and got tangled, and he fell down. After about a quarter of an hour of this Simon had had enough – he sat in the snow and sulked.

Hilary crouched down beside him. "I'll never do it, Mum," he wailed, "The skis are too big and too long!"

Hilary smiled, "They're not, Simon, look, they're much shorter than mine. They're wider too and shaped to help you to balance – you've only just started. You will get the hang of it, I promise, it just needs practice and patience. Think how much further ahead you'll be than the others when we get there!"

Simon thought for a moment and then he pulled himself up; he gritted his teeth and concentrated very hard and this time he managed it – a perfect snowplough. "Yes!" he shouted, punching the air with his ski pole, and promptly fell down. He and Hilary burst out laughing.

When they finally trudged home in the late afternoon, the whole family felt tired but happy and when Jack suggested hamburgers and chips for tea, Hilary raised no objections.

The next day was the day of the big slush. Jack went to work, but progress was slow on the roads – there were floods everywhere, and some roads were still closed. He did what he could, but on the whole, it was a frustrating day, and he headed for home early.

The house was empty. Hilary had gone to the sales with the kids and so he grabbed the opportunity and climbed on the scales. He was stunned – half a stone more than last time! No wonder he was panting yesterday! Only two weeks to go to his medical. Panic gripped him and he got out the rowing machine, but it took him an hour to assemble it and by then, Hilary, Simon and Anna had arrived back, loaded with bags.

"Hi, Dad," his daughter shouted, "Look what I've got!" and she proceeded to give him a fashion show of all her new gear.

Jack was not in a good mood. The thought struck him that if he lost his job those might be the last new clothes she had in a long time.

He put the rowing machine away again – he just wasn't in the mood.

Three more extremely busy days followed and on New Year's Eve, Jack was late home again. He and Hilary were going to Karen and Geoff's for New Year. Jack was never thrilled about Hilary's 'work do's ' as he called them but he hadn't been given any choice about this one.

Half way through the evening, he found himself in the kitchen, surrounded by teachers, all earnestly discussing the latest government proposals on education.

"Well I think it's a great idea," one young woman was saying, "If we go for purely academic subjects from eight until one, we can really push them on – they can get more contact time for the basics and we can have the afternoon off."

"Don't kid yourself," an older man said, "they'll never give us the afternoons off, we'll end up doing two shifts or something, it will mean less non-contact time, more marking and more preparation."

"Well, I think it's a brilliant idea," Karen said, "a whole afternoon of non-academic subjects, we can have a ball, and we can have the mornings off to do shopping and have medical appointments and so on." She turned to Jack. "What do you think, as a parent, Jack?"

Jack thought about it for a moment. "It sounds alright in theory, but I'm not sure about the practicalities – for instance, would the children be occupied every afternoon? Because otherwise, if parents were working, where would they go? Anyhow as far as I'm concerned it's just another government directive we could do without!"

"Why are you so anti-government, Jack?" Geoff asked, "There are a lot of advantages, you know."

"Such as what?" Jack challenged him.

"Such as giving the kids who are less academic the chance to learn more skills."

"What good will that do if they can't get a job?" Jack came back.

"That's the whole point. They can learn practical skills so they can get a job."

"Says who? Most of the kids who aren't academic don't want to work anyway."

"That's just not true, Jack. Those kids do want to work, but they don't know how to go about it; their parents can't help them but we can."

Hilary had joined them. "The trouble with Jack is that he just doesn't have any experience of the sort of children we're talking about. He thinks they are all ungrateful yobs who think the rest of us are stupid."

"That's not true!" Jack insisted.

"Yes it is, Jack. You've always been the same. You don't look behind the scenes at the kind of home life these kids have. You've been brought up in a cosy protected environment by Charlie and Alec and you've no idea what it's like in the world outside!"

"Food! Everybody!" Karen shouted.

Jack stayed quiet as Hilary turned away. He knew she was right. He had to admire her for the job she did and for the way she cared about her pupils.

They all piled into the food, which was actually delicious – Karen was a dab-hand at Asian cuisine, as it happened; so the table was laden with samosas, curries, sate, rice and noodle dishes and it was quite a while before anybody did anything else but eat.

Later on in the evening, as the New Year approached, Jack wandered into the lounge, which was now a dancing area. He stood and watched Hilary dancing with Dai Evans– she had always been a good dancer, and tonight was no exception. She moved rhythmically and sensuously to the music, her body encased in a clinging, long black dress. It had a kind of sheen to it, which caught the light as she moved. She had grown her hair recently and had it highlighted and Jack had to admit that he was married to a very attractive lady. He watched her laughing at something that Evans bloke said and wondered for a split second if there was anything between them, but then it was gone again. Hilary was far too self-controlled to have a fling with her boss. He put his beer down and walked over to claim his husbandly rights and dance with his wife – as he took her in his arms for the last dance of the year, he vowed that next year he would treat her better.

CHAPTER 10

Jack headed north – he wasn't looking forward to today one bit. He'd managed to lose 5lbs since Christmas, but it wasn't enough! He was still 2lbs heavier than he'd been at his October medical and his target had been to lose half a stone. He'd just have to complain that this meeting was two weeks early and there had been Christmas in between and hope that they'd give him another chance; he really thought he could do it now.

The traffic was bad – he was making slow progress, despite his early start. It seemed there was one hold-up after another from south of Birmingham right up to Manchester – he sighed and resigned himself to crawling slowly northward.

By the time he arrived at Holme Farm, it was already 9.30a.m., half an hour late. He made his way into the lecture hall and sat at the back. Bernard Holmes was coming to the end of his New Year pep talk.

"And I want to make this the best year ever for Holme Farm Products. We are expanding even further into Europe, with a particularly lucrative deal on offer in Italy and we have some exciting new products to show you. I am very enthusiastic about the future and I am sure that with your continued dedication and hard work, we will go on to even greater things."

He sat down and the chief accountant gave a summary of the balance sheet to date, stressing that they must make an extra push before April.

Jack made his way to the dining room – he definitely needed a coffee. He sat on his own, lost in thought and didn't even see Don approaching.

"Well, well, well, you don't look a happy person, has she jilted you then?"

"What!"

"Your lady friend, Angie, has she jilted you? Word is, her husband's back from abroad."

Jack could cheerfully have thumped him.

"No, she hasn't jilted me – there is nothing going on, so it's not necessary."

"Ah, come on, Jack! I wasn't born yesterday – you were having a fling! It's no skin off my nose you know. In fact, it's made me see you in a new light – quite a dark horse, you are!"

Jack didn't say anything; he wasn't in the mood for this. He sipped his coffee and glowered at Don, who, of course, didn't even notice.

"Just be careful though, if Hilary finds out, you might end up with a few broken bones, she's a fit lady!"

That was it! Jack slammed his coffee cup down and leant across the table so his face was nearly touching Don's.

"Hilary won't find out because there is NOTHING to find out! The sooner you get that through your thick head, the better!"

Don raised his hands in a gesture of submission. "OK. OK. Keep your hair on! Whatever you say."

Jack sat back and took a deep breath, and both men cast furtive glances round the room – no one seemed to be taking any notice.

"Well, what about tonight then? What do you fancy?"

Jack realised he hadn't even thought about it – showed how preoccupied he'd been, and he felt a pang of guilt, as he always used to enjoy their nights out.

"I don't know," he said as pleasantly as he could, "what have you got in mind?"

"Well, there's a good pub near the university where they have live groups apparently. I haven't been yet but word is that it's got a good atmosphere."

"OK. I'll meet you in the bar at the Fellside. I've got my medical this afternoon, so I might need cheering up!"

"Oops! Christmas got the better of you eh?"

"You could say that," Jack moaned as he stood up.

"Your medical won't take all afternoon, will it?"

"I don't know, why?"

"Because we are due at a team-building session later on. 'How to be a successful Sales Team' by Robert S. Simpkins, Sales Manager."

"Oh God! Are we? Oh well, I'll see you later then!"

The medical was worse than he feared. It was with the new young doctor, Dr Anderson. He was conscientious and very earnest in his views, unlike old Dr Evans, who everyone knew smoked like a chimney and drank like a fish.

The young man tutted constantly as he went through the tests and punched figures into the computer.

"Well, Mr Baker, it isn't looking good I'm afraid! You haven't met your targets by a large margin and I'm going to have to report to that effect."

"What does that mean?" Jack snapped.

The young man looked at him sternly. "It means that you'll have to attend another health and fitness seminar and attend counselling, so we can ascertain what your problem is and—"

"My problem is," Jack interrupted him, "that I was given these targets at the most difficult time of the year and this medical is two weeks before it was scheduled to be! Given two more weeks, I'd lose the extra weight and I wouldn't have to be here listening to you wittering on about counselling. Which, by the way, I refuse to attend!"

He simply was not in the mood for young pipsqueaks like this to start telling him how to run his life.

"I'm sorry, Mr Baker, but those are the rules! The seminar is in two weeks' time. Frankly, it seems very unlikely that you are going to reach your targets by then, but counselling is inevitable anyway. All these records go through to the insurance company, and they don't see people, just figures!"

Jack got dressed in stony silence and snatched the papers out of the young doctor's hands before storming out of the medical centre. There was no way he was going back into the lecture hall now – he simply wasn't in the mood for 'team-building exercises'.

He headed for his car and drove to Morecambe, thinking that a walk along a windy seafront would do him good. Morecambe in January was not the busiest place in the world, but he managed to find a lonely ice-cream booth and bought a defiant ice-cream cone with a chocolate flake. He ate it as he walked along, watching the waves break against the prom – the tide was in for once.

There was nothing for it, he'd have to starve for two weeks. Better to starve for two weeks than starve for the rest of his life, without a job.

"Where did you get to this afternoon? I had to cover for you with Simpkins. I told him you had a stomach bug!"

"Oh, thanks, Don." Jack was genuinely grateful, as he didn't want to get on the wrong side of Simpkins, he was in enough trouble already.

"So what's the problem, Jack?" Don looked genuinely concerned for once. "Come on, Jack – it's that woman isn't it?"

They were sitting in the bar at the Fellside. Don had a pint, but Jack, with new determination, was drinking diet coke.

"No, how many times do I have to tell you, Don? There's nothing going on between Angela and me, we are just friends!" He was glad he could say it calmly and with conviction this time. "It's my medical, I've got to lose half a stone in a fortnight, but what's worse, I've got to go for counselling! That bloody little upstart Anderson, I could wring his scrawny neck!"

Don nearly choked on his beer and laughed out loud, "You – in counselling! God, this I'd like to see!"

"Well you won't because I'm not going! I told him straight out." Jack was feeling even more indignant than he had that afternoon.

Don looked serious again for a moment. "Look, you can do it, Jack, not the counselling, but the weight, and Hilary will help you. It will be simple really!"

"It might be simple for you, but my body is particularly resistant to losing weight," he moaned, "Still, you're right, it's lose the weight or lose the job, so I haven't got a lot of choice!"

"That's the spirit! Now, let's see what that new pub has to offer." Don downed his pint, but the diet coke didn't have quite the same kudos so Jack just left it on the table.

Becky Abbot was itching for a fight. She marched up to the front entrance of Carrisbrook Middle School, heels clacking determinedly. She was going to see the Head, if it was the last thing she did.

Her determined assault was halted by the implacable stare of Doris Bates, and a stand-off ensued.

"Can I help you?" Doris was always polite.

"I want to see Mr Robinson," Becky stormed.

"I'm afraid that's impossible, Mrs Abbot – he's in a meeting with a parent and it could take some time. I can make you an appointment if you'll just give me some idea what it's about."

Doris was well practised at diffusing steaming parents. Becky, however, was not to be deterred. She had no plans for the day, other than to speak to the Head – she was prepared to sit in the foyer for hours if necessary.

"I don't want to discuss it with anyone except Mr Robinson – it's to do with the ski trip and my son Sean!" she spluttered, realising she'd already said more than she'd intended. She stood there, arms folded, face flushed and her high-heeled boot tapping impatiently on the carpet.

Doris, on the other hand, was in complete control. She had the information she needed.

"If you'll just take a seat, Mrs Abbot, I'll see what I can do for you."

Doris loved moments like this – she had a mission and that was to keep irate parents away from the Head at any cost. Having expertly ascertained the nature of Becky Abbots' complaint, she knew exactly what the problem was and exactly who to look for.

Doris knew that Dai Evans did not want Sean Abbot to go on the ski trip. He had very good reasons for his decision – Sean was a loose cannon, he could be very, very good, or he could be very, very bad, and there was no knowing from one lesson to the next how the mood would take him! School trips were always a big responsibility and Dai, as Head of P.E. was used to that, he accepted it as part of the job, but he tried to minimize risks as much as possible and Sean Abbot *was* a risk. He'd discussed it with his department. Hilary, of course, thought Sean should be given a chance, but she'd always had a soft spot for him. Karen was noncommittal; she said she'd go along with the majority. Dave Morris, a science teacher but keen sportsman, was adamant that Sean should not go. Dave was a strict disciplinarian, just the sort of teacher Sean liked to play up. Give Sean a rule and he'd break it – he didn't learn much science, spending most of his time outside in the corridor. Dai needed Dave Morris on the trip, he had to have at least two male members of staff and he basically agreed with him anyway, Sean did not deserve to go.

Doris quietly manoeuvred Dai to one side of the staff room and quickly put him in the picture. He raised his eyebrows, set his jaw and made his way purposefully towards the foyer.

"Mrs Abbot, I'm David Evans, Head of P.E. I understand you have a problem regarding Sean and the ski trip."

"I want to see the Head," Becky said defiantly – she was beginning to lose her nerve. She'd never liked school herself, and sitting cooling her heels in the foyer had reminded her of times spent sitting outside the headmistress's office when she was a headstrong teenager. She owed it to her Sean to persevere though. Dai saw the nervousness and used his most persuasive tone.

"Well, Mrs Bates will make you an appointment, but it may take a while, so in the meantime, perhaps you and I could have a chat?"

She warmed to Dai's gentlemanly manner and nodded her head. "OK."

"We'll go in the interview room, through here."

When they were settled, Dai began, "Now – what is the problem, Mrs Abbot?"

"The problem is that my Sean wants to go on the ski trip. We've got the money, I've saved it up, and he applied in time, but he came home yesterday and said he couldn't go! He's really cut up about it, been practising for weeks over at Tamworth, me brother takes him and he says he's really good, snowboarding and everything." She paused for breath and brushed a stray hair from her face. "I don't know why he can't go, I expect it's his truanting and everything but I just know that if he doesn't do this then all this hard work and getting him to come to school and everything, it will just be wasted, he'll just give up!"

Dai sighed, "I see. Well, I'll have to be honest with you, Mrs Abbot. I made the decision that Sean couldn't come."

Becky opened her mouth to say something but he held up his hand. "Just a minute – let me finish. I made the decision based on Sean's behaviour. I agree he's been coming to school regularly, but when he is here, his behaviour still leaves a lot to be desired. A ski trip is a dangerous situation, lives are quite literally at risk, so, children have to be prepared to toe the line and do as they are told instantly. Their lives may actually depend on it. Sean could endanger his own life or that of other children or staff if he decides to mess about." He stopped, waiting for the onslaught, but it didn't come. Becky was thinking – she knew only too well how headstrong Sean could be, and she realised that what Mr Evans was saying was

124

true. She would have to have a serious talk to Sean because she didn't want some snotty parent accusing her son of causing an accident.

She looked back at Dai and smiled. "I know Sean can be a handful, Mr Evans, but he's never had his heart set on anything like he has on this. The thing is, he's good, you see and he's never been good at anything before. It could be his one chance at showing some of these other lads that he's not just a thicko, that he can do somethink. Please give him a chance! You can send him home if he plays you up. I'll come and fetch him myself, but I swear he'll be good as gold. I'll talk to him beforehand. Please, Mr Evans," she pleaded with him.

Dai felt his resolve melting away. It was the part about proving he could be good at something. That rang so true and he didn't want to be the one who was responsible for consigning yet another kid to the scrap heap.

"I'll tell you what, give me a couple of days and I'll talk to the other teachers and see what I can do, but I'm not promising anything."

He thought she was going to kiss him, but she just stood up and clapped her hands together.

"Thank you, you won't regret it, I promise."

Dai made his way to the science lab. *I hope you're right, Mrs A*, he thought ruefully, *because if you're not, then I'm in big trouble.* He sighed; now all he had to do was convince Dave Morris.

CHAPTER 11

A ngela and Carla sat hugging mugs of hot soup. They were relaxing in Angela's kitchen after a Saturday afternoon's shopping.

"Ah, come on, Carla, I can afford it, we'll call it a belated Christmas present."

"We don't buy each other Christmas presents," Carla reminded her.

"I know, but look, you'll be doing me a favour. I won't go on my own and I need a pick-me-up."

Carla looked back at the brochure and considered her friend's offer. Angela wanted a day out at the Lakeside Springs, a new health spa that had opened in Windermere, and she was willing to pay for her friend to join her.

"It does look very nice, look at that pool." She pushed the brochure back across the table and Angela gazed at the picture of the pool room, all marble and tropical plants, surrounding the sky-blue water.

"I know, it's supposed to be marvellous, come on, you know you'll enjoy it."

"Of course I'll enjoy it but I like to pay my own way and it's way out of my league!"

Carla's elfin face and slight figure disguised an iron will.

"Well, just promise me you'll think about it. You know I need cheering up at the moment."

"Yeah. Men! I'd like to get my hands on Jack Baker, first sign of trouble and he's suddenly the perfect family man, scurrying back to his wife and kids. Typical!"

"Well, he never tried to deceive me," Angela reminded her, "He was honest from the start, so I can't complain."

"Yes, but how long would it have gone on for if Pete hadn't walked in that morning? I bet he wouldn't have been in such a hurry to end it if that hadn't happened!"

Angela stood up. "I've told you, it was over before Pete walked in, he just wasn't the sort to have an affair."

"Yes. Quite. I wonder if he realises what a state he left you in. I bet he's got no idea, and I bet he's not fretting that he was no good in bed, or he needs to lose half a stone, or have a new hairstyle!"

Angela smiled. "It's not because of Jack that I need cheering up, it's because Pete's gone back and I'm lonely again."

"Well, I hope you've learned your lesson. Don't go getting involved with any more married men."

Angela pulled a face. "I don't intend to. I'm not cut out for it any more than Jack was, it was definitely a one-off! Anyhow, talking of getting involved, how about you and Danny? You've become quite an item, haven't you? I've hardly seen you all Christmas!"

Carla smiled. "He's lovely," then she said sternly, "He's not married though!"

"No, I know. Actually, I'm really pleased for you – I knew you had an ulterior motive for coming on that weekend! Anyway, stop changing the subject. Are you coming with me or not?"

"I'm thinking about it," was the stubborn reply.

"Come ON, Simon – we'll be late!" Hilary was getting impatient.

"I'm coming," shouted a disembodied voice from somewhere upstairs.

Simon appeared at last, taking two stairs at a time and tumbling into the hall. His hair was still wet and he was trailing a holdall behind him.

127

"Now, are you sure you've got everything?"

"Yes, Mum."

"Well your ski-gear is all in the car, so go and give that bag to your father and then we can be off."

Simon trudged outside – he wasn't sure this was a good idea after all, Mum had been at her bossiest ever since he'd got home from school.

He gave the bag to his father, who was trying to rearrange the boot into some kind of order. He had offered to do it as an excuse to get out of the house, as Hilary seemed rather fraught. He looked at Simon. "It will be alright once you're on your way, Mum doesn't want to be late, because she's got to stay fairly close to the minibus for the journey up in case there are any problems."

"I know, but she's been nagging me for hours now, Dad. I hope she's not going to be like this all the time we're away."

"Why don't you ask if you can travel in the minibus with the other kids?"

"Well that would leave Mum on her own."

"She's done it before, she always takes her car up in case of emergencies."

"I'll see." Simon hopped from one foot to the other in obvious discomfort.

"Come and give me a hug, Mr Responsibility."

Jack hugged his son; he knew that Simon wouldn't leave Hilary by herself, he was a good kid.

They were travelling up to Scotland overnight, to avoid traffic and make the most of their skiing time; they always did it, but this was the first time that Hilary had had the added responsibility of her son to think about.

Finally, they were both ensconced in the car, and Jack and Anna stood ready to wave them off.

"Now don't forget to pick Anna up from music practice tomorrow night and from Jenny's house on Friday."

"I won't forget, just relax and concentrate on your driving," Jack told her.

"When are you taking her to your parents?"

"On Friday night, we're both staying there and I'm leaving from there early Saturday morning."

"It's such a nuisance, you having to go to that seminar this weekend, of all weekends."

"I know, but it can't be helped – it's all arranged now."

Hilary sighed, "OK, then, be good, you two," and she kissed them both through the car window.

"Bye, Mummy. Don't let Simon break a leg." Anna grinned cheekily at her brother, who just raised his eyes heavenward and settled down into his seat.

Father and daughter waved them off and then hurried back into the warm house.

"Mum says I've got to make sure you only have healthy foods and that you do your exercise every day," Anna announced with authority.

Jack smiled, "Don't worry, I'm not going to blow it now. I'm nearly on target."

"What are we going to have for tea then?" Anna was obviously not convinced.

"Well, you can have whatever you want, poppet – but I'm having a grilled fish steak with loads of vegetables."

The nine-year-old grinned at her dad and said, "Can I have pizza please?"

"No problem."

They ate in companionable silence and then Anna said, "I hope Simon gets on alright, he gets really uptight if he can't do something."

"Yes, I know what you mean," Jack agreed. He'd spent a lot of time over the last two weeks persuading Simon that it was worth persevering with the skiing. Hilary had taken him to Tamworth twice, and each time he'd been less than pleased with his efforts, even though Hilary had assured Jack that he was improving; the trouble with Simon was that he was a perfectionist.

"Maybe he'll be better when he gets an instructor up there," Jack tried to reassure Anna, "He always wants to impress Mum, so he tries too hard."

"Maybe." Anna looked doubtful. "Anyhow, you've got to do some exercise," she announced, poking him in the ribs.

"Give me a chance, I've just eaten! We've got to clear up first and then, after a rest, I'll get on that dratted machine!"

"Yes, you will, because I'll tickle you to death if you don't," Anna warned him.

"Like mother, like daughter eh?" Jack advanced, hands outstretched for tickling and Anna ran squealing out of the kitchen.

We're lucky with the weather, Hilary thought as they progressed northwards. The night was cloudy, so there was no frost and the roads were relatively traffic free. They were making good time.

It could take anything between eight and ten hours to get up there. Now, they were about to stop at the Tebay Services on the M6. She followed the minibus into the car park and looked forward to a hot coffee. Simon woke up as the car stopped.

"Where are we?"

"Tebay Services, sleepy head. Are you ready for something to eat and drink?"

"Yeah. I'm starving!"

Hilary smiled to herself. Simon was always starving these days. He was growing fast.

They joined the others and the kids all thronged into the toilets and the restaurant area. Hilary met up with Dai and Karen.

"How's it going?"

"OK. We've only had one sick bag so far." Karen pulled a face.

"And who dealt with that, I wonder?" Hilary looked meaningfully at Dai, who had the grace to look defensive.

"Karen was nearest, and it was a girl!" he told her. One look at Hilary's face made him add, "If we get any more, I'll see to them. I promise."

They all sat together to eat and drink, and Simon joined them. Hilary hoped that eventually he would make friends with some of the others, but it was early days yet.

The pupils started to drift off towards the well-equipped shop and Hilary volunteered to supervise them. She watched them wandering about in twos and threes and then it occurred to her that Sean wasn't there. She searched the shop and the amusements section; where was he? Then she had an idea. She walked outside and found him, leaning against the fence and smoking.

"Give the cigarettes to me please, Sean." She said it quietly but he still jumped and turned round.

He surveyed her out of eyes older than his face; he was tall for a twelve-year-old, but skinny, and he looked incongruous in his ski-jacket, his legs sticking out of the bottom. Like a hot dog out of its roll. He recovered his composure and looked defiant.

"They're mine. I paid for them."

"Yes, I know they are and you'll get them back at the end of the trip, but for your own sake, give them to me now and don't buy any more please!"

He handed them over reluctantly but carried on smoking the one he'd lit. He turned away again and leaned over the fence. Hilary went and leant next to him. She kept the same quiet tone of voice and said, "A lot of people have stuck their necks out for you, Sean, including me. I was one of those who said you should come on this trip. Don't go letting me down now."

He kept on smoking and she followed his gaze out over the blackness that surrounded the services. It was as if they were on an island of light in a black sea. She saw his shoulders relax and he said,

"I know, me Mum told me, but I'm not doing anyone any harm. I'm only having a fag."

"True, you're not harming anyone else but yourself, but you are breaking rules, and if Mr Morris catches you, there'll be trouble."

"I'm not scared of him." Sean was scathing.

"Maybe not, but he could insist that Mr Evans sends you home and we're not even there yet. Look, Sean, you like skiing don't you?"

"Yeah," he said defiantly, as if he was saying 'so what'.

"Well, you need to be fit to ski well, you'll see when we get up there. Smoking damages your lungs and stops you getting all the oxygen you need, especially if you start as young as you are."

He didn't say anything, but he threw the cigarette on the ground and crushed it under his boot.

Hilary knew better than to say any more. "Do you need anything from the shop? It will be a while before we stop again." He turned round to look at her and grinned, "A can of lager would be nice."

She pretended to cuff him round the ear, her hand deliberately missing his head, and he ran off laughing. She followed him, smiling to herself, at least he had a sense of humour – mind you, she wouldn't put it past him. She hurried into the shop.

Back in her car, Hilary felt refreshed and ready for another bout of driving. She knew she'd be tired by the time they got to the guest house, but at least they'd get a few hours' sleep before hitting the slopes and doing it this way, they got an extra day's skiing.

Her thoughts turned to Sean – she was going to have to watch him like a hawk, more for his own sake than anyone else's. Dai had had terrible trouble persuading Dave Morris to agree and in the end, he'd made it perfectly clear that he would take no responsibility for the lad whatsoever.

Dai had no problem with that, but he'd left Mrs Abbot in no doubt that at the slightest provocation, he would send Sean home. They all knew that Hilary was the only one who could handle him and so she was left with the task, but it wasn't going to be easy.

Jack and Anna sat back from the table with a sigh of satisfaction. Charlie had excelled herself, as always, with a vegetable lasagne and fresh fruit salad.

"That was delicious, Mum," Jack told her, "and before you ask, yes, I've lost weight. I'm on target so it will be OK."

Charlie looked relieved and Alec nodded in approval. Jack looked at his father and said, "You look tired, Dad. What have you been up to?"

"Oh, this and that, you know." Alec looked uncomfortable.

"He's been moving his tank into place, that's what!" Charlie scolded, "I told him that it was too much for him and Jack and that they should get help, but no, he's too stubborn!"

"Oh stop fussing, woman," Alec retorted, but in a gentle voice, "It's done now and nobody got a hernia or blew a gasket, so you can stop worrying."

Charlie just tutted and carried on clearing the table. Jack looked thoughtful. "I told you I'd help you when the time came, why didn't you phone me?"

"Because we could manage! I don't know what all the fuss is about. I'm going to watch some telly!"

He stumped off into the other room and Jack, Anna and Charlie exchanged glances.

"He's always like that when he knows he's in the wrong. You know how stubborn he is, Jack, take no notice!"

"Don't worry, Grandma, I won't let him do anything silly while I'm here this weekend."

Charlie smiled. "Good for you, little one – now, what would you like to do this evening?"

"Can we have a film night with popcorn?" she asked.

"Yes, course you can. Go and choose a DVD."

Jack sighed and went to join Alec in the lounge, but when he got there, he was fast asleep and snoring loudly in competition with the TV.

Angela was busy with the mail – she always enjoyed it, something to do with opening other people's letters she supposed. Bernard Holmes placed a great deal of trust in her and she always opened everything addressed to him.

Yet another missive from 'Perma-Care' the health insurance for a secure future. She ran the advert in her head – happy, good-looking family, husband, wife and two kids, all bouncing with health, cavorting on a beach somewhere, 'we leave you free from worry – to pursue the future of your dreams' – yuck! Then she stopped and re-read the page. "Oh, God," she said out loud and she sat down heavily in her chair.

There was a list of names, people the insurance company thought, were a bad risk, so their premiums would be going up. Employers were entitled to deduct the increases from salary and for some people, that left them very little to manage on. On top of that, Bernard had been known to use it as an excuse not to renew contracts, although he could never admit that to the employees, he always found another excuse.

The names that had caught Angela's eye were Jack Baker and Danny Hodgson.

There's something fishy going on here, she thought. Danny, she could understand, but Jack? No, she'd seen him at close quarters, as it were, and although he had to lose some weight, he didn't fit into this category, so what had happened?

Think, Angie girl! Well first of all, this letter wasn't getting to Bernie until she'd had a chance to do some digging. It would have to be passed on eventually, but she'd buy some time. Next, she needed more information from the insurance company. She shut the letter in her desk drawer and carried on with her work, but her brain was racing.

Half an hour later Angela put through a call to Perma-Care.

"Hello. Norma? It's Angela Carter. Yes, fine thanks. Listen. Mr Holmes has a few queries about that last letter."

Norma was the woman Angela usually dealt with; they'd spoken to each other many times over the years and built up quite a rapport.

Angela discovered that the reason Jack's name was on the list was a letter they'd received from Dr Anderson, stating that his attitude was very negative and, in his opinion, the weight would not be lost.

"Mr Holmes values Mr Baker as a salesman and he wants to know how we can help him to get back on the lower premium list, Norma." She crossed her fingers and held her breath.

"Well," Norma hesitated, "In the past, a letter from either the doctor, or John Fielding, stating that the employee has lost the weight and improved their attitude, has done the trick."

"Thanks, Norma, I'll pass that on. Now, tell me about your daughter, she was pregnant, wasn't she? How's she doing?"

After ten more minutes of chat, Angela put the phone down. She was seething with that snotty little upstart, Anderson. Who the hell did he think he was, playing God with people's lives, he'd got a reputation for being a nasty piece of work. Not like old Dr Evans, he'd been there for years and was a lovely man, but he was getting near to retirement now and Anderson could smell power coming his way. *Well, you've met your match now, Robert my boy.* She set her teeth and marched over to the personnel files. She wasn't going to risk bringing anything up on computer.

Carla downed her second gin and tonic and lit her third cigarette. They were sitting in the local pub – Angela had suggested it, knowing Carla would need somewhere away from work to vent her fury, when she found out Danny's name was on the list.

"That bastard!" she snarled. "I'd like to get him up a dark alley on a cold night."

"Why a cold night?" Angela asked.

"So it would hurt more when I kicked him in the balls."

Angela nearly choked on her drink, "Remind me never to upset you," she said with feeling. "Now calm down, we need clear heads for this one."

"It's alright for you – you're not about to lose your job, but Danny is."

"Danny and Jack," Angela reminded her.

"I don't care about Jack – it serves him right," she snapped, "but Danny has been working hard, he's lost five pounds and he *needs* this job."

Angela was quiet for a moment. "I care about both of them, they both need their job."

Carla looked up at her. "I don't know why you're bothering, Angie, he's done nothing for you."

"He did do something for me; he's a friend and I am going to help him."

She looked her friend straight in the eye, her own brown eyes flashing defiance, and Carla knew better than to argue, so she just took another drag on her cigarette and raised her eyebrows.

"So, what's the plan?"

"Well, first of all, I've got to warn Jack. He's due to come for another session, and he's got to look willing to do anything to lose that weight, then maybe John Fielding can write a letter."

"How are you going to do that? He'll just think you want to start things up again."

"I'll leave him a message to contact me and tell him it's about work."

Carla looked dubious, but she didn't want to discuss Jack, she wanted to know how to help Danny.

"I'll have to warn Danny as well, but he's got a lot further to go than Jack; he might be out of a job before he can make any real progress. What about Anderson? Isn't there anything we can threaten him with?"

"Not a thing – he's squeaky-clean. Married, with a baby daughter, wife was a nurse. Qualifications check out and so far he is turning out to be the perfect citizen."

"What are we going to do?" Carla moaned.

"Well, I'm not sure yet, but somehow I've got to persuade our Bernie and subsequently Perma-Care that our perfect Dr Anderson got it wrong somehow and made a mistake."

Carla snorted, "Well, that's not very likely is it? He's too bloody conscientious. I bet he double-checks everything!"

Angela suddenly smiled, "That's it! He's too conscientious, that's his weakness!" She sat back in her chair. "Would you like one more for the road? 'Cos I've got a plan!"

"Come on then, don't keep me in suspenders, what is it?"

"Well, it involves a friend of yours actually."

"A friend of mine? Who's that then?"

"Helen Freeman."

"Helen Freeman? The nurse!"

"Yes, she works with Anderson doesn't she?"

"Yeah, but I've known Helen for years, she's as straight as a die. She'd never do anything even remotely shady."

"She doesn't have to – all she has to do is to tell our dear doctor about this wonderful new restaurant she's heard about."

Carla looked blank. "What are you talking about, Angie? I think you've finally flipped!"

Angela sighed. "How do you think our conscientious young doctor would react if he came across a restaurant that broke all the rules on healthy eating?"

Carla grinned; realisation was dawning. "The foodie bar," she whispered.

"Precisely! He would make a big fuss, wouldn't he? Because he's like that. After all, it's right on his territory, undermining all his hard work with his patients, besides being against the law. He'd be bound to go to Bernard about it – and then BINGO!"

Carla just looked blank. "I don't understand. How will going to Bernie about it help Danny and Jack?"

Angela grinned,"Because Bernie owns it!"

Carla looked gobsmacked. "Bernie owns the foodie bar!"

"Yes. He put up the money for his sister and her husband to buy it."

"Angie, you're a genius!" Carla leapt up and hugged her friend. Then she stopped and sat down again.

"But what if he gets rid of Anderson and still lets Danny and Jack go as well?"

"Don't worry, I'll sort something out, the first thing is to make Bernie think that Anderson is trouble. Our Bernard won't let anything stand in the way of his business interests and he's making a packet out of that place."

"Yes, Anderson won't have a clue that Bernie owns it. I didn't know!"

"Very few people do."

" God! I hope it works."

"It will, Carla, it will." Angela spoke with the utmost confidence.

CHAPTER 12

Hilary was shattered her whole body ached and yet, she hadn't even had a pair of skis on yet. All that had been achieved so far was to get everyone kitted out with the appropriate sized boots and skis and to get them all labelled.

Now, they were all having something to eat and drink before going off for their first run.

Karen had elected to stay with the beginners, and Dai and Hilary were going with the more experienced skiers.

So far, the weather was good, fine and sunny, but it could change dramatically up here in a very short time, so they were all keen to get going.

"Are you all set then?" Hilary asked Simon.

He was sitting quietly beside her, stirring a cup of hot chocolate round and round; he didn't appear to have drunk very much.

"Yes, I'm fine."

"Are you looking forward to it?" She tried again.

Simon carried on stirring. "A little bit."

"You'll be fine, you know. The instructors here are very good and you already know a lot more than most of the beginners."

Simon just nodded.

Hilary sighed and just patted his arm; she knew there was nothing more she could do, he'd just have to get on with it.

Dai stood up and announced that he wanted everyone outside in five minutes for their final briefing.

Simon listened to the instructions carefully.

"Stay with your group at all times. No skiing off-piste."

Not much chance of that, Simon thought to himself. *I'll be lucky if I do any skiing on-piste*!

Dai was continuing. "Do as your instructors tell you at all times and if anyone is caught disobeying, then they won't ski for the rest of the trip."

Simon thought this sounded a bit harsh, but it didn't matter to him, he didn't intend to disobey anyone.

"We'll all meet back here at twelve-thirty for lunch; Oh and one last thing. Don't break any legs!"

Everyone laughed and started to drift off. Twelve-thirty seemed like a lifetime away to Simon.

Hilary waved at him and then walked towards the ski lifts with the established skiers and Karen walked towards him. *Ah well*, he thought, *here goes nothing*.

The morning actually went far better than he'd imagined. He managed to stay upright most of the time, and by lunchtime, he had skied down the gentle slope and successfully come to a halt several times. Several members of his group were not as competent and were asking him for help, just as Hilary had predicted.

One lad, Justin Copeland, was having real difficulties just staying upright. He was rather overweight and not very well co-ordinated. Simon felt nothing but sympathy for him as he struggled to his feet after each tumble. His own confidence though, had increased to such an extent, that he decided to sit with some of his group at lunchtime instead of sitting with Hilary and the other staff.

Justin was tucking into a huge plate of spaghetti; shovelling it into his mouth with a great deal of concentration, as two boys sauntered past; one was tall and thin with curly dark hair and the other was shorter, red-headed and had a permanent grin on his face.

The taller one shoved Justin in the back as he went past and they both looked back, laughing.

Justin didn't seem to mind too much, and simply carried on eating with a singlemindedness which amazed Simon.

"Who are they?" he asked the girl next to him.

"Gareth Thompson and Mark Allen. They're a real pain – think they own the place." She glowered after them.

By the time the two boys came back, Justin had demolished his spaghetti and progressed to a dishful of fruit salad and ice-cream. With one quick movement, Gareth pushed his head down and Mark sneered,

"Oh look, Justin's in the snow again."

Lots of the kids were giggling as Justin wiped ice-cream off his face with the back of his hand.

Simon was incensed. "Leave him alone. He's not doing you any harm!"

The table went quiet as the two boys slowly made their way up towards Simon. They were glancing in the direction of the staff table, as they moved, one on either side of him.

Gareth bent down, and putting his face really close, he said,

"What's it to you? You his brother or something?"

"No."

"Then why should you care?"

"I don't like to see people being bullied, that's all."

"Right little teacher's boy you are." He glanced up at his partner in crime, who was jerking his head in the direction of the staff table.

"Get lost, you two." The girl sitting next to Simon gave them a contemptuous glare as they started to move away, but at the last moment, Gareth turned back.

"Don't think Mummy can protect you all the time, Baker's boy. You just watch out," he said as he waggled his finger under Simon's nose and walked away.

"Don't take any notice of them," the girl said, "they're all talk."

"I'm not scared of them," Simon told her, sounding much more confident than he felt.

The afternoon went as well as the morning, and by the time they all piled into the minibus to go back to the Guest House, Simon was feeling very pleased with himself. They'd had a very good instructor and even Justin had managed a few runs without falling over.

The guest house had a cellar converted into a games room, and after tea, all the kids tended to gather down there, playing pool, listening to music, or watching TV.

Simon and some of his newfound friends had gathered in a corner playing cards, and the two miscreants from lunchtime were having a game of pool. Every now and again, they would look over and then put their heads together and laugh. He knew what they were trying to do and he knew that he must ignore them, but it was hard just the same.

Mr Evans came in at about ten o'clock.

"Right then, let's have this place cleared up and then I want everybody in bed. Lights out in half an hour."

The majority of the group began to drift away in dribs and drabs, but as Simon left, he noticed the two playing pool seemed in no hurry.

Simon was sharing a room with two other boys; they had the bunks and he had the bed. He decided to try and get into the bathroom before the rush, but when he looked for his washbag, he realised all his stuff was missing.

"Have either of you two seen my things?"

They both looked up innocently enough, and even helped him look, but it was no good, everything was gone.

It didn't take Simon long to realise who was responsible. He raced back downstairs and confronted the two pool players.

"Where is it? What have you done with my things?"

They both carried on calmly playing and ignored him.

Simon was beside himself with anger. "I'm talking to you. Where's my stuff?"

"Have you lost something?" Mark asked with an innocent look on his face.

"You know very well that I have. I won't ask you again. Where is it?"

Gareth swung round suddenly and held the cue across Simon's chest.

"We don't know what you're talking about, Baker's boy. Now push off back to Mummy and stop interrupting our game."

"Is this what you're looking for?" a calm voice asked.

All three boys froze and turned round to see Sean standing in the doorway, with Simon's belongings hanging from his arms.

"Yes, that's it. Where did you get it?" Simon was still suspicious.

"I watched these two goons stashing it away earlier on."

He turned back again to look at the other two and all the attitude had gone out of them; their heads were down and he realised that they weren't going to challenge Sean.

"Thanks," he said as he gathered everything from the other boy, and, with one last glare at the other two, he made his way back up the stairs. Consequently, he didn't hear the older boy's choice words of warning to the other two to leave 'that kid' alone.

Sean was desperate for a cigarette. He had a packet hidden in his bag; that wasn't the problem, it was where to smoke it. He didn't want anyone squealing to the teachers and he didn't want them smelling the smoke.

He decided to find somewhere outside; it would be cold, but at least he'd get some peace and he'd be able to think

His mum wasn't answering her phone. Sean told himself that it didn't mean anything, they were probably just at the pub, but it made him uneasy. He didn't trust his father. He took another drag of the cigarette. He'd just have to try again tomorrow, that was all. Once he'd spoken to his mum, he'd feel better. He stubbed out the cigarette, and, hunching his shoulders against the cold, he made his way back up the steps leading to the back door.

All the teachers and the majority of the children were asleep before eleven, so most of the party felt refreshed and raring to go by Friday morning. Only the dark circles under Sean's eyes gave away the fact that he'd lain awake most of the night. Finally, he'd got up early and managed to talk to his mother before she went to work. She'd told him she was fine and not to worry, just to enjoy himself, so, although tired, he felt a lot more cheerful, and managed to eat a hearty breakfast.

Simon had another good day, and when Hilary managed to get away to sneak a look at him, she was very impressed with what she saw. He was coming on in leaps and bounds, both in confidence and ability.

At the end of the day, they all piled onto the minibus and Karen and Geoff led the singing. Hilary noticed Sean was sitting on his own at the back just looking out of the window. She wondered if he was enjoying himself; it was certainly hard to tell. He'd performed very well on the slopes and showed obvious enjoyment then, but she wasn't sure that he enjoyed anything else.

"He hasn't been any trouble so far, has he?" She turned to Dai, who was sitting next to her. Too late, she realised that he'd had his eyes closed.

"Who?"

"Sean."

He sat up and rubbed his eyes. "No, not as far as I know. I just hope it lasts." He glanced towards the seat occupied by Dave Morris.

"You look tired."

"Not sleeping very well, that's all."

Hilary nodded; she knew perfectly well why he wasn't sleeping.

"Praps a nightcap would help," she ventured.

Dai turned to her and grinned, "Is that an invitation?" and she felt herself blushing.

It had been a long day and Dai was tired, both mentally and physically, but he simply couldn't sleep, despite the nightcap. This had turned out to be a few glasses of red wine with Hilary, Karen and Geoff, but it had done no good; he was as wide awake as ever. He kept thinking about Harry and how much he missed him. Spending the odd day taking him out and having meals in fast food joints just wasn't the same. He missed Linda too, but he was still so angry with her that he daren't even think about her. He had almost stopped thinking about women entirely. He turned over onto his back and then he heard the sounds; muffled giggles and sssssh's accompanied by the rustling of paper.

He climbed out of bed and, pulling on some clothes, he made his way on tiptoe out of his room and in search of the culprits. He didn't have to go far, in fact, he couldn't help but smile to himself at the stupidity of some kids – they were right next door.

"What's going on here?"

As Dai opened their bedroom door, the boys scattered towards their respective bunks, leaving a pile of crisp packets and cans of coke piled in the middle of the room. A discarded torch was still rolling around. He snapped the light on and they all squinted in the brightness.

"What are you lot up to?"

"We were hungry, sir," the boy nearest to him said.

"I don't see how you could be hungry after what you all ate at teatime."

"Yes, but—" Dai had heard enough. He held up his hand to stop the boy and bent down to gather up the crisps and coke.

"I'll take this lot, thank you, and I want you all dressed and waiting outside the dining room before breakfast. I'll make sure you're all far too tired for midnight feasts from now on."

He switched off the light and closed their door before his face cracked into a grin. He enjoyed being an ogre on occasions like these. The question now was, would he be able to get to sleep?

"Hilary! Are you awake?"

She knew who it was straight away – she'd recognize that voice anywhere.

"Yes. Is there a problem?" She started to get out of bed.

He shut the door and came and sat on her bed.

"No, there's no problem – well, nothing you need to get up for anyway."

"What's the matter then?" She was wide awake now and put on the bedside light so she could see Dai's face. He looked as lean and handsome as ever, sitting there in his fleece and jeans with his hair all tousled from tossing and turning.

"I'm the matter, Hils. I can't sleep, and it's because of you."

"Why? What have I done?"

"Nothing. You don't have to, something just happens to me when you're around. It's no good, Hils. I can't keep on ignoring it. I've been in love with you for a long time now."

She pulled him to her and stroked his hair. "I know. I feel the same, but it's no good; I'm married and so are you and there are enough complications in your life at the moment."

He didn't answer, just lifted his head and kissed her, long and tenderly, and before she had time to think, she was kissing him back. Their tongues explored each other's mouths and their hands explored each other's bodies.

He took off his clothes and she was lost; his body was in superb shape, lean and fit. He climbed in beside her and she tried to say something, but he put a finger to her lips and then kissed her again, and after that she was too busy enjoying the sensations to bother protesting anymore.

He began to massage her and she couldn't believe how good it felt as he turned her over onto her stomach and began to manipulate her flesh with expert fingers.

He straddled her and she could feel his erection caressing her buttocks as he worked on her shoulders, driving her crazy with the bites and nibbles he was giving her neck and ears. She could hear her own sounds of pleasure, but it was as if they were coming from someone else. Surely she wasn't capable of such sounds?

With strong arms, he lifted her up and round until she sat facing him in his lap with her legs crossed behind his back.

"What was it you were saying?" he mocked her, but she just kissed him passionately in reply whilst he lifted her up again and impaled her, his hands underneath her buttocks.

.He moved her backwards and forwards, slowly at first and then faster, until she picked up the rhythm and made it her own.

She came again and again, and was left sweating and panting for breath, like an animal after the hunt.

She lay like that for quite some time, her hand still clasped between her legs, relishing the release.

When her breathing had calmed down, she turned and looked at the clock. Six-thirty! Why had she woken up so early and felt so randy that she'd had to indulge in one of her favourite fantasies?

She fetched herself a glass of water and propped herself up on the pillows, sighing deeply. It was probably because she'd spent the previous evening drinking wine with Karen, Geoff and Dai. All the kids had seemed tired and were mostly settled in their rooms by about ten o'clock – if not asleep, then at least just quietly talking, so this was a good opportunity for the staff to get together for a bit of relaxation.

They had gathered in Karen and Geoff's room and for some reason the conversation had got round to 'first loves'.

"Mine was girl at school who used to play in the netball team," Dai revealed, "I just loved her long legs in that short pleated skirt."

"Right! No more netball practices to be covered by you then!" Karen teased him. "Mine was a boy I met on holiday with my parents. We were staying in this cottage in southern France and I used to offer to go and fetch the fresh croissants every morning so we could meet up and make our plan for the day. Ummmmm! He was really yummy."

"Was he French?" Geoff was looking slightly peeved.

"No, course he wasn't. He came from Macclesfield."

"Did you see him after the holiday?"

"This won't work if people start getting jealous, you know," Karen scolded him, but Geoff was undeterred. "Did you see him after the holiday?"

"No I didn't." Karen sounded decidedly edgy, but then she looked round to see Hilary and Dai propping each other up because they were laughing so much that they couldn't sit up, and she started to giggle, "You're jealous!" she accused Geoff.

"No I'm not. I'm just curious, that's all." He got up and poured himself another glass of wine.

"Alright then; tell us your first love and stop asking Karen questions," Hilary challenged him.

"OK. Mine was a busty sixth-former called Susan Whitehead. I used to worship her from afar until she pushed me into a corner at the school disco and started snogging me!"

"Then what?" Karen asked.

"Then I went off her 'cos she had bad breath."

They all burst out laughing and Karen threw a pillow at him. "You're still the same now; you can't stand it if I've had garlic. Anyhow, you remembered her name!" she accused him.

"What about you, Hilary?" Dai changed the subject before another row ensued.

"Mine was a young man who used to mow the next door neighbour's lawn. He used to strip to the waist and his back was all tanned and muscly. I used to watch him from my bedroom and lust after his tight buttocks in denim shorts."

"Ummmm, very nice," Karen agreed, "then what?"

"Then I went off him when my mum told me he'd been arrested for pushing drugs!"

"Well, it just goes to show you," Dai said.

"What?" the others all said at once.

"Love is blind." They all nodded sagely and took another sip of wine.

Hilary thought he might be about to open up, but it didn't happen and they all just drifted off back to their rooms soon afterwards. She felt so sorry for Dai, she could only guess at the pain and rejection he must be feeling; she wanted to take them away, but she knew she couldn't.

Maybe that was why she'd chosen that particular fantasy. She thought about Jack; she missed him. Sometimes she told him her fantasies and he found them a turn-on; she wouldn't be telling him that one!

She heard footsteps running along the landing and giggling outside her bedroom door – no more time for fantasies now.

CHAPTER 13

The alarm went off at 5.30a.m. Jack crawled his way up to consciousness. For a while, he was completely disorientated and couldn't figure out why he was in a single bed, then his brain began to function and he remembered he was at his parents' house. He must get up and go on the dreaded fitness weekend. He dragged himself out of bed with a heavy heart – there was nothing worse than having to get up at the crack of dawn on a cold, dark, winter's morning.

Finally, with the heater blasting, he was on the road. There had been a heavy frost and his headlights turned the verges into silver beards, edging the roads. Thank God for heated screens, he thought; he could remember when only rear screens were heated, but at least nowadays, the vital windscreen didn't take forever to defrost. Hopefully, the roads would be clear at this time of day and he'd have a good journey.

He made good progress for about an hour and a half and then he noticed the heater had packed up.

He fiddled with the controls, but it was no good – he was destined to feel the chill for the rest of the journey. *Typical! I've only had the car a couple of months and there are problems already.* He put the radio on for company – nothing – dead as a dodo. Now he started to get concerned, and tried the indicators – they seemed OK but no other electrics seemed to be working. "Shit! – That's all I need, car trouble, today of all days!" he said out loud.

A series of options ran through his head and he decided to take the car into the garage nearest to head office. They valued their Holme Farm account and therefore they'd pull out the stops to get the job done quickly, he reasoned. He checked his watch – he should be there as they opened, hopefully they'd lend him a car, or give him a lift to the office, as it was only about a mile away.

The mechanic was on his back, fiddling under the dashboard; he had a voltage meter and was probing in the depths with the leads, rather like a doctor with a stethoscope. Jack was tempted to ask if it was a boy or a girl, but he refrained. Instead, he wandered over to the glass-fronted office and went inside. The young woman behind the desk smiled apologetically. "We won't keep you long, Mr Baker, I'm sorry we haven't got a car for you, but Colin will run you over to Holme Farm in a few minutes."

Jack grunted, as he was too fed up to be civil, even though he knew she was being as helpful as she could. He checked his watch again – 9.05 – he was already late, which wasn't going to help matters at all. He picked up his mobile to ring and explain, when it rang – it was Anna.

"Hello, Daddy, it's me."

"Hello, poppet. How are you?"

"I'm fine. I just want to know if I can stay over at Jenny's tonight, she's just asked me to and Grandma says I have to have your permission."

"Oh, I don't know, why do you want to stay?"

"Because I'm going out with them for a meal and then the cinema and her mum said it would be easier."

"Put Grandma on, will you?"

"Hello, Jack, got there alright have you?"

"Well actually, no, but I'll tell you about that in a minute. Are you happy about Anna staying over?"

"Oh yes, love. It's no problem, Jenny's mum said she'll bring her back in the morning and she's picking her up this afternoon, so it's no trouble."

"OK then, tell her she can stay."

"What's happened to you then?"

"Oh, I'm having problems with the car. I'm at the garage now and I'm hoping to get it fixed, but they haven't got another one for me, so I might have to hire one to get home tomorrow."

"Oh dear. Well, let's hope they can fix it. Phone me before you leave tomorrow and let me know."

"OK then, bye."

Jack looked up just as a red-faced young man came rushing into the office. "Mr Baker? I'll give you a lift to Holme Farm now," he announced breathlessly.

Jack gathered together all his belongings and as they were walking over to the car, he said, "Have they found the problem yet?"

"No, they're still testing, but the boss says if you phone at lunchtime, we should know more then."

Jack sighed – it was obviously going to be one of those days!

When he arrived at Holme Farm, he trudged over to the Reception desk. "Jack Baker. I've got an appointment with John Fielding. I'm sorry I'm late, I had car trouble."

"Ah, yes, Mr Baker, Mr Fielding is in the gym, if you'd like to go down. Oh, and there's a message for you." She handed him an envelope with his name typed on the front. He opened it at once and read:

Dear Jack,

It is very important that I see you tonight. This isn't personal – it's to do with your health insurance. I've got some important information for you. Please phone me as soon as possible!

Angela

152

Jack put the note away and made his way to the gym. What was all this about? Was it to do with his insurance? Or was Angela trying to start things up again? He pushed it out of his mind for the time being. He was right about it not being a good day.

John Fielding looked up and smiled as he walked through the door; he was over the other side of the gym with a group of people.

"I'll be with you in a minute, Jack, just take a seat will you?"

Jack slumped down and looked at the note again. To do with health insurance – Angela wouldn't use that as an excuse, there must be something in it. He got out his mobile, and she answered straight away,

"Hello, Jack, I'm glad you phoned. Look, I've come across your name on the increased premiums list. Dr Anderson wrote a letter to Perma-Care about you and it doesn't look good!"

Jack was stunned. "That bastard! I'll wring his bloody neck when I see him."

"Don't do anything until I've seen you, I think I've got a plan – you must impress John Fielding today, make him see you've been trying hard."

"I have been trying hard, I've reached my target anyway." He looked up – it was obvious that John was finishing up and would be over any minute. "I'll have to go, where shall we meet? I've had problems with the car today and I don't know if it will be back or not." There was a moment's silence while Angela thought quickly.

"I'll pick you up at Holme Farm at six o'clock and we'll sort something out. OK?"

Jack could see John approaching. "OK, see you later," he said hurriedly and switched off.

"Morning, Jack. How are you doing?" He held out his hand.

"I'm fine, thanks, reached my target weight, ready for anything." He shook John's hand firmly and tried to look more confident than he felt.

"Well, that's good news! Let's go and do some tests then."

Half an hour later, Jack was beaming – he'd actually lost 9lbs in the fortnight and his fitness scores were improving. He sat down with John in his office, paying close attention to what he was saying.

"Well, weight-wise, only another six or seven pounds to go, Jack, and you'll be well within the acceptable range for your build. The rowing machine seems to be doing the trick too, because your muscle tone is improving, but we need to work on your stamina. You need something like aerobics or jogging to increase your staying power."

Jack nodded and tried to look enthusiastic. "What about today?" he asked.

John looked a little embarrassed. "Well, you've got an appointment with Claire, our weight counsellor, in ten minutes." Jack pulled a face.

"I know. I'm not sure that the appointment is necessary myself, but Dr Anderson has booked it for you, so we'd better go ahead."

Jack almost growled at the sound of Anderson's name. "He's got it in for me, John."

"Yes, it looks like it. What did you do to upset him?" John stood up, smiling.

"He caught me on a bad day," moaned Jack.

"Well, to be honest, he's not the easiest of blokes to get on with, but, after today, I can write a favourable report on you that will, hopefully, get him off your back."

Jack wasn't so sure, but he nodded and said, "So, what's the score after my counselling?"

"Well, there's an aerobics class after coffee, you can join us for that, and then, this afternoon, I think I'll spend some time in here with you, working on the machines which will improve your stamina the most. How does that sound?"

"Fine by me." Jack was just grateful to feel as if he was getting somewhere at last.

The weight counsellor turned out to be a pretty young woman, who agreed with Jack that he didn't really need the session.

"You know what you should be doing and you've achieved a significant weight loss in two weeks, Mr Baker, so I see no need to book another session and I shall inform Dr Anderson and Perma-Care to that effect."

She went on to hint to Jack that Robert Anderson was not a popular fellow within the health department. This information cheered Jack up immensely and he went off to coffee feeling much more positive.

He actually enjoyed the aerobics session with John's group and realised that his regular rowing and loss of weight had made a difference. He phoned the garage at lunchtime, to be told that there was a short circuit in his electrics and a couple of parts needed to be replaced. The mechanic was confident that they could get hold of the parts and deliver the car to the Fellside later that evening. Things were looking up. He set off to the gym with a spring in his step.

Charlie was baking. She was never happier than when she was in the kitchen, creating something.

She knew Anna liked carrot cake and she'd found a low-fat recipe, which still tasted delicious – when Jack came to pick Anna up tomorrow night, she'd give them this for dessert. There was something very satisfying about feeding carrots into the food-processor and watching them come out all shredded; she didn't know why that was, and it was probably not a good idea to think about it in too much detail. She hummed to herself and mused about her loved ones. Jack looked much better for his weight loss, and he and Hilary seemed more relaxed with each other, thank goodness. She fretted over all her offspring, but Jim and Susan had always seemed more capable somehow. When they were children, it was always Jack who got into trouble at school, usually because other, more devious friends, made suggestions and then got out of the way when trouble loomed, leaving Jack to face the music. He was also accident prone, getting into silly scrapes, like falling into the sewerage works when they were on holiday in Scotland. They were staying in a caravan and Jimmy and Susan had come running back, saying Jack was all smelly. They'd had to borrow a hose from the site-owner and hose him down before they could even take him to the shower-block. She chuckled out loud at the memory. He was always the most loving though, always wanting or giving a hug, always the one who remembered to bring her little presents back when he'd been anywhere.

She was lost somewhere, back in the past, when she heard the sound. It was almost imperceptible really, but some sixth sense rang alarm bells in her head. She switched off the processor and listened – there was nothing unusual, just the sound of the television. Alec was in the lounge, watching some Saturday afternoon sport. She decided to ask if he wanted a cup of tea, and wiping orange hands on a tea towel, she walked into the room. He was lying on the floor, where he'd fallen, one arm outstretched. Instinct made her run to him, feel his neck – he was still alive but he seemed to be unconscious. She thought, *heart attack*, and ran to the phone, dialling 999 with shaking hands. She answered questions as best she could, knowing it was important, but all she wanted to do was get back to him. She ran back and knelt by his side, stroking his face and talking to him. "Oh, Alec, I told you not to do so much, you're so stubborn, please don't die, don't you DARE die and leave me alone!"

Jack sank back into Angela's settee with a sigh of satisfaction. He was physically exhausted but mentally alert. The session in the gym had been pretty intensive but he felt he'd got somewhere and had come away with a useful programme, which he could take to his local fitness centre.

Now he was showered, changed and resting. Angela was rustling something up in the kitchen; she'd assured him that there was no danger of them continuing their physical relationship, she just wanted them to be friends, so he felt relaxed and pampered.

She appeared with two mugs of tea and sat down opposite him.

"How did you get on today?" she asked.

"Very well. I've lost nine pounds – only another six to go before I'm well within acceptable range, and my fitness has improved!" He was obviously very pleased with himself.

"What did John Fielding say?"

"He said he'd write a letter to Perma-Care, describing my progress and saying my attitude was good. He said Anderson was not a good man to cross, typical of me to be the one to upset him. The weight counsellor said he was very unpopular as well. She was going to write to Perma-Care as well, more or less saying he'd been wasting her time!" He sipped his tea and looked across at Angela; she looked very relaxed, slimmer than she had before, but she still had a gorgeous figure, shown off by a clingy sweater and jeans. She was obviously deep in thought, so he didn't interrupt; then she said, "Well, that's all good news, with all those good reports about you, persuading Bernie that Anderson's a vindictive bastard shouldn't prove too difficult – now we've just got to put a few nails in the coffin." She told Jack her plan. He was speechless when he heard that Bernard had an interest in the foodie bar, but when he'd had time to think, he wasn't so surprised.

"He's such a canny beggar. He probably uses all the surplus fat from the factory to make the cream they use!"

"Oh yes, he's up to that and more. I've worked for Bernard for a long time and I wouldn't put anything past him."

Jack had the same worry as Carla where Danny was concerned. "Bernie could get rid of Anderson and still not keep Danny on."

"Don't worry. I'll have a word with our dear boss – he owes me a few favours."

"Why are you doing all this, Angela? You don't owe any of us any favours."

"I told you before, I think you're a nice man, so is Danny and you don't deserve to lose your jobs just because some arrogant young doctor likes playing God." Her face was flushed with righteous indignation and it made Jack glad she was on his side.

"Well, all I can say is, I'm glad you feel that way," he smiled affectionately at her. "Don't go losing *your* job over any of this though, will you?"

"Don't worry. I can take care of myself – now let's stop talking business and enjoy what's left of the evening. I've prepared a chicken stir-fry and stuffed, baked apples – all very nourishing and healthy," she announced.

"What! No custard?" Jack quipped.

"Actually. There is custard, made with skimmed milk, so there!" She stuck her tongue out provocatively and Jack felt tempted by more than custard.

Charlie was feeling tired and, unusually but not surprisingly, weepy. She knew she needed some hot, sweet tea and probably something to eat if she could face it, but she couldn't find her way to the café. She seemed to have been walking for miles, following signs and getting no nearer. She was getting tired and panicky – the latest sign seemed to be pointing up some stairs and along the corridor at the same time. She looked around helplessly and saw a man in a green uniform coming out of a door. "Can you tell me how to get to the restaurant please?"

"Of course, love." He looked at her for a moment and then said, "I'm going that way myself, I'll show you the way if you like."

The relief flooded over Charlie – how did he know that was just what she wanted him to say? They walked along together and within a very short time, she was telling Malcolm all about Alec's collapse. By the time they reached the restaurant, he knew every detail. He was a nurse, so he was able to reassure her about the tests they would be doing and that her beloved husband was in good hands. He made her sit down and brought her a cup of hot, sweet tea. She could hardly drink it because there was such a knot in her stomach and she felt nauseous, but she sipped it and began to feel a little better. She was so grateful to him. It was comforting to know that people could still be so kind to strangers.

She had phoned all the kids, but Jack and Hilary hadn't replied yet.

Her mobile rang and when she heard Hilary's voice it all came out in such a rush. Charlie hardly stopped for breath – "and I can't get hold of Jack, they say he's booked in but he's not there yet and he's not answering his mobile, he had car trouble this morning, anyway, I've left a message, but he might not be able to make it 'til tomorrow anyway." And so it went on.

Hilary, at the other end, was momentarily numbed with shock about Alec, but then her brain kicked into action. "Don't worry, Charlie, I'll pick him up on my way down, I'll leave right away. What about Anna. Is she with you?"

"No, she's staying at Jenny's tonight and they're bringing her back in the morning."

"Well, that's one good thing anyway. What time are Jimmy and Susan due to arrive?"

"Well, they both said they'd leave straight away. I phoned them about half an hour ago."

Hilary did a quick mental calculation. Charlie would be on her own for about one, to one and a half hours – too long, if she got bad news.

"Look, Charlie, why don't you phone Mary-next-door, she'd come over and sit with you."

"Oh, I couldn't do that, she'll have settled down for the evening."

Hilary bit her lip. "OK, but don't worry, I'm sure Alec will be fine, we'll be there as soon as we can, you go and sit down somewhere until Susan and Jimmy arrive."

She said goodbye and put the phone down. Her mind was racing and she took the stairs two at a time, nearly knocking Karen over, as she was on her way to the shower room.

"Karen – I've got to get home – Alec's collapsed and Charlie's on her own at the hospital – the others are on their way – but I've got to get Jack, he's had car trouble, it couldn't have been at a worse time, normally we'd have been there, but we're so far away." It was all coming out in a rush, but Karen got the gist. "Look, you get your stuff together and I'll find Dai – are you taking Simon?"

Hilary stopped in her tracks. "I don't know, I ..." She carried on into her room and sat down on the bed. "I've got to get someone to be with Charlie, she's all alone, supposing she gets bad news, she won't phone Mary-next-door." Karen hadn't the faintest idea who Mary-next-door was, but she put two and two together.

"Have you got her number?" By now, Hilary was throwing things into her bag.

"Whose number?"

"This Mary-next-door person."

"I don't know – yes, I might have it in my address book somewhere."

"Well, I'll get Dai and Simon so you can see if he wants to come and you try phoning Mary."

By 5.30p.m. Hilary and Simon were ready to go, Mary-next-door was on her way to Walsgrave and Dai was assuring Hilary that they could manage without her.

"We've only got two more days to go, Hils, Karen's here for the girls, Geoff is an extra pair of hands for the rest of the weekend, and some of the better ones can keep an eye on the beginners. We'll be fine, you drive safely now."

Simon had insisted on coming – he adored his grandfather, and he wanted to be there. He sat next to his mother in silence as she drove, his face white and his young eyes troubled. He had a million questions going round in his head but he knew that now was not a good time to ask them.

Jack got up and stretched. "I'd better be going back, Angela, if you don't mind, I've got another long day tomorrow, aerobics again, then swimming and aqua aerobics and then I've got to drive home. Mind you, that's if I've got a car." He frowned. "I hope they've fixed it."

Angela drove him back to the Fellside. They were both quiet and felt awkward – Jack was very grateful for all she was doing for him, but he still wasn't a hundred per cent certain *why* she was doing it.

They pulled into the Fellside and Jack saw his car parked there. "Thank goodness for that," he breathed. "That's one less problem to worry about." He turned to Angela. "Thanks for tonight and all you're doing for me."

"That's alright, I enjoy it, I told you why." She pulled the boot release and Jack got out and collected all his gear. He went round to the open driver's window.

"Take care of yourself."

"I will, don't worry – I'll email you on developments."

"OK." He bent down and pecked her on the cheek. "Bye for now."

She pulled the car into a U-turn and waved as she drove past. Jack started walking over towards his car, and then he noticed someone standing by a car parked right in front of him. The person and the car looked familiar, and for a second he couldn't think why, then horrific realisation dawned as a female voice called his name.

"Jack."

"Hilary! What are you doing here?"

CHAPTER 14

*C*harlie sat alone on a hard chair in the waiting room and faced widowhood. She had wondered about it many times before, fleetingly; when a friend had been widowed or she'd seen something on the news about an accident or disaster, but she had never really given it any serious thought.

She sat now and took it from that dark corner of her mind where it lurked and she really looked at it, and she was appalled. She put her hands up to her face, perhaps in an effort to wipe away the image of herself at the funeral; surrounded by family, but already feeling the loneliness.

"Here you are, dear – drink this, it will make you feel better." Mary-next-door stood next to her with a steaming cup of tea. "Wait a minute now, I've got something else here somewhere."

The older woman reached into her handbag and took out a miniature brandy, which she emptied into the plastic cup, all but a drop which she kept for her own.

Charlie made no objection and found the mixture of the steamy liquid and the alcohol a comforting combination.

"Ever since Albert died, I've always kept some handy, you just never know." She sipped her own drink and stared into space.

Charlie was shocked to realise that this kindly woman, her next-door neighbour, already occupied the awful kingdom of widowhood, which she'd been contemplating a minute before. Mary-next-door, they called her. Mary was already a widow when she and Alec had moved to their present home and Charlie couldn't remember when she'd said her husband had died, she didn't think it was long before they'd move there, but she wasn't sure – she was horrified with herself, that she'd taken so little notice of this traumatic event in Mary's life. She remembered that he'd died of a heart attack, but that was all. They just didn't talk about it – they didn't talk much at all really, just exchanged comments on the weather and their state of health, gossiped about the neighbours occasionally, and did small kindnesses for each other. Now here they were, sitting together at what could be the gateway to Charlie's new world. She shook her head to clear her thoughts.

"They'll be back soon to let you know the results." Mary patted her on the shoulder and carried on sipping her tea.

The automatic doors opened and Charlie recognised her eldest son. He came in quickly, scanning the room; she saw him before he saw her. Her heart lurched, because he was so like his father, taller and balder than Alec, but the face was just a younger version, and she felt the tears well up as he hurried across and sat on the other side of her, his arm across her shoulder. She couldn't stop the tears then, it was the first time she'd cried since it happened, and she didn't think she'd ever stop.

Jimmy was asking her questions. "Where is he? What have they said? Is it his heart or what, Mum? Please don't cry, he'll be alright, Mum. How long have they left you here like this?"

All this, while Charlie carried on sobbing – she hadn't answered anything.

"It will do her good," Mary announced. And Charlie smiled within and despite herself at the perplexed look her eldest son gave her neighbour. "Always does you good to let it out, doesn't do to bottle it up, you know."

Charlie blew her nose and turned to her son. "They've taken him off for some more tests, they've kept me informed

163

and I've had plenty of hot tea. It's not his heart, could be a stroke or a cerebral haemorrhage, they'll know soon." She heard her own voice and was amazed at how calm it sounded.

Jim didn't say anything at first, it was all just sinking in, then he said, "Bethany sends her love, I've got to phone her when we know what's happening – where are the others? Have you phoned them?"

"Yes. Susan's on her way and Hilary is driving down from Scotland with Simon. I can't get hold of Jack, he's on a fitness weekend, Hilary's picking him up, he had car trouble this morning."

Talking about familiar people and things calmed her. Mary tapped her on the shoulder. "There's that nice young doctor again, dear."

A young woman in a white coat walked across the room; she had long blonde curls tied back from her face, and calm, blue eyes. She was smiling as she approached and Charlie took that to be a good sign.

"We've completed all the tests, Mrs Baker, and you can come and see Alec now – he's conscious and we're just popping him into bed."

The relief washed over her in a wave and Charlie felt quite literally light-hearted.

"Why was he unconscious?" Jimmy asked.

"He has had a stroke, Mr, er?"

"This is my son," Charlie explained.

"I thought so, I can see the resemblance." The young woman smiled. "Alec has suffered a stroke to the right hemisphere of the brain, there is some paralysis to the left side but we don't think it is too severe, it's early days yet. The physiotherapist will do an assessment tomorrow, we'll know more then."

"Why have the tests taken so long?" Jimmy was taking control now.

"When someone comes in with Alec's symptoms, Mr Baker, we have to ensure that there is no bleeding inside the brain, because the drugs we give to counteract the effects of a stroke can actually make bleeding worse, whereas they will help to disperse a blood clot. Now we know that Alec has no bleeding, we can treat him with clot-busting drugs, which hopefully will minimise the effects of his stroke."

Charlie was already standing up, eager to get to Alec.

Mary stood up stiffly. "Ah well, that's good news then." Jimmy looked puzzled again; he couldn't quite figure out how Alec's stroke was good news, but then she went on, "He's right-handed, so he won't be so helpless – it's when they're helpless that they're such a burden." She tutted and shook her head. "I'll be off then, Charlie."

"Thank you so much for being here, Mary, I'll come and see you tomorrow." She kissed the wrinkled cheek, and the other woman said, "No rush, dear, you just concentrate on Alec for a while, give him my love, I'll see you when you have a minute – no rush."

The two women walked to the door and Jimmy watched them – women in a crisis were an enigma to him. They became like alien beings, doing and saying strange, inexplicable things, which only they understood. He'd been through it a lot recently with Bethany and her sisters and their reactions to their mother's illness. She'd recently undergone heart surgery and seemed to be recovering very well now, but during the weeks before her operation and immediately after, he'd witnessed these strange rituals. They seemed to consist largely of long and frequent phone calls and hushed conversations in the kitchen over copious amounts of tea.

Charlie came back to join him and they walked together to Alec's ward.

Hilary concentrated on her driving; she told herself that she must get to the hospital safely and see Alec and Charlie. Then, she could think about what she'd seen – then, she could tackle Jack and ask all the questions that were fighting to be asked. There would be a perfectly rational explanation, there had to be, the alternative was too awful to contemplate. She blinked back the tears – she was incredibly tired. Simon slept beside her, and she felt like a lioness protecting her cub. Nothing would threaten her children and their security, she'd see to that!

She pulled off the road, into the services. Jack had told her to stop. "At least promise me you'll stop on the way for a coffee, you look exhausted." His eyes had been full of concern because she'd insisted that he should drive his car back, she could see them now, but she could also see the look of blind panic when he'd realised it was she who'd called his name.

She drank strong coffee and ate a sandwich, trying to answer Simon's questions as calmly as she could.

"I wish I could drive, Mum, and then you could have a sleep, you look very tired."

Hilary smiled at him. "I'll be alright, one day you'll learn to drive, and I'll enjoy you driving me around, but for now, it's up to me. Come on, let's get going, it's not far now, you'll have to stay awake and talk to me!"

"OK. I'll ask you questions."

"Oh no, not questions." They both laughed and walked hand in hand back to the car, something Simon would only contemplate in the dark and where nobody knew him.

Jack drove on autopilot – he was numb with shock, how could his father have collapsed? He was stronger than anyone he knew and had never been ill in his life. He couldn't die! That just wasn't going to happen. When he got to the hospital, Alec would be sitting up in bed, and being incredibly grumpy because everyone was making such a fuss. And what about Charlie? She'd be devastated, she worshipped him, they worshipped each other. She was strong in lots of ways, but not this way, Alec was her rock and without him, she would crumble.

Oh, God, why did this have to happen while I was so far away? Usually we're so close by.

Then there was Hilary – she'd looked totally destroyed, was it because of Alec? Or was it because of what she'd seen?

Jack gritted his teeth. He was so angry with the fates for what they had done, now, after it was all over – now Hilary would suffer when she didn't need to and that would mean he would suffer too. She hadn't said anything, but Jack knew Hilary, she was in shock at the moment, it would come out later. If only he hadn't switched his phone off, he would have got Charlie's call, he could have been back with Alec and Charlie before Hilary was half way. He'd have been home and dry.

As it was he was drowning.

He sighed. Ah well, all that would have to be dealt with when the time came – first of all, he must get to the hospital.

It was after one in the morning, when he arrived at the hospital. Walsgrave always reminded him of an airport for some reason – it certainly looked like one now, a tall building, all lit up and surrounded by cars. He found a space and made his way to reception. After what seemed like an eternity, he found the right ward.

Alec was propped up on pillows and surrounded by tubes and paraphernalia – he was sleeping. Charlie and Susan were sitting next to each other, propping each other up like two rag dolls, their heads lolling as they dozed.

Jack stood for a moment, looking at his father – he looked old and frail suddenly, not the vibrant, strong man that Jack had visualised. Life could be very cruel.

Charlie stirred and looked up. "Jack, you've made it. Where's Hilary?"

"She's following, Mum, my car was OK so I came on ahead." He was whispering.

Susan stood up and rubbed her neck and Jack walked over and kissed his mother.

"How is he, Mum? What have they said?"

"He's had a stroke, love. They will know more tomorrow after he's had an assessment, but it's the right side of his brain that's been affected so his speech should be alright, thank God."

Jack was stunned – a stroke – he couldn't really take it in.

"Does anyone want a drink?" Susan asked.

"Yes please," they said in unison.

Susan just looked at them both, eyebrows raised and Jack said, "Coffee please."

"Tea, please, dear," Charlie followed.

Jack sat down and held his mother's hand. "How are you feeling?"

"I'm alright, tired, but at least he's alive, and I know what it is now, it was the not knowing that was the worst part."

"How did it happen?"

"Well, I was making a carrot cake, for you and Anna, and I heard a noise, so I went into the lounge and there he was, lying on the floor. It was awful, I thought he was dead." She shook her head again to get rid of the picture. Jack patted her hand and looked at Alec.

"What have they given him?"

"He's on this clot-busting drug and he's had a mild sedative – he's been sleeping for quite a while now. When Jimmy and I first saw him he was awake and he smiled at me and squeezed my hand."

"What are all these tubes and things?"

"They look worse than they are, love, he's got oxygen and the clot-buster and a catheter for now and ..." She stopped and pushed her hair back and Jack could see the tears in her eyes.

"Why don't you go home, Mum, you need to sleep."

"Everyone's said that, but I want to stay until he's had his assessment in the morning and then I'll have a sleep. Jimmy's gone back to our house and he'll be back in the morning. I wouldn't sleep anyway at the moment." She rubbed her eyes and looked over at Alec.

Susan came back with steaming plastic cups and they all drank in silence, then she looked at Jack and jerked her head in the direction of the door. Jack got up reluctantly because he knew his sister. He could guess what was coming. "We've got to get Mum out of here, she's exhausted," Susan hissed.

"I've just tried, but she's adamant that she's staying with Dad, she says she'll go after the assessment, and Jimmy will come back in the morning."

Susan tutted, "Next thing we know, she'll be ill."

Jack smiled. Susan hadn't changed, she'd always been impatient.

"She'll be fine, they're both tougher than you think."

"Where were you anyway? Mum tried your mobile but it was switched off." She looked at him accusingly. Jack gulped; this was so typical of Susan, she could change tack so quickly it took your breath away.

"I was in the gym – it's difficult to talk on the phone and pump weights at the same time, then I just forgot to switch it back on," he snapped back.

Good job we can both think quickly, sister dear.

At least she seemed to accept his explanation.

She leant against the wall and sipped her drink. Jack thought she looked pale, but otherwise she was the epitome of the young career woman – designer trousers and cashmere sweater, her shiny dark hair, cut into a business-like bob. She was slim, well-groomed and efficient looking, just what one would expect from a successful young accountant. She turned back to Jack.

"This is going to change everything, you know."

"What do you mean?"

"Well, think about it. Mum and Dad have always been a partnership, happily pottering in their own little domains and mutually supporting each other. Now, all the pressure will be on Mum, she'll become the prime carer and she'll need help."

"They haven't even done the assessment yet – we don't know how Dad will be affected, don't write him off too soon, Sue."

She gave him one of her 'you're so stupid' looks just like she used to do when they were children.

Even though she was three years younger than him, she'd always acted older and she'd always thought he was an inferior being.

He turned away and walked back into the room to sit next to Charlie. She smiled at him and he wanted to hug her and take all her worries away, as he took her hand and squeezed it. They both sat in silent companionship, watching a man they loved as he slept.

Then Jack heard familiar voices outside, and Hilary and Simon crept into the room. Hilary went straight to Charlie and hugged and kissed her, and Simon came and stood next to Jack; he hugged him close to his body and found the contact comforting. The boy stood and stared at his grandfather, his young face showing such concern that Jack led him gently outside.

"Grandpa's had a stroke. It's a blood clot that stops the flow of blood to the brain for a while. He's not going to die, Simon, the doctors will give him some drugs and he'll get better."

Simon just nodded and Jack hugged him again.

Susan had been standing looking out of the window when her brother and nephew came out of the room. She'd watched Jack explaining so gently to his son and it had melted her heart. She was strong and she'd coped up to now, but it was as if, once her defences were breached, she let all the feelings rush in and the tears poured down her cheeks. She stood where she was, arms crossed over her chest, and let them come.

Hilary came out of the room, and, without looking at Jack, she said to Simon, "Come on, let's take you home, we'll come back to see Grandpa in the morning."

Simon looked at his father. "Aren't you coming, Dad?"

"Yes, I'll follow you, I'll just say goodnight to Grandma and then I'm coming home." He looked at Hilary, but she'd already turned away and he knew there was trouble brewing. He sighed and walked over to Susan.

"Do you want to go and get some rest? I'll stay with Mum if you want."

"No, you go. I'll stay with Mum and sleep tomorrow."

"Where's Geoff?"

"He's at home. He has to deliver a paper to this conference in Edinburgh tomorrow – it's the culmination of about two years' work, so I told him not to come."

She was still hugging herself and she looked tired and vulnerable; very unusual for Susan. Jack leant forward and kissed her on the forehead and as he held her, he could feel the tension in her arms, and could see she'd been crying.

"He'll be alright, you know, he's a tough old bugger. I bet you that by tomorrow, he'll be driving us all mad."

Susan smiled. "I expect you're right – off you go now, you've had a long drive, I'll catch up with you later tomorrow."

Jack said goodnight to Charlie and promised to come back in the morning, then he headed home.

When he got in, the house was in darkness and he realised how tired he was – he just wanted his bed. He undressed in the dark and climbed into bed. It felt cold and empty as he reached across in the dark but there was no one there. Hilary's car had been outside, so he knew she was back. He lay in the dark and sighed deeply. He was right, trouble was brewing, but right now he was too tired to think about it.

CHAPTER 15

Jack woke up with a start. He'd been dreaming; he couldn't remember it but he knew it wasn't pleasant. He was sweating and he had a headache. He reached for the clock – 9.30. He listened for sounds of life – nothing. He struggled up and put on his dressing gown, made his way to the bathroom and grabbed the headache pills. The phone rang just as he was swallowing them.

"Hello."

"Jack?"

"Hi, Jimmy. How's things?"

"Look, I'm just off to see Dad. Do you want me to pick you up? I heard you had a long drive last night."

"Yeah, that would be great. I'm not feeling on top of the world this morning."

"OK. I'll be right over."

Jack put the phone down and felt reluctant to move. He felt as if his life was out of his control and running away with him. He went in search of his family but there was no one around – the beds had been made and the kitchen was all tidy. God! Hilary must have been as tired as he was. How had she managed to get up early enough to have done everything and get out, with Simon as well, he must be shattered too. What was she up to? He dragged himself back upstairs to get ready.

By the time Jimmy arrived, Jack was sitting at the kitchen table sipping coffee and his headache was beginning to subside. They greeted each other with a handshake; Jack would have hugged his brother willingly but he knew it would make Jim feel awkward.

"Want a coffee?" Jack asked.

"No thanks, I think we'd better get on, I want to get Mum home as soon as she'll leave. Where's the gang?" Jimmy was looking round. *Good question!* Jack thought.

"To be honest, I don't know. They left me sleeping."

"You're lucky! My lot would have made sure I was awake."

Jack was relieved that he'd dismissed it so lightly. He nodded and they made their way out to the car. As always, it was the latest model, there had to be some perks in working for a motor company, Jim always said.

"How was the old man when you saw him last night then?"

Jack sighed. "Well, it was hard to tell, he was sedated, tubes everywhere, but stable, we were told."

"About the same as when I was there then; he'll be alright you know, he's a tough old bugger."

Jack smiled. "That's what I told Susan, she was getting all dramatic, saying things would never be the same and Mum would need help and so on."

"You know Susan, she'll invent a crisis and then pretend she's solved it, so she can go back to her ordered little world and be smug about it."

"That's a bit harsh, she adores Dad, she was very upset actually."

Jim had the grace not to reply, he just concentrated on his driving for a while.

You never got on, Jack thought, *too much of an age gap for one thing but also you're too much of a chauvinist, big brother – never liked the idea of little sister earning more than you.*

Jack broke the silence and asked, "How's your lot then? How's Bethany's mother doing?"

"She's picking up quite well actually, it was touch and go for a while though. The others are fine, kids costing me a fortune!"

"Tell me about it." Jack groaned.

"Bethany is thinking of going back to work."

Jack was surprised. "Really. I thought she always said she wanted to be a full-time wife and mother."

"She did, but we need the money. We bumped into her old boss at a party the other week; they got talking, and he persuaded her to try part-time for a bit first and see how she gets on. She starts tomorrow – that's why she didn't come with me, too much to organise."

Bethany used to work for an estate agent and had been a very smart young lady when Jim had started going out with her. Jack could remember how proud his brother had been, introducing this vibrant, sophisticated young woman to his family. Jack had found her extremely attractive and had been quite envious of Jimmy. She was slim and petite, but she'd always worn high heels to add to her height. She'd had a sleek, short haircut, which emphasized her huge eyes and she'd always been immaculately turned out, nail varnish, the works. Jack had always loved her soft, husky voice and the fact that when she spoke to you, you felt as if you were the only man in the world.

Nowadays, after three children and sixteen years of marriage, she looked decidedly frumpy, her hair was long and lank, she'd put on weight, and most of the time, she wore shapeless ensembles, which made her look even bigger. Jack couldn't imagine her being an asset to any business.

"It will do her good," he said with feeling.

Jim jerked his head round. "What's that supposed to mean?"

Jack hadn't realised that his thoughts had added such vehemence to his words – he was always doing that. "Oh, nothing, just that she's probably been bored, you know, she'll probably enjoy getting out and about again."

Jim didn't say anything and Jack looked out of the window. There was a fine drizzle falling and it was bitterly cold – the sort of day when people just huddle up and get wherever they are going as quickly as possible, no time or inclination for any niceties.

They had to stop at a pelican crossing, and a young mother with a pushchair and a toddler in tow hurried across the road. She had on jeans and a short jacket, no gloves, no hat; her hair was sticking to her face in rat's tails and she was pulling the toddler, his feet hardly touching the ground. Her face was set grimly and it looked blue with cold. *Probably a single mother*, Jack thought, *poor thing – maybe, if Hilary divorces me, I can find another family to take care of, one that will appreciate me.* He was horrified at his thoughts and shifted in his seat. Jimmy must have sensed his disquiet because he asked, "What about your lot then? Is Hilary as fit as ever?"

"Oh yes, still jogging and eating muesli, generally in control – she's just been on a school skiing trip took Simon with her, but they had to come back in a hurry last night."

"Was he enjoying it?"

"I haven't had a chance to ask him yet," Jack retorted bitterly. He desperately wanted to see his kids, feel their unconditional love, it was becoming a growing need. Where were they? Surely Hilary wouldn't just take them off, simply because she'd seen him kiss another woman on the cheek!

Jim was talking again. " Listen, once we've seen the old man and got Mum safely back home, why don't we go for a pint somewhere, it's been a long time since we've spent any time together, what do you think?"

"I think it's an excellent idea – we'll get Mum home and then go to Dad's local, they do a good pint in there."

That being decided, Jack cheered up – he was just being paranoid, Hilary had never done anything impulsive in her life. He was tired and worried about his father and that was making him imagine things.

When they reached Alec's room, Susan was standing outside, sipping a hot drink. She looked up and smiled when she saw them and they both kissed her.

"I see the cavalry have arrived," she quipped.

"Don't you be so cheeky," Jimmy scolded, "How's things then?"

"Well, at the moment the doctor's giving him the once over, but the news isn't too bad."

"What do you mean?" Jack was looking around for Charlie. "Where's Mum?"

"Hilary's taken her home for a sleep – once the assessment was made, we persuaded her to go."

Jack looked stupefied. "Hilary?"

"Yes, didn't you know? She said she'd left you sleeping and gone to pick Anna up. She wanted to see her grandpa, so she came here and took Mum home – she looked shattered, but competent as ever."

Jack just nodded; Jim gave him a sideways look and then said, "What did you mean, 'the news isn't too bad'?"

"Well, the speech therapist and physiotherapist have assessed him – his speech will be OK.

It's the right side of his brain that's affected, so his left side is partially paralysed, but they can work on that. Mainly, he will have trouble with things like dressing himself, co-ordination, walking, of course and short-term memory. They can work on all these things, it will be a long process they say, but eventually he should get back to almost normal. Oh, one other thing, he will probably try to do too much – he won't realise that he *can't* do certain things and this could lead to falls and obviously to a lot of frustration. They've given us a few booklets to read."

Both men looked shocked – they knew their father only too well, knew what he liked to do, how independent he was, and they were both appalled at the struggle he had ahead of him.

Susan carried on drinking her coffee and waited for it all to sink in.

Jack spoke first. "Oh, God. He's going to be unbearable!"

"Yes, quite," Susan nodded, "As I said last night, Mum will need all the help she can get and the patience of a saint!"

Jimmy had the grace to look sheepish.

The door of Alec's room opened and a young man came out, followed by two nurses. Susan introduced her brothers.

Dr O'Reilly smiled. "You'll all be pleased to know that Alec is doing very well. His condition is stable, we've got him on clot-busters and blood-pressure reducers, but other than that, there's no need for any other medication. We'll probably be able to stop the blood pressure ones in a couple of days. He is still a little confused, but that is perfectly normal, and it will diminish soon. If he carries on as well as this, we can move him to the rehab unit in a couple of days and start his programme. You've got the booklets haven't you? Good – well if you have any worries don't hesitate to ask any of the staff. I'll be back to check him again in the morning." And he walked quickly away.

Another nurse came out and said, "You can go in now. Alec might drift off to sleep now and then, but that's perfectly normal, so don't worry."

This time, Jack thought his father looked slightly better. He was propped up on pillows – he still had a few tubes, but not so many and he had more colour. He smiled in recognition as they all trooped in. They all kissed him, even Jimmy, which surprised everyone.

"Where's your mother?" Alec asked.

"She's gone home to have a sleep, Dad, she's been here with you all night and she's very tired," Susan told him.

"I didn't see her," he said stubbornly.

"Well she *was* here, with me, all night, and she'll be back this afternoon."

He looked extremely dubious, so Jack said, "Have you had breakfast?"

"Breakfast?"

"Yes, Dad. Have you eaten anything?"

Susan intervened. "He could only have liquids until the assessment because they have to check the swallow reflex, but they said he could have baby food at lunchtime."

Alec screwed up his face and Susan smiled, "It's only for today, you'll soon be back to normal."

"Where's your mother?" he asked again.

Susan repeated what she'd said before and Jimmy walked over to the window. Jack could see he was struggling with his emotions, and he turned to Susan. "What about you? It's about time you went to get some sleep too."

She nodded. "Yes, I'll drive back to Mum's and crash there for a while, and then I'll pop in tonight on my way back down to London. I'll keep in touch and be up again at the weekend. Keep an eye on Mum, won't you."

"You know I will," Jack told her.

She bent down and kissed her father. "I'm off now, Dad, to get some sleep, the boys will stay with you for a while."

"OK, OK. I'm alright, you know."

Susan smiled at him and blew kisses to her brothers before going out of the room.

Jack looked around for a television, desperate to find a distraction, but there was nothing.

The three men were silent, all locked in their own world.

Jack sat by the bed and Alec closed his eyes, mercifully drifting off to sleep. Jimmy turned away from the window and looked at Jack. "What do we do now?"

Jack shook his head and looked at his watch – 11.30. "I don't know, we've just got here – Mum and Susan were here all night. What did they do?"

"God knows, slept, I suppose." He paced around the room for a while and then sat down, opposite Jack; both men watched Alec sleeping.

"I can't get over it," Jimmy whispered, "One minute he's fine, strong and healthy, working on all his projects and now this." He gestured towards the bed angrily, as if Alec was something disgusting. Jack felt protective. "It can happen to anyone, it could happen to you, it's not his fault. I bet you anything you like, he'll be back to normal in no time."

"You always were naive, little brother," Jim said bitterly and he started pacing again.

Jack knew how Jimmy was feeling, so he didn't pursue the conversation, besides, he wasn't sure that Alec couldn't hear them. Jimmy turned round. "Look! Why don't we go for that pint now? He's sleeping, so we can't do anything, we can come back later this afternoon."

Jack hesitated. He felt he should stay, and yet, like Jimmy, he didn't know what to do – he felt awkward and restless.

"Won't they expect us to be here?"

"Who?"

"Well, Mum and Susan for a start."

"I don't see why. They're sleeping anyway."

"But what if something happens?"

"Like what?"

"You know – what if he gets worse or something?"

"He's fine now, he's on all these drugs, he'll probably sleep the rest of the day."

Alec opened his eyes and looked at them. "Where's your mother?"

"She's sleeping Dad, she's been here all night and she's sleeping now, she'll be back later," Jack told him.

"Shouldn't you two be at work?"

Jack smiled, "It's Sunday, Dad, we'll be back at work tomorrow."

"I'm bloody thirsty, call that nurse, will you."

Jimmy jumped up, happy to be doing something and made for the door. "Wait a minute." Jack stopped him. "It's here by your hand, look. You press the button when you want the nurse, Dad."

Alec dutifully pressed the button, and shortly afterwards a nurse appeared.

"He's very thirsty," Jim announced.

"OK, Alec. Let's see how we go."

She held what looked like a baby cup to his lips and he managed to take some sips.

"The water is here by the bed, Alec, you can reach it with your right hand, look." She showed him that he could reach it, checked the tubes and monitors and was just going towards the door when Jim cleared his throat. "Um, we were thinking of going now, so he can sleep, just to let you know he'll be on his own, um ..." he tailed off.

"That's fine, Mr Baker, we're checking him regularly, he'll probably be moving into the main ward later today, so he won't get lonely."

"Oh, OK."

The nurse left and Alec closed his eyes. "We're going now, Dad, so you can sleep," Jack said, but there was no response. Jimmy jerked his head towards the door and both men tiptoed out.

Sitting in the pub a while later, with pints in front of them, the brothers began to relax.

"God, that tastes good." Jimmy sighed.

"I bet Dad would enjoy one," Jack said, "I hope it won't be too long before he can join us again."

"I think it will be a while – he's still so confused, isn't he? Keeps asking for Mum. I expect it's the drugs as much as anything."

Both men sipped their pints and sat in silence for a while and then Jack asked,

"How's the job going?"

"Plodding along – we're working on a new prototype at the moment."

"Anything you can talk about?"

"Not really, except to say that it's a hybrid." Jimmy smiled.

He worked as a development engineer for a major car manufacturer and he was always at the stage where he 'couldn't say'; then when a new model came out and Jack had read all about it in his car magazine, Jimmy would phone and tell him all about it.

"Most car manufacturers are working on electric or hybrid these days, or at least, they say they are – that's not giving any secrets away."

Jimmy smiled. "Sorry, that's all I can say. How's the dairy business? Old Bernie still as canny as ever?"

"Old Bernie's alright – he's not the one I'm worried about."

"Oh?"

"No, it's me I'm worried about. I've been told to lose weight and get fitter or else my premiums will go up – some super-keen doctor took a dislike to me." Jack sipped his pint.

"You look alright to me," Jimmy commented with brotherly solidarity.

"I might look alright but I've still got six pounds to lose. I made my original target on time, but our dear doctor saw fit to assume I wouldn't and wrote to Perma-Care."

"Well, that's a bit much isn't it? Is that why you were up at this fitness thing then?"

"Yeah, partly." Jack hesitated – he badly needed to offload on someone and maybe Jimmy would be able to give him some advice. He took a deep breath and ploughed in – half an hour and another pint later, he finished his tale. His brother sat back and pronounced his verdict. "What a bloody mess, Jack! What in heaven's name possessed you?"

No sympathy here then. "I don't know. It just happened."

"And you think she's helping you out of the goodness of her heart! Just because you gave her a good seeing-to. Bloody hell, man! She's not going to let you go now, she's unhappy with hubby, for all you know, he might have already have been sent packing – you've only her word for it that he hasn't and now Hilary knows, *she* might send *you* packing too."

"It's not like that, Jim, and yes, Hilary might want to send me packing, but I want to stay with my family, I want to carry on as I am."

"Bit bloody late for that, mate – you'll lose your kids and probably everything else you have, and for what? A one-night stand! God! What a weekend! My dad in hospital and my brother in shit!"

"I should have known better than to think I'd get any useful advice from you," Jack said bitterly, "Come on, I've got to get back." He stood up, and Jimmy's shoulders slumped.

"Come on, Jack, you can't blame me – it's been a shock that's all, look, sit down again and we'll talk about it."

"There's nothing to talk about is there, Jim? It's my problem and I'll sort it." He stood there glaring down at his brother and the other man got up reluctantly. They walked to the car in silence and after a minute or so, Jimmy said,

"You won't tell Mum and Dad about this, will you?"

"Of course not," Jack snapped, "What do you take me for? Don't you tell anyone about it either, particularly Bethany. Hilary doesn't know all the details yet and I want to talk to her before she hears it from anyone else."

"You're not going to tell Hilary everything, are you?" Jim screeched, "You must be mad! For God's sake Jack, have some sense, if you must tell her something, say it was a moment of madness and leave it at that."

There was silence while Jack thought about it – there was some sense in what his brother had said.

"I'll see," he muttered.

Jimmy sighed, "Well, that's something, I suppose."

When they got back to Jack's house, there was still no sign of life.

"Do you want that coffee now?" Jack asked.

"No, I'd better not. I'll go back round to Mum's and take her back to the hospital this afternoon, then I'd better be getting back home." He looked uncomfortable.

"Look, Jack, if you need to talk any time, just give me a ring – I'll be to and fro to see Dad in any case, so we can get together."

Jack sighed; he knew this was Jimmy's way of saying he was sorry.

"Don't worry, I'll get it sorted, but thanks anyway, I'll see you when you come to see Dad, take care now."

They waved goodbye and Jack went into the empty house – he headed for the kitchen and made himself scrambled eggs because it was quick and easy, and was just finishing it, when he heard a car. He held his breath as the front door opened and let it out with a huge sigh of relief as he heard Simon and Anna chattering away. They came into the kitchen clutching shopping bags and were already arguing about what they wanted for lunch.

"Hi, Dad." Anna said it so naturally that he wanted to hug her.

"Hi, poppet, how was your sleepover?"

"It was great! Jenny's mum didn't know, but we stayed up until one o'clock. We were surfing the net for music videos. We couldn't find one we liked for ages, there were all sorts of weird things, but eventually we found the one we wanted."

"What was that?" Her father hardly dared to ask.

"The recording of Cole Train's last concert, of course."

Both parents breathed a sigh of relief. Jack looked at Hilary, whose mouth was set very grimly and back at Anna, who was already busy unpacking food. He didn't know what else to say.

Simon piped up, "Didn't Jenny's parents have a block?"

"I don't think they know," Anna replied.

Jack and Hilary knew they should have checked, but with all that had been happening, they had been very remiss.

Simon then added, "Peter found out his dad's last password, and for a while, we could get into the system, but then his mum found out and it's changed again now." He said this as though some great injustice had been done.

Brother and sister had extricated their favourite snack foods from the shopping bags and made their way out of the kitchen as if they had said nothing out of the ordinary.

Jack was stunned. "Do we need to talk about this?"

"What?"

"The fact that our eleven-year-old son and possibly our nine-year-old daughter have been watching highly unsuitable movies in the middle of the night!"

Hilary stopped what she was doing and looked at him. "Yes, Jack, we probably do need to talk about it, but there are one or two other things I want to talk about first."

Jack sighed and turned away. "I thought there might be."

CHAPTER 16

*A*ngela was sweating – she was so hot, she thought she might spontaneously combust and all that would be left would be a sticky mess of melted cling-film and green mud on the floor of the treatment room. Why had she decided to have this particular treatment? She could have had an aromatherapy massage, or a bust treatment, or hydrotherapy, but no, she had to go for the detoxifying body mask.

It had been quite pleasant at first, when the mud was smeared on, but once the cling-film was on and the heat applied, it became decidedly unpleasant. She'd never feel quite the same about the Sunday roast again. She sighed and blew out through her mouth, as if this tiny exhalation of breath might cool her, next she threw off the blanket that protected her modesty – she was so hot now, she didn't care if the whole world saw her mummified state. Her next step would have been to start tearing at the cling-film, but luckily, the door opened just then and the beautician came back in.

"Oh, thank goodness, I think I must be cooked now."

"Don't worry, once I've unpeeled you, there's a nice, cooling shower to follow."

Angela didn't think a simple shower would ever be as welcome again.

Later, wrapped in towelling robes and sipping health drinks in the conservatory, Angela and Carla were in relaxed mode. They'd been scrubbed, rubbed, pampered and preened and now, all that remained was for them to relax before the final hurdle of facials and hairdo's. Oh, and the bill of course.

"I'd come again. Would you?" Angela murmured, stretching out on the rattan chaise lounge.

"Oh, yes, when I can afford it." Carla was gazing out at the landscaped garden – it was beginning to get dark again and yet there were patches of frost in the shadows that had never melted; it was a bitterly cold day, but inside, the temperature was almost tropical.

Angela followed her gaze. "You can come for a weekend you know, just think, a whole weekend of pampering." She closed her eyes in delicious anticipation.

"Oh, I couldn't. I'd never want to go back to work again."

Her friend giggled, "You could bring Danny, I bet he'd love it, there are more men here than I thought there'd be."

Carla smiled. "I might try a massage on him, he's such a big softy, I bet he'd love it."

"How's his weight going?"

"Very well really, another three pounds off last week. He's really getting into it now. Trouble is, I've started losing it again, I have to keep remembering that I'm supposed to eat all the things he can't have."

Angela smiled. "You are made for each other you know, the perfect couple, 'Jack Spratt could eat no fat, his wife could eat no lean'," she quoted.

Carla laughed. "Talking of which, how's Jack the lad getting on? What was it like seeing him again the other night?"

Angela thought for a moment. "Not too bad – the old chemistry reared its head a couple of times."

Carla raised her eyebrows and they both burst out laughing. "You know what I mean." Angela was still giggling.

Carla gave her an old-fashioned look. "So, you still fancy him then."

"Yes, I do, especially now he's lost some more weight, but we were very controlled and we've gone back to being friends."

"What did he think of the plan?"

"He was all for it, he's already convinced John Fielding to write to Perma-Care so he might not even need the extra help."

Carla looked alarmed, but Angela held up her hand. "Don't worry. I'm still going through with it, our delightful doctor deserves it."

Carla sat back again and sipped her drink. "I'd love to be a fly on the wall when he goes there."

"You could be."

"What do you mean?"

"There's nothing to stop us going there the same night, once Helen lets us know when it is he's going. How's she getting on?"

"Well, it worked out perfectly because it's his wife's birthday soon and he was asking about places to go, so Helen told him about the Italian and as soon as he's booked it, she's going to let you know, so you can change the booking to a special table."

"Great. Did you have any trouble persuading her to do it?"

"No, she can't stand the bloke, says he's a pig to work for."

Angela smiled. "I love it when a plan comes together. That's settled then, as soon as we know when, we'll go along."

"Oh, no, it's too dangerous, he might recognise us."

"Not if we go in disguise, it would be a laugh, it's dark down there anyway, there's only candles for light, and we could make sure we sit well away from him. Ah, come on, Carla, you've always said you wanted to go – let's go for it, it would be fun."

Carla looked extremely dubious but Angela thought that with a little bit of persuasion, she'd agree in the end.

Carla, for her part, just wanted to change the subject. "What's happened about the Perma-Care report, the one with Danny's name on? Has Bernie seen it yet?"

"No, the gods are working in our favour, he's off to Italy for a week, so I don't need to show it to him until he gets back, and hopefully, by then, Anderson will have walked into the trap. Also, Perma-Care should have John Fielding's letter about Jack, so it's all coming together."

"Yes, but he hasn't written one about Danny yet," Carla moaned.

"No, but he's still losing weight, isn't he? So by the time Bernie gets back, the plan will be well on its way. Don't worry."

"Yeah, I suppose so."

"Come on, it's facial and hair time." Angela got up.

"I didn't think I had any."

"Any what?"

"Facial hair," Carla quipped.

They both laughed, and as they walked away, Angela said, "I'm sure I feel thinner already you know, that cling-film thing might have been awful, but I think it works."

Becky Abbot knew she had to get to a hospital – her face didn't feel as if it belonged to her.

She dragged herself over to the sink and looked in the mirror – she could hardly see into it, her eyes were slits, her mouth swollen and bloody and her cheeks bruised. As she had pulled herself up using the washbasin, the pain in her side had been excruciating, so she guessed she had a few broken ribs as well. She couldn't cry – she was beyond it – she knew what she must do, she must get away.Before he killed her.

Last night had been the worst attack so far, thank goodness Sean was away. They'd gone to the pub together and everything had been fine, but once they got home he'd started again – she'd been giving that bloke the come-on, she was a slut, she was a whore, and each insult had been underlined with a punch. In the end, she'd dragged herself up to the bathroom and locked the door, curled herself up in a protective bundle and stayed there, waiting for him to fall into a drunken stupor.

Now it was light and her mind was racing; she didn't want to go out, didn't want anyone to see her in this state, but, if she didn't go, the same thing would happen again – he would say he was sorry, he would be good to her for a while and then it would happen again.

Last time she'd walked out, and it had given him a fright; he'd been good for quite a time and she'd thought it was over and he'd learned his lesson, but now she knew he'd never learn his lesson. This time she must go for good, for Sean's sake, she must go. Her handbag was downstairs, that was all she needed.

She lifted water to her face and tried to comb her hair, but every movement was agony.

She unlocked the door and crept down the stairs, hardly daring to breathe, it hurt too much anyway. There was no sign of him, he must be asleep on the bed; she picked up her handbag and coat and walked out of the front door, closing it without a sound. This time, she wouldn't be coming back.

Hilary was crying, lying on her bed and sobbing into her pillow. She felt ashamed of herself, but she couldn't help it. When she'd started the conversation with Jack, she'd felt in control – she was prepared, calm and collected, but the minute he admitted that he had kissed the woman and so acknowledged that there was something between them, all resolve had melted away and she'd run from the kitchen, crying uncontrollably.

Jack had followed her and tried to reassure her that it was just a harmless flirtation; it had been over before it had begun. He was just saying goodbye, etc. etc., but Hilary had screamed at him that he was a lying, cheating bastard, that he was to get out of the house and she never wanted to see him again. Finally, he had given up and gone away.

If anyone had ever told her that she would react like that to her husband's infidelity, she wouldn't have believed them. In fact, she wouldn't have believed that Jack would ever be unfaithful to her, but she had to believe it now – that was the trouble!

She knew the children had been concerned and she had heard them asking what was the matter, but she hadn't heard Jack's reply.

When she lifted her head to listen, everything was quiet. She lay there, hugging her pillow until it began to get dark and then she dragged herself to the bathroom, to wash her face and comb her hair.

What a sight she was! But she didn't care – her mouth was dry and her eyes were stinging, and she badly needed a cup of tea. She ventured out of the bedroom tentatively, like she used to do as a child when she'd been punished. *Don't be ridiculous, Hilary, you've done nothing wrong*, she told herself.

The house was empty, so she made herself the tea and went and sat by the fire; she was so cold.

Later, when she tried to remember, she couldn't say what time Jack came back with Simon and Anna. She remembered them creeping in after she'd gone back to bed, and looking at her, but then they were gone again.

She remembered Jack bringing her another cup of tea, which she drank, and he'd asked her if she wanted something to eat, but she'd refused. After that, it was all a blur, she remembered hugging her pillow again as if it would prevent her world from falling apart and drifting in and out of sleep. She knew Jack didn't sleep in their bed, but she didn't care one way or the other.

When she woke up, it was morning, only it wasn't; it was lunchtime and it was Monday. Oh my God, she should be at work, she should be getting the kids off to school, she had responsibilities!

She flung her robe on and ran downstairs. Jack was sitting at the kitchen table, doing some paperwork. She stared at him. "Why didn't you wake me? What will they think at school? Where are the kids?"

"I phoned Doris and said you wouldn't be in today because of Dad. They weren't expecting you anyway and had you covered because of the ski trip. I also got the kids off to school. I'm quite capable, you know," he told her in a calm voice.

"What did you tell them?" She sat down opposite him.

"Who?"

"The kids."

Jack sighed. "I told them that you saw me kissing another woman and that you were very cross with me."

"What did they say?" Hilary was amazed.

"Anna asked me why I kissed the other woman and Simon said it was a stupid thing to do."

Hilary snorted. "That would be right. How did you answer Anna?" She stood up and started making herself a drink.

"I told her that she was a friend and I was saying goodbye."

Hilary didn't say anything, she carried on making coffee and then she asked, "How's Alec?"

"He's OK. They've moved him onto the ward and started physio on him, but there's a long way to go yet. He and Mum were holding hands like a couple of teenagers when I left."

"You didn't tell them about all this, did you?" Hilary waved her hand between them and sat down again.

"Of course not, and I told the children not to say anything either."

He stood up. "Do you want anything to eat?"

"Yes, but I don't know what."

"How about an omelette?"

"OK."

While he was busy, she looked around her; everything looked the same, safe, secure and familiar but it was as if it was all in a parallel universe, out of synchronisation with her.

"What have you told them at Holme Farm?" she asked.

"I've got a couple of days of compassionate leave, because of Dad – I'm going back on Wednesday."

"It's going to be a long process you know, Charlie is going to need a lot of support."

"Yes, I know."

He carried on cooking and Hilary suddenly felt restless, so she got up and set the table, her mind turning to household chores. "There's washing to do," she muttered.

"I've done it."

She looked at him, he looked different somehow, older, wiser maybe, but more than anything else, he looked calm – she hated him for it and yet at the same time, she found it reassuring.

They ate in silence and then she went to get dressed, feeling somehow vulnerable, still in her robe.

She had a long soak in the bath, and later, with a big fleecy towel wrapped around her, she started to feel slightly better. She looked in the mirror, and the face that looked back seemed quite composed – it was amazing that she could look like that on the outside and yet be in such turmoil within.

She heard Jack come up to the study – she thought it was ridiculous, and yet she was glad he was there, glad he hadn't taken her at her word and left. She didn't want him to touch her and she didn't feel strong enough to have any more discussion about the other woman, so she didn't particularly want to talk to him, but, if she was honest with herself, she found his physical presence comforting, and that was really annoying.

She got dressed and pottered about in the bedroom for a while but she was still restless and as she walked past the study, she could see the bed-settee was made up and somehow it made her want to get out of the house.

"Shall we go and see Alec?"

Jack looked up, obviously surprised. "Yes, if you want to."

"I do, I didn't see him yesterday and I want to know if there's anything we can do for Charlie."

Jack drove and they hardly said a word but there was a strange calm between them that Hilary couldn't define; it was enough that it was there.

Charlie was sitting next to Alec's bed and she smiled as they came in. Alec appeared to be sleeping.

"How is he?" Hilary whispered.

"Well, he's had some physio again this morning, but he tried to get out of bed just before lunch, and it was as if he'd forgotten he couldn't walk and he fell over and got very upset, he was crying, I've never seen him cry. I tried to comfort him as best I could but he wouldn't touch his lunch, the nurse told me it was perfectly normal for stroke victims and I've read about it in the booklet but it's very hard." Her face looked drawn and anxious.

Hilary took hold of her hand and squeezed it.

"What about you? Have you eaten anything?"

"Yes, I had a sandwich and a cup of tea about an hour ago."

"What about breakfast?" Jack asked her.

"No, I didn't have time. I had to catch the bus."

Jack and Hilary exchanged glances. "You should have phoned us," Jack scolded her.

"I can manage, you have your own lives to lead and besides, once you're back at work, I'll *have* to manage on my own." She jutted her chin out determinedly.

"Well, we'll take you home anyway," Jack told her.

"Who's taking you home?" Alec opened his eyes and looked at them all.

"We're taking Mum home soon, Dad – she's still very tired and we'll cook her a nice meal."

"Good idea," Alec muttered.

Charlie looked between son and father and gave them both a withering look. "I will go home when I'm ready to go home and I don't need a meal, thank you, I've got something prepared." Then she softened her tone. "How are you feeling, love?"

"A bit groggy and thirsty but I'm alright." He squeezed Charlie's hand. "I'd be a lot better though if they'd just leave me in peace – they're forever doing something – check this, check that, drink this, swallow that, it drives you mad."

Jack smiled to himself; that sounded more like his dad.

They talked a little while longer and then Charlie decided she would have a lift after all, but she wouldn't have anything to eat. They dropped her at home and on the drive back to their own place, Jack decided that he would cook a batch of freezer meals, so that at least Charlie wouldn't have to cook after she got back from the hospital each day.

"Charlie will have to start driving again," Hilary announced.

"She hasn't driven for years."

"I know, but she used to and Alec won't be able to drive again for months, if ever, so she'll have to take it up again."

Jack realised it was true, but the thought depressed him terribly – his father's independence had gone with one fell stroke. He gritted his teeth at the irony of that expression.

Simon and Anna came home from school very subdued; they both kept looking at their parents, checking to see their expressions and although Jack and Hilary tried to be as normal as possible, they realised what an added strain it was going to be.

Jack got busy cooking and Hilary suggested that the rest of them watched a DVD. They sat on the settee together, cuddling up and watching a Disney classic. Jack came in for a while, and although he was glad to see them there, he also felt a pang of jealousy that he wasn't with them.

Later, when he went up to kiss the children goodnight, they didn't say anything except, 'Night, Dad,' and Anna turned her back on him and pulled the duvet up around her ears. Simon was reading and hardly took his eyes off the page; Jack felt a physical pain in his chest at the thought that he might be losing their love, but he knew better than to push things.

He and Hilary sat watching television, or, at least it was true to say the television was switched on, but whether either of them was watching it was another matter, both were lost in their own thoughts.

"Are you taking Charlie into the hospital tomorrow?" Hilary broke the silence.

"Yes, I said I'd pick her up at ten."

"Then what will you do?"

"I haven't thought about it really, I suppose I'll stay and visit Dad for a while and then, later on, I'll come back here and do some work, prepare a meal for us all." He broke off and looked across at her, to see she was biting her lip. "Why? Is there something you want me to do?"

"No, it's more that I *don't* want you to do something."

"What do you mean?"

"I don't want you contacting that woman."

"Oh, for God's sake, Hilary," he snapped in exasperation, "I've told you – it was a goodbye kiss, a kiss between friends. I won't be contacting her."

"I've only got your word for that, you could be lying, you've obviously lied before."

"I haven't lied to you," he said levelly.

"Oh, yes you have, saying you were going to those fitness weekends when you were going to see her – no wonder you weren't losing weight! A good cook is she?" She was warming to her subject now and had leant forward in her chair, her face flushed and her eyes shining with indignation.

Jack sighed; he'd been waiting for this and had already decided he must not rise to the bait, as to lose his temper would be fatal.

"I did go to the fitness weekends, I *didn't* lie to you, I met her on the weekend, it wasn't prearranged."

"Oh, I see – overweight is she?" Hilary sat back, arms folded, glowering at him.

"Well a little bit I suppose." He hesitated. "Anyway, I don't want to talk about her, I told you it's counter-productive. What's the point?"

"What's the point?" Hilary hissed. "The point is that you've been screwing another woman and I want to know why, I want to know what you see in her, what she can offer that I can't."

Jack visibly flinched at the words. "I didn't say I'd been screwing her," he snapped back in alarm.

"No, you didn't, but I know you have, I can tell."

She looked at him, challenging him to deny it, but he couldn't, he felt like a rabbit caught in the headlights – his mouth was paralysed and he just stared at her.

"You've destroyed this marriage by your actions, Jack. When I think back, you've probably been having this affair since we got back from holiday. That's when you changed." He opened his mouth to deny it, but she held up a hand to stop him. "I've been a bloody fool, but not any more – you can carry on sleeping in the study, I never want to sleep with you again. As far as the future is concerned, I want time to think about it, I think you owe me that," and she got up and stormed out of the room.

Jack rubbed his eyes and stared at the television. *Well, welcome back, Hilary!* Jack got up and poured himself a whisky. This was it then, he was supposed to stew until her ladyship decided what his fate should be! He took a gulp and smiled; mind you, he preferred her like this to the weeping willow she'd been the day before, and he settled back in his chair and closed his eyes.

Upstairs, Hilary lay in the darkness, wide awake and enveloped in rage.

CHAPTER 17

Dai Evans put his phone back in his pocket with a sigh – there was always something! The Head had phoned to tell him about Becky Abbot. Sean would now have to be placed on the 'at risk' register. The local police had been to the school and asked that Sean not be told anything until he was back there, then he'd be collected by Becky and a social worker and taken to a safe house to wait until his father could be prosecuted. Poor lad, he didn't have much luck – maybe his life would improve from now on.

The Head had also told him that Hilary's father-in-law had had a stroke, but was stable, and she'd be back at work tomorrow. That was good news, she'd be around to help if Sean threw a wobbler.

Dai gritted his teeth and made his way back upstairs. He'd have a word with Dave Morris, maybe if he knew the situation, he'd lay off the lad a bit. God, he felt tired, this five days felt like a lifetime, all he really wanted to do was sleep for a week.

Hilary had never really looked upon Carrisbrook Middle School as a sanctuary before, quite the opposite on occasions, but on this particular Tuesday morning, that was exactly what it felt like. The familiar smells, sounds and faces were like balm to her troubled soul and she could feel normality creeping back. People were very sympathetic about Alec, and she was able to tell them about his progress, glad to have something to discuss that wasn't connected to her marriage. She didn't feel that she wanted anyone to know about that – it would be better that way, then she could always come to work to escape.

The ski party were due back before the end of school, and the other staff wanted to know how it had gone up until the time she'd left; they were particularly interested in Sean Abbot in view of the developments with Becky. Hilary was horrified as Doris filled her in with the gory details. "He'll be devastated," she told Doris, "he'll blame himself for going away."

"Well, Dai asked if you could hang around after school for a while, in case anyone needs to talk to him, because he trusts you."

Hilary sighed. "Yes, I'll be around," she said and wandered back to her classroom, feeling rather ashamed – her own problems seemed trivial compared to Becky's.

Just before the final bell, Hilary watched from her classroom window as the ski-trippers trudged wearily across the playground, staggering under the weight of their holdalls and equipment – they all looked tired and bedraggled. She spotted Sean, as always, sauntering along, alone, at the back of the group. Poor lad, she thought, he'd already had to cope with more crises than most people cope with in a lifetime, yet he was only twelve.

She quickly dismissed her class and made her way to the front office. Doris spotted her and gestured towards the parents' interview room.

Becky Abbot was sitting inside; her face black and blue, her eyes still half-closed. There was a baseball cap and sunglasses on the chair next to her and, as always, she was twisting the strap of her handbag between her fingers. Hilary smiled as reassuringly as she could. "Hello, Mrs Abbot, I've been asked to be available if needed, in case Sean needs some support. Is that OK?"

Becky nodded. "Yeah." She was having difficulty speaking. "He'll be alright though – he won't give no trouble if I'm here."

"No, I know he won't. Where's the social worker?"

Becky jerked her head in the direction of the window. "In the car."

A sensible one, for once, thought Hilary. "Alright, I'll leave you in peace then – he was very good up there, by the way, he's a natural and he was also very kind to my son."

Becky smiled as best she could, and Hilary closed the door quietly; she hovered around the entrance area, keeping her eye open for Sean, and finally, she spotted him, coming down the corridor with Dai. He looked rather like a caged animal, trapped, yet aggressive. Dai saw her and nodded but they didn't speak as they walked past. She watched as they went into the interview room and then Dai came out again, shutting the door softly. He ran his fingers through his hair and then came to join her.

"You should have seen his face when he saw her, he tried to hug her but she yelped in pain and he said, 'I swear I'll kill him one day Mum, I swear.' I hope to God he doesn't."

"She'll talk some sense into him," Hilary reassured him.

Dai turned to her. "How's things with you?"

Hilary felt a lump coming up in her throat and she swallowed hard. "Alec's partially paralysed, left side, his speech is OK and I think he's going to be alright but it's going to be a long haul."

Dai nodded, studying her face but he didn't say anything. They both just stood leaning against the wall, waiting for Sean and Becky to come out of the room.

Finally they came out, Becky had on the baseball cap and the glasses and they walked defiantly, heads held high, nodding to Hilary and Dai as they passed on their way to the front door.

"What now?" Dai asked.

"Well, there'll be a case conference soon and then we'll see. I just hope to God he keeps coming to school, that's all." She shook her head. "Well, I s'pose I'd better get home," she sighed.

Dai just nodded and watched as she walked back to her classroom – she looked incredibly tired.

The rest of the week just seemed to happen. Jack went back to work, Charlie kept visiting Alec, who had been moved to the rehab unit, and Hilary enjoyed the security of her school routine. Simon and Anna gradually began to act more normally around their parents but they got into the habit of having nightly meetings in their bedrooms to discuss the situation.

"He's still sleeping in the study," Anna whispered.

"Yes, well, Mum hasn't forgiven him yet. I expect they'll have a romantic dinner and a sloppy, snogging session like those mushy films and then he'll move back into their bedroom."

Anna wasn't convinced. "They might not, I heard Mum say she never wanted to sleep with him again."

"Yes, but she was very angry, she'll get over it," her brother assured her, and with that they got down to the far more interesting business of who they thought they'd get Valentine cards from.

As far as Jack and Hilary were concerned, they managed to keep very busy and avoid each other as much as possible.

Jack got into the habit of visiting Alec each evening on his way home from work, thus putting off his homecoming.

Hilary, for her part, always found plenty of schoolwork to do in the evenings which, unbeknownst to Jack, she only started when she heard his car. They ate separately, slept separately and managed to exchange any essential information very quickly in the mornings, just as they were on their way to work. They both communicated with the children more than usual and were more affectionate with them than usual, but they didn't seem to notice, or if they did, they didn't comment.

Jack felt like a man on Death Row – he'd been given a temporary reprieve but he didn't know how long it would last. It was driving him mad and he just had to talk to someone, so he phoned Jimmy.

"How's it going then?"

"It's awful!"

"You didn't tell her everything, did you?"

"No, of course not, but she's convinced I slept with Angela and that I've been having the affair since we got back from holiday last October. Why would she think that?"

"God knows. Ours is not to reason why in these matters, you know women. Once they get an idea in their heads you've had it. She hasn't thrown you out then?"

"No, I'm sleeping in the study, she says she never wants to sleep with me again and she needs time to think about the future."

"That's a good sign."

"Is it?"

"Oh, yes. She'd have contacted a solicitor by now if she wanted to get rid of you."

"She might have, for all I know," Jack moaned.

"Come on, look on the bright side, the worst is over now, she knows about it and you're still at home – just ride out the storm."

"That's alright for you to say – that bed-settee is bloody uncomfortable!"

Jimmy laughed. "You've got to experience some pain for your pleasure. Personally, I think you've got off quite lightly so far."

"You would!" Jack retorted, but it was said in a playful way and he did feel better after talking to Jimmy – he was right, it could be worse, *patience, Jack, patience.*

That evening, after his shower, he stepped onto the scales out of habit and was amazed to see that he'd lost another five pounds without even trying.

Well, there had to be some compensation for what he was going through. He was due to see John Fielding again at the end of the month, but he mustn't run into Angela – in his present celibate state, it just might be too much of a temptation! Then, he realised, she didn't know! She had no idea that Hilary had been there and she didn't know about Alec's stroke. So much had happened in the last week that he hadn't even thought about it. Well, he had to phone her anyway, to see how the plan was going.

The next day, Jack sat in a supermarket car park, a diet coke and salmon sandwich on the seat next to him, and phoned her at work.

"Oh, that's terrible," she groaned. "I'm so sorry about your father. Isn't that just typical that she should have been there, life can be such a bitch at times. What are you going to do?"

"What can I do? I'm sleeping in the study and we're barely talking." Jack was enjoying the sympathy.

"She doesn't know it was anything more than a kiss though, does she – just tell her we're friends."

"I've tried that, but she doesn't believe me, she's convinced that we've been having a full-blown affair since the holiday in Malta in October."

"That's ridiculous, you'll have to convince her somehow, you can't let her think that after all the care we've taken, it's not true and it's not fair."

"I know but I've tried and she doesn't believe me, it's awful, she said she needs time to think about the future, and I feel as if I'm living under a death sentence."

"Well, snap out of it and do something. You can't just do nothing at a time like this – you've got to fight for what you want. Look, I'll have a think but I've got a lot on at the moment, Bernie's away in Italy and he's left me to organise the monthly meeting. He's having an Italian evening –DVD Italian foods, wine-tasting, fashion show and so on, it should be really good, you'll enjoy it."

"I'm not coming."

"Why not?"

"I can't, can I? She'll think I'm seeing you and we'll have the whole thing all over again."

"Jack, you can't stop coming to the monthly meetings – you'll be missed and questions will be asked."

Angela was getting annoyed now, and she had felt a sense of mounting irritation throughout the conversation – was she really sticking her neck out for this wimp?

"No, not all of them, but I thought I'd miss this one, plead sickness or something."

There was silence.

"Angela. Are you still there?"

"Yes, I'm here, I was thinking. Look, Anderson is booked into the foodie bar next week, Carla and I are going along. I'll phone you on your mobile and let you know what happens, shall I?"

"Yes, please. Look, I'm sorry, I'm not helping much am I? My life is just upside down at the moment, that's all, thanks for what you're doing."

"That's alright. I understand. I'll be in touch. Bye."

She stared at the phone for quite a while. Why was she bothering? Had she thought he might leave his wife and come to her if she helped him? Well, he certainly wasn't doing that! Maybe his wife would leave him though and he'd have no choice. She fantasised about meeting his children, taking them out for treats, and cooking special meals for them, she was just at the point of buying Christmas presents for them, when the office door opened and Carla stuck her head round.

"Are you coming for a coffee or what?"

Angela came to with a start. "What? Oh, yes, I'm coming."

"Well, you're a bundle of laughs today," her friend commented, having watched her stare into her coffee cup for at least ten minutes, "what's up?"

Angela looked up. "Jack phoned, his wife saw us, the other night when I dropped him off at the Fellside, she was there."

"What did she see?" Carla was gaping.

"She saw him kiss me goodnight."

"Is that all? What was she doing there anyway?"

Angela explained the whole situation about Jack's wife and his father and she finished by saying, "And he says he daren't come to the monthly meeting. Can you believe that?"

"I don't blame him."

"Why?"

"Because he's in deep trouble, that's why and he doesn't want to rock the boat any more. Why do you want him to come anyway?"

Angela thought and then she replied, "I don't know really. I suppose it's because I'm sticking my neck out for him and I think he should be prepared to take a few risks too. Besides, he'll get into trouble if he doesn't."

"In case you've forgotten, he's already taken his risks and he didn't ask you to help out over this insurance thing, none of us did, it was all your idea. Why are you doing it anyway?"

Angela looked exasperated.

"I don't know any more. You've changed your tune. You were calling him all the names under the sun last week."

"Yes, I was, but that was before his marriage was in danger. I don't think you're over him, you still have feelings for him."

"That's not true!"

"Well, why are you so bothered about seeing him then? Seeing him will only make things worse for both of you. He needs your help and understanding now more than ever and Danny still needs your help." She emphasised the last sentence by saying it more slowly.

Angela looked up again. "You're right, don't worry, I'll still do it. As you say, nothing's changed. I don't know what I thought, maybe I hoped he'd be so grateful to me for saving his job, he'd leave his wife and come running. Oh, I don't know. I'm confused now."

"Aren't we all," Carla retorted, rolling her eyes heavenwards.

Angela smiled. "OK. OK. Point taken, a good job I've got you isn't it? A good dose of realism is what I need." She stopped and thought for a moment. "Those poor kids, their granddad in hospital, their mum and dad not talking – they must be so confused, bless them. Oh dear, what a mess!'

"Yeah, it's always the innocent who suffer, poor mites."

Angela stood up. "Well, at least we can make sure that they don't have Dad's redundancy to add to the list," she said determinedly.

Carla drained her cup and stood up. "That's the spirit! That's the Angie I know and love! I'll see you after work then." Angela looked blank. "You haven't forgotten, have you?" Still no recognition. "The disguises for the foodie bar."

"Oh God, I had forgotten, I told you I had too much on – OK. I'll meet you by my car at five-thirty."

Angela meandered back to the office, deep in thought; how would she feel if she found out Pete was having an affair? She really didn't know, she didn't let herself dwell on things like that because he had so much opportunity in his line of work, but if she was presented with the visual evidence, if she'd actually seen him with another woman? She shook her head, it didn't bear thinking about.

Hilary had started the week with good intentions; she didn't want anyone at work to know about Jack, but she hadn't reckoned with her own nature. She thought she could cope with it on her own, but by Thursday lunchtime, she needed to talk to someone and when Karen came into her classroom and asked how Jack was coping with his father's stroke, she cracked.

"I don't know and I don't bloody care," she said, and burst into tears.

Two mugs of coffee and half a box of tissues later, Karen was pretty much in the picture.

"So, what are you going to do?"

"I don't know." Hilary sniffed.

"Well, do you want to stay married to him or not?"

Hilary stopped and looked at her. "Is that the only choice, married or not?"

"Well, yes, really, I mean if you're going to stay together as a married couple, then you'll have some rebuilding to do, if not, then the sooner you split, the better, for Simon and Anna's sake."

Hilary shook her head. "I don't know, it's such a mess at the moment, there's Alec's stroke, Charlie needs us, and she and Alec would be devastated if Jack and I split. Then, as you say, there are the kids to consider, we both love them so much, it would be impossible."

"So you want to stay with Jack then."

"I didn't say that."

Oh yes you did, in so many ways, Karen thought, but she said, "Well, does Jack want to leave you?"

"Oh no, he's sworn that it was a moment of madness, that it's over, and he wants to stay with me and the children."

"Do you believe him?"

"Yes, I do."

"Well, I don't see the problem then."

"You don't understand, I don't know if I can ever trust him again and at the moment, I can't even bear him sleeping in the same bed, never mind touching me."

The bell rang, and Karen stood up. "Look, you need to do some serious thinking, the worst thing for all of you is this limbo situation that you're in. You look shattered, take a day off, go off on your own somewhere and get yourself together. OK?"

Hilary just nodded, she had felt relieved that she'd been able to offload on someone, but she thought Karen couldn't possibly understand how she felt. She was newly married and didn't have any children. How could she understand? She felt more isolated than ever.

Hilary had sworn Karen to secrecy, and she'd kept her promise, but she told Geoff of course, because he didn't count, he was her husband, and he didn't teach at Carrisbrook in any case. Geoff kept it quiet as well, just as Karen had told him to, but later in the week, after football practice he had a few beers and told his mate John – after all, John didn't know Hilary from Adam. It so happened though, that John's wife Catherine thought she did know who he was talking about.

When Catherine went to yoga, she told her friend Joanne, whose children went to the same school as Simon and Anna, and so it was that by the end of the next week, the news was widespread and various. It ranged from Jack was having an affair and had left Hilary for the other woman, to Hilary had caught Jack and his mistress *in flagrante* and had thrown him out.

Jack and Hilary, of course, knew nothing of these stories and might have remained in blissful ignorance; if it hadn't been for the fact that Simon came home from school with a split lip, having obviously been in a fight.

The week had not been a good one for Jack. He was beginning to show signs of stress; He had forgotten a couple of appointments and had to field irate phone calls from clients who had been left twiddling their thumbs. He had locked his car keys in the boot of his car which meant he and Charlie were too late to visit Alec one night; this had not gone down well with either of his parents. Finally, he had narrowly escaped being beaten up by an angry motorist in a car park. The motorist in question didn't appear to know how to use the ticket machine at the entrance to the multi-storey and Jack had impatiently hit his horn, only to find, a few seconds later, that the man was banging on his window asking him what the problem was. Jack just told him he'd hit it by mistake and breathed a sigh of relief when he went away.

Apart from the incident with the car keys, he'd visited Alec every night. Charlie kept telling him it wasn't necessary, but she was glad of the lift home all the same. Susan and Jimmy and their respective partners were coming at the weekend, so he thought he might get a break, but Charlie had looked so happy at the prospect of a family gathering on Sunday that he didn't have the heart to disappoint her.

This Friday was Valentine's Day and he'd bought flowers and a card for Hilary, with the hopes of melting the ice a little, so it didn't fit in with his plans at all when he got home to find his son nursing a split lip and his wife on the phone to another parent, obviously having a blazing row.

"Well, it's his word against Simon's and I know who I choose to believe, Mrs Barnes. Your son has been in trouble for this kind of thing before, he's got a foul mouth and one can only assume it is an inherited trait."

She then lifted the phone away from her ear and after a few seconds she shouted, "and the same to you!" before slamming it down.

Jack put the flowers and card on the kitchen table, where Simon was sitting looking decidedly dishevelled and miserable. Hilary came marching back. "Right then, young man, let's wash your face. I'll have to come and see Mrs Brown on Monday now, to make sure this doesn't carry on any further."

Simon pulled a face. "It's alright, I'll wash it," he said, and stood up.

Hilary rounded on Jack. "This is all your fault."

"Why, what have I done?"

"You know very well what you've done. Simon got into this fight because a boy at school told everyone we were getting divorced!"

Jack turned to Simon. "Is that true?"

Simon hung his head. "Yes, he said Mum had caught you in bed with another woman and you weren't living at home anymore and he called me a liar when I said it wasn't true – so I hit him."

"Good lad, I hope it was good and hard!"

"JACK!" Hilary shrieked and she ushered Simon out of the room.

Jack sat at the kitchen table and put his head in his hands. God what a mess, if he could just turn back the clock.

Anna came and sat next to him. "Are these for Mummy?"

"Yes, poppet."

"I'll put them in water then," she announced. "I got three Valentine's cards."

"Did you? Do you know who sent them?"

"Oh yes, they told me."

Jack smiled; life was really very simple when you were nine years old, if only it were that simple now.

Anna placed the flowers very carefully in the centre of the table and then began rooting about in the freezer.

"What are you looking for?"

"I'm going to give Simon an ice-lolly, they're good for swollen lips. Do you want one?"

"Yes please."

Hence, when Hilary came back into the room; it was to find her husband still in his heavy winter coat, sitting at the table sucking an ice-lolly. She didn't say anything, just picked up the card and opened it. Jack had agonised over what to write and had finally settled on,

With all my love
Jack

"I haven't bought you one," she said quietly.

"I didn't expect you to."

She touched the petals of one of the tulips, her favourite flowers, and sighed. "Thank you," she almost whispered. Then she looked at him and grinned, "You look ridiculous."

"I know but I don't care," he grinned defiantly, "I'll go up and speak to our errant son if you like, I swear I haven't said anything to a soul, so I don't know how that story's got around."

"He'll be alright. I must admit I'm quite pleased really that he thumped that Barnes lad, he is an obnoxious little so and so."

"Well, we're in agreement then, that can't be bad. What would you like to eat tonight?"

"I don't know, surprise me," she said, and smiled at him as she left the room.

Jack took his coat and jacket off and rolled up his sleeves; he hadn't heard her say that for a long time, maybe things were looking up at last.

CHAPTER 18

*C*arla's sides ached and her eyes streamed, she couldn't catch her breath and she was in grave danger of wetting herself. Angela was in the same predicament – they were both collapsed on her bed, helpless with hysterical laughter.

"Ooh, I've got to go to the loo," Carla gasped and waddled off, clutching her stomach.

"Hurry up, I've got to go too," Angela wailed.

They had been trying on outfits to go with the wigs they'd bought for their trip to the foodie bar. Carla had chosen a long, black Cleopatra style with a fringe, and Angela's was blonde, shoulder-length with soft waves, reminiscent of Marilyn Monroe.

It was these associations with famous characters that had prompted them to dress up accordingly. They had outlined Carla's eyes with black kohl pencil and found her a gold choker, straight black skirt and a geometric top – she looked decidedly glamorous and Angela was quite jealous, so she delved into her wardrobe with renewed vigour. She managed to find a very sexy, strapless little number, made from a satin-like material and she struggled into it triumphantly. Unfortunately, she'd put on weight since she had last worn it years ago, and when Carla was zipping her up, the zip stuck about halfway up and no amount of pulling or pushing would release it.

"Breathe in," Carla told her for the third time.

"I am breathing in, you silly tart!" Angela snapped. "If I breathe in any more, I'll suffocate. Let me do it!" and she had pushed Carla away, and putting two hands behind her back, tugged at the zip as hard as she could.

Suddenly, there was an ominous ripping sound, and the back central seam, which had been under considerable pressure, split open like a banana skin. It was then that the two friends had collapsed in hysterics.

When they finally regained their composure, Angela threw the offending garment in the bin and announced, "Ah well, I never liked it anyway," which set Carla off again.

Eventually, they managed to get back into their jeans and tops and made their way down to the kitchen for a glass of wine.

"Have you booked the 'special table' yet?" Carla mumbled through a chocolate biscuit.

"Yep. I phoned up yesterday and altered it, said it was a surprise. They're booked for eight o'clock, so I'll pick you up in the taxi at seven. I want to be sure we're there before them."

"I'm quite nervous about it."

"Why?"

"I don't know – partly because I want it to work for Danny's sake, I s'pose, and partly because I don't want him to recognise us."

"I can assure you he won't recognise you in that lot." Angela jerked her head towards the ceiling. "I, on the other hand, will have to find something else to wear," and they both started giggling again.

Charlie was fed up – she was tired, wet, cold and yes FED UP.!!!

She dumped the shopping bags on the kitchen table and kicked off her wet shoes. *What I need is a change of clothes and a hot cup of tea*, she told herself.

Once she was changed and dry and warm, sitting by the fire cradling a steaming mug in her hands, she felt a lot better, but she was still fed up.

All the family were arriving to see Alec tomorrow, and then coming back to her for a meal.

It was her fault, she'd invited them, but without Alec to take her shopping in the car, it had become a major task for her. She'd had to wait at bus stops, carry heavy bags whilst getting soaking wet and now she still had to clean the entire house and prepare the meal, because she'd be visiting Alec in the morning.

All three of her children had told her not to do it, that it was too much trouble and they would all eat out somewhere, but she always enjoyed doing it, it was just that this time, she hadn't realised just how much trouble it would be.

On top of all that, Alec hadn't taken too kindly to the fact that she wasn't visiting him this evening. He'd sulked, and refused to speak to her anymore once she'd told him – there didn't seem to be any appreciation of the fact that she'd been in twice every day since his stroke.

She sighed deeply and tears of self-pity began to slide down her cheeks – her life was never going to be the same now in any case, Alec wasn't like the man she knew and loved, he was moody, childish and self-centred, and he'd never been any of those things before. The nurses told her it was early days yet and that he was making excellent progress, particularly with his walking. She could even *see* the progress, but her strong and capable husband was still an invalid and the thought of spending the rest of her life caring for him filled her with horror. She let the tears flow and wash away her self-pity and after a while, she felt calmer and she felt ashamed. She loved Alec and she knew that if the tables were turned, he would be there for her, not always patiently perhaps, and she smiled to herself – but he would be there, and so would she. Enough of this, she had work to do.

"Jack and I will pop down to the off-licence for you, Mum," Jimmy offered.

"Oh, would you, love, I just forgot all about beer, I couldn't have carried it anyway."

Once they were in the car, Jimmy laughed, "Nicely manoeuvred, eh? Now then, how's things?"

"Well, a little better, we are being civil to each other, I'm still on the bed-settee, but there's been no mention of divorce, in fact, in a funny way, it was Simon who broke the ice a little." And he went on to recount the tale of the split lip.

"Good lad!" Jimmy was obviously proud of his nephew. "Oh, she'll come round now, I'm sure. In a funny kind of way, it was a good thing it happened when Dad had his stroke, because she won't want to upset Mum and Dad anymore."

Jack didn't like to remind him that if Alec hadn't had his stroke, it wouldn't have happened at all, so he just murmured, "Uhhm – well, it has meant I've had an excuse to be out of the house more than usual. My biggest worry is, what if she'll never sleep with me again and I'm condemned to a life of celibacy?"

Jimmy spluttered with laughter. "She won't want to do without it forever, women have needs too – just be patient."

Jack sighed, and they carried on for the beer.

"Shall we get Dad a bottle? Do you think they'd let him have some?" Jimmy asked as they wandered round the shop.

"It's worth a try," Jack told him. He decided to buy some chocolates for Charlie because Jimmy and Bethany had bought her flowers and he'd felt rather guilty.

"I thought he looked a lot better today, much more like his old self." They were walking back to the car, and Jimmy was obviously feeling more positive than he had been the last time Jack had seen him.

"Yes, I think so, but I see him every day, so it's more difficult to see the progress – it certainly gave him a boost to see us all together."

"I get here as often as I can you know, I'm not just round the corner like you."

Jack realised that he'd done it again, said something that could be misconstrued, so he hurriedly put Jimmy's mind at rest.

"I know you do, Jim, I didn't mean anything by it, just the way it came out, that's all."

Jimmy looked slightly mollified, and they drove home.

When they got back, the Sunday roast was just about ready, and Geoff, being the only male on the premises, had been designated as carver. Why did a man always have to carve, Jack thought, did it go back to caveman days when the hunter got the honour of sharing out the kill? Maybe, but it wasn't quite the same somehow, when the 'beast' had been cornered at the meat counter in the supermarket.

Charlie buzzed about during the meal, and after several tries at getting her to, 'sit down, Mother' the younger generation gave up and concentrated on enjoying the roast beef and all the trimmings, followed by bread and butter pudding. Simon and Anna were a bit disappointed that their cousins weren't there – one of Bethany's sisters had volunteered to have them for the day – so they disappeared off at the first opportunity to watch some television.

The adults were enjoying each other's company and some lively conversation.

"How's the car business then, Jim?" Susan asked.

"Oh, can't complain, you know."

"He let me in on a trade secret the other week," Jack said mischievously.

"What was that then?" Susan was all ears.

"That the car he was working on was a hybrid."

Susan chuckled, "Come on, Jimmy, all cars are going that way these days."

Before Jim could answer, Geoff piped up, "No they're not, Sue, all new cars are, but there's still a lot of old ones around."

"Yeah, but they're just an investment and a toy for middle-aged men – anyway, it will all be academic soon, the car is on its way out," she pronounced.

"That's a rather sweeping statement," Jimmy said menacingly, "What factual evidence do you have to base that on?"

"Well, it stands to reason, it's so blooming expensive to run one now. Where we live, in London, nobody owns one anymore. It's cheaper to hire one when you need it, like we did today. By the time you've bought the thing itself, paid for the owner's permit, the parking permit, the insurance, the tax, the petrol, maintenance costs, road tolls etc, you're virtually bankrupt!"

"That's just in London though, where the public transport is so good anyway, up here it's different," Jack pointed out.

"It's beginning to change though," Hilary intervened, "quite a few people I know are dropping down to one car, or, like Susan says, hiring one when they need to – a lot of companies are providing transport to and from work, because the government incentives are so good."

"Well, I'm going to take a refresher course," Charlie announced.

"Are you, Mum? That's the spirit," Susan encouraged her.

"You could manage without it, you know, Mum," Jimmy said, "the hush-buses are very good round here."

"Yes, I know, and I'll use them as much as I can, but it's still not the same as having transport outside your front door. Your father's got the car out there and he's not going to be fully mobile for a long time, if ever." She stopped for a moment and then went on, "He hates buses and I'll have to get him to the health centre for his physio regularly, but apart from that, I still want to visit people like Aunty Barbara and Bunny, so I've got to drive again."

"You go for it, Charlie." Hilary gave her an encouraging smile. "Good for you!"

"So, what do you think, Jimmy? In view of what Charlie's just said," Geoff asked, "Is the car on the way out?"

"In the cities, possibly; air pollution is a big issue now – all city vehicles, taxis, delivery vehicles, council vehicles and, of course, buses, have to be pollution-free and it's deliberate government policy to discourage private cars from entering city centres, or even, in some cases, residential areas, but, outside the cities, there's still plenty of cars around."

"The permit system will kill them off eventually," Susan announced.

"Why should it?" Jack asked, "I need a car for my job, all sales personnel will still get automatic permits, all doctors, firemen, ambulance drivers, policemen etc. etc. – the list is endless, those people won't have to pay for their permits."

"Yes, but people who can't prove they one need for their job will have to pay, and that's an awful lot of people, Jack, particularly as so many people work from home these days."

"I'm not so sure," Jimmy told her, "I think people will always be prepared to pay for the convenience, they might become a rich man's prerogative though."

"Well, I disagree. The government will realise that there are people other than the rich who need to have a car – look at Mum," Jack pointed out.

"It will mean yet another means test," muttered Charlie.

"Anyway, I love the hush-buses," Susan said emphatically.

"Why?" Jack was amazed.

"Because they're so quiet and clean and comfortable. Whenever I need one, there's always one there; I just step on, sit down, close my eyes and that soft voice tells me where I am, so I don't even have to look, and then I just step off again and I'm home."

"They sound better than a man," Bethany quipped and everybody laughed.

"Yes, but that's in London," Charlie pointed out, "round here, you have to wait in the rain and more often or not, when they arrive they're full and you have to stand up!"

"You're right, Mum, London has got it sussed, there are waiting areas outside all the tube stations and they are all undercover, plus, there are so many buses that it's just a continuous stream, so I never have any trouble getting a seat."

Jimmy looked unconvinced, but Susan went on. "The whole process is so much easier than it used to be when

I drove; getting stuck in traffic jams and fretting that I'd be late for work. Breathing in all those poisonous fumes, searching for a parking space and not finding one, then having to walk for miles or get a taxi anyway because I had to park so far away, and then I'd be late anyway. It was a daily nightmare."

The other women nodded and then Charlie said, "Well, at the moment there are three cars on our drive and one in the garage, so they haven't disappeared yet."

"Yep, I'll have a job for a while longer, I think." Jimmy looked content at the thought.

"Oh, yes, without a doubt, big brother, after all, men aren't going to give up their status symbols in a hurry are they? All that macho charisma, driving around in a wimpy little hush-bus just doesn't have the same appeal as a Ferrari does it?"

The women all laughed and Geoff gave his wife a reproving glance, but he was smiling, all the same.

Jimmy scowled and changed the subject. "Anyway, Mum, never mind cars, what about computers? What you need is a laptop."

"Yes, I know I do, Mary's son is going to come with me next weekend to help me choose one."

There was a stunned silence.

"Mary's son! Why didn't you ask us?" Jack sounded mortified.

"Well, he works in computers and Mary and I were talking about it and she said she'd ask him. Well, he popped round last night and he was ever so helpful, so we arranged to go next Saturday afternoon."

The family all exchanged glances – the three younger women stood up and started clearing the table, while Charlie took chocolate bars into Simon and Anna.

"I don't know what's got into her," Jack muttered, "she never asks us for help, it's as if she doesn't think we're capable."

Don't be silly!" Susan snapped, "She hasn't changed, she's always been independent, it's you who suddenly wants to do things, that's all, or rather thinks you ought to."

Jack was thinking about this later, as Hilary was driving them all home.

"Am I being unfair to Mum, do you think?"

"What do you mean?"

"Well, like Susan said, am I expecting her to ask for help now, just because I feel I ought to be doing something?"

"I think there's an element of that, yes, we all want to do something practical to help because it makes us feel better, but Charlie has always been very capable and she'll ask for anything she needs."

Jack thought back to his childhood – his mother had always worked, she was an educational psychologist and one of his abiding memories was of her sitting at the dining room table in their old house, surrounded by files and scribbling away, writing some report or other. Alec had travelled abroad frequently and Charlie had coped with the three of them plus her job, without any outward signs of stress.

Hilary interrupted his thoughts. "Anyhow, once she's got the laptop she'll probably need help getting used to it, so you'll still be useful."

Simon leaned forward from the back seat. "Grandma was asking me about my laptop today and I told her I'd help her once it's all set up."

Jack smiled. "Good lad, she'll probably take instruction better from you anyway, you've got more patience than I have."

Cleopatra and Marilyn Monroe sat, nervously sipping wine in the foodie bar. Not literally of course, in fact, no one else would have made the connection – both women had decided on unobtrusive outfits in the end, because they wanted to blend into the background. The wigs stayed though and both had assured the other one that they wouldn't be recognised.

"What time is it?" Carla hissed.

"It's ten past eight, five minutes later than when you asked me last time."

"Ooh, I knew this was a mistake," she wailed, "I'm so nervous, I can't eat a thing anyway and if they don't turn up, I won't be able to sleep either."

"Just shush and drink your wine." Angela wasn't feeling very different but she didn't dare admit it. "Wait, there's someone coming now, yes, it's them, DON'T turn round, I'll do a running commentary for you."

"Oooh, I can't stand it." Carla was jigging up and down in her seat. "Trust you to sit so you can see and I can't."

"God, she's HUGE!"

"Who?"

"His wife, she's tall and she is BIG, fat, ginormous, oh, my God, this could turn out to be a disaster!"

Angela took a slug of her wine.

"Why should it be a disaster because she's fat?" Carla couldn't see the connection.

"Because, she'll love the food won't she and it's *her* birthday, she might be so pleased with her surprise that he won't do anything about it."

"Oh, God. Why didn't you think of this before?"

"I can't be expected to think of everything – who would have thought that the perfect Dr Anderson would be married to anyone less than perfect." Angela knocked back some more wine in disgust and kept watching.

"They're looking at the menu, oh, she's spotted Louisa, her eyes are out on stalks and she's saying something to him, he's turning round to look."

Angela put her head down and pretended to look in her handbag.

Louisa was her usual strutting self, dressed in black, a long-sleeved, low-necked, tight-fitting sweater and skin-tight trousers, cropped at the knee – she looked like half bull-fighter, half siren, but the effect was stunning, especially when you added high-heeled mules.

Robert Anderson was re-adjusting his tie – Angela could just imagine that he felt hot under the collar – he turned back to the menu.

"Oh, he's not happy, he's turning it over to look on the back."

"There's nothing on the back," Carla informed her.

"I know – uh oh, he's calling Louisa over, this is getting interesting, Louisa's shaking her head."

Carla swivelled round in her chair. "Oh, I've got to look. I can't stand the strain."

She turned round just in time to see Robert Anderson stand up, as Louisa tossed her head and walked away, but his wife didn't move, except to reach across the table and grab her husband's wrist, pulling him back down onto his chair. She was saying something, and from the look on her face, she wasn't pleased.

Carla turned back again and rubbed her hands together.

"Ooh, this is getting good, he wants to go and she doesn't, it could be better than we thought, if he has a really bad evening, he'll hate it even more."

The waiter brought their own meal then and they managed to eat some food, whilst still keeping an eye on the situation behind them.

Angela reported that Dr Anderson was drinking wine and his wife was tucking into what looked like a plate of steak and kidney pie.

"Isn't he having anything to eat?" Carla couldn't believe it.

"No, he's drinking plenty of wine though. WOW. I bet they're in for a humdinger of a row when they get home," she chuckled wickedly, "this is brilliant."

The girls started to relax and tuck into their own food and then Angela suddenly stopped.

"Hang on, he's getting up. Oh my God, he's messing about with his pager."

Carla couldn't stand it and turned round just in time to see him saying something to his wife and walking out of the restaurant.

"He's gone on an emergency call," she whispered.

"Oh, she doesn't look happy," Angela hissed back.

The next thing they knew, she was tucking into the sticky toffee pudding that Louisa had brought like a woman possessed. She called a waiter over and barked out some order and as Angela and Carla watched in fascination, she continued to demolish three more desserts, followed by an Irish coffee.

"Wow, she can eat!" Angela commented with admiration.

As the friends were finishing their own puddings, Angela looked up and said, "Uh oh, he's back." And once again, Carla couldn't resist looking round just as the waiter arrived with the bill.

Mrs Anderson stood up with a Mona Lisa smile on her face and watched the look of horror on her husband's face as he looked at the total.

"You've got to be joking! This is extortionate. We haven't had all this food!" he roared, looking at his wife for support.

"Oh yes we have, darling, or rather I have. Thank you for a wonderful birthday. Now I really must go and powder my nose." And with that she swept towards the Ladies room, leaving her husband gawping after her.

Angela and Carla had to physically stop themselves from applauding.

After the doctor and his wife had left, Angela ordered brandies to celebrate. "We might as well make use of the fact that we've come by taxi."

"Suppose it still doesn't work." Carla slurred a little after a while and was beginning to get melancholy again. "Then what shall we do?"

"We'll worry about that if it happens." Angela was much more confident. "But I don't think we'll need to, I think it worked like a dream." She raised her glass. "Here's to Mrs Anderson, long may she reign!" she toasted.

CHAPTER 19

*H*ilary parked her car outside the Abbey Centre and checked her watch – five minutes late, mind you, judging from what colleagues had told her, case conferences never started on time. There was a fine drizzle falling as she ran up the steps to the front door, brushed herself off and went inside. The receptionist behind her glass screen didn't even look up.

"Hilary Baker, for the Abbot conference."

The young woman checked her list, nodded, and pressed a button to open the security door. Hilary walked through to the inner sanctum of the social security offices.

The place seemed deserted as she walked down a corridor, but then she found an open door and popped her head in – there was a circle of empty chairs set out in the middle of the room, and Becky Abbot was standing at the back of the room with her head out of the window, smoking a cigarette.

"Hello, Mrs Abbot."

Becky jumped, but then smiled when she saw it was Hilary.

"Hi, I'm glad it's you, these things make me so nervous."

"Oh, I'm sure it will be fine, after all, you've done nothing wrong; everyone only wants what's best for you and Sean."

The young woman nodded and flicked her cigarette away, just as three more people came into the room.

After about ten minutes, the seats were beginning to fill up – the social worker, police child-protection officer, educational welfare officer and the manager of the hostel where Becky and Sean were staying, had all arrived. The meeting was opened and apologies read out from the school doctor and the educational psychologist, but they'd sent reports.

The police officer read the apology from the casualty doctor who had attended to Becky and also his report on her injuries. He also read a report from her G P listing various other injuries she had received treatment for in the past.

Hilary found it hard to believe that this frail looking woman had put up with so much abuse for so long

Time went on, and various other reports were read. Hilary was asked about Sean and his behaviour, and Becky was asked some very personal questions about her relationship with Sean's father; Hilary was left with nothing but admiration and respect for the way she handled herself throughout the proceedings. When the professionals were asked for their opinion, she felt it was so presumptuous of them to be deciding on the future of this woman and her child. Yet she knew it had to be that way if Becky was to get the help she needed and Sean was to be protected. The conference decided to put Sean on the Child Protection Register for the time being, but to meet again in a month's time to review the situation. As long as Becky didn't return to live with her husband, then it wouldn't be necessary, but despite Becky's assertions that she wouldn't, she'd done it before, and they wanted to be sure this time.

The police said that he would be prosecuted and probably be put in prison, but it would take time and meanwhile, Becky must be kept at the hostel, where she and Sean would be safe.

"Can I give you a lift?" Hilary asked as they were on their way out, "I know you've been meeting Sean across the road from school."

Becky smiled a little sheepishly. "How'd you know that?"

"Well, I had to rush over to the shops straight after school the other day, and I saw you together, plus, when I was on duty, I noticed he hurries over there."

"Yeah well, I didn't want to embarrass him and come to school, but we like to spend a bit of time together, away from the hostel, you know."

"Yes, I know. We're just pleased he's still coming to school."

"Oh, he'll come, he knows I've got enough on my plate, I don't need no more trouble from him."

Hilary pulled in by the shops and Becky got out. "Thanks for the lift and all you've done for him, he's always liked you."

"And I like him, you take care, I'll see you in a month."

She drove back to school, thinking again how lucky she was – Becky and Sean faced an uncertain future. Ah well, half-term next week, a chance for a rest and a bit of serious thinking.

Alec was enjoying himself – this pretty young physiotherapist had given him a rough time to begin with, but they had got each other's measure now and he knew she liked him because she always winked at him as she walked past. Today, she was manipulating his left arm, massaging it, and applying heated pads – it was very pleasant, she was touching his body with hers and he could smell her perfume. He felt something stirring, thank God for that! He'd been worried that he might never have sex again, now he had some hope.

Consequently, when Charlie arrived for her morning visit, she found her husband in a cheerful mood and when she went to peck him on the cheek, he turned around and gave her a mouth-to-mouth kiss and then grinned at her quite cheekily.

"My, we're feeling perky this morning," she smiled back at him, "I've brought you the magazines you asked for."

"Thanks, yes I'm feeling quite cheerful today, they say I'm making good progress and I might get home sooner than they thought, they've got to do an assessment of the house first though."

"Oh, that's wonderful news." Charlie felt tears prick her eyes. She knew he could walk using a stick now, but it was his left arm that was proving to be difficult, it was stiff and uncooperative and they'd told her that he must be able to dress himself before they'd let him come home.

"Simon and Anna are on half-term next week," she told him, "and Hilary said she'd bring them in to see you, they're also going to come and show me how to use my new laptop."

Alec smiled. "They'll have to do it all over again when I come home."

Charlie was most indignant. "No, they won't, I'll be able to show you!"

Alec chuckled, "OK then, clever clogs – you can show me," and he took her hand and squeezed it. "Thank you for all you've done for me."

Charlie blushed and looked away. "I haven't done anything really, that will start when you come home."

A shadow passed over his face. "Yes, I shan't be much good at anything."

"Don't say that, you will, you'll be amazed what you'll be able to do before long."

"I hope so." Alec sighed and looked into the distance.

Charlie squeezed his hand, and prayed that she was right.

The phone rang and Angela jumped – she'd been trying hard to listen to the conversation she knew was going on in the office next door, but so far, she'd been unsuccessful. The call was from Italy, and she knew it was important, Bernie had told her to put it through whatever was happening – she transferred the call and then got up and paced around the office. Robert Anderson had been in there for half an hour already and she hadn't heard any raised voices. She did what work she could until, about ten minutes later, Anderson walked out of Bernie's office, totally ignoring her as always. Almost immediately, Bernie's phone was in use, and, using her usual trick, Angela ascertained that he phoned the foodie bar and then the local council offices.

Well, something was happening at any rate! Five minutes later, her boss came bustling out. "I'm off out for about an hour, Angie, now, are you sure everything's OK for tomorrow night?"

"Yes, everything's under control," she assured him.

"Good, what would I do without you eh?" and he bustled off.

Angela looked at her watch – coffee time, she was bursting to tell Carla.

"Well, I don't see how you can say that's good news, anything could have happened." Carla looked decidedly glum.

"I have every confidence that Anderson is on his way out – Bernie made two phone calls, one to the foodie bar and one to the council offices, that means he's had to warn them off and that won't have made him happy."

"Yes, but you said Anderson walked out calmly, he wouldn't have done that if Bernie had given him the push, would he?" She took another sip of her coffee and lit a cigarette. "Danny's been trying so hard, Angie, another three pounds this week."

Angela reached over and patted her arm. "Just be patient, it will be fine, I promise. When is he due to see Anderson again?"

"That's just it, today. God, I hope he's in a good mood."

"Well, he's met his target hasn't he? So Anderson can't say anything."

"Yes, but you know what he can be like and anyway, Danny's still got a long way to go to reach his ideal weight."

"Look, we'll worry about it, if and when it happens, so just calm down."

Carla took another drag of her cigarette.

"You've helped him a lot you know, he wouldn't have done it without you," Angela told her.

"I know, he told me that since he's been living with me, it's been so much easier to eat sensibly. He doesn't stop at service stations anymore because I give him a packed lunch and if he has to stay away, he goes into a supermarket and buys the low-fat sandwiches and salads. It's certainly working, even his asthma is better."

"Good, now don't worry, it will be fine."

Angela didn't feel quite as confident as she sounded, but there wasn't anything else she could do, so she decided to change the subject.

"Are you going to the Fellside tomorrow night?"

"Yes, we'll meet you there after the Italian evening. Are you nervous?"

"In a way. It's the first time I've organised anything quite as complicated, but I'm pretty sure it will go well. I'm looking forward to the fashion show, have a stiff drink ready for me, just in case."

The Italian evening was very important to Bernie, and Angela knew he would not be pleased if anything went wrong, so she was nervous, but she'd done all she could, so she'd just have to sit it out and have faith. She seemed to be doing a lot of that recently.

Jack was moping. He'd cried off the monthly meeting successfully enough – family commitments, which was true tonight anyway, Hilary was at a parents' evening. He was restless though and wished he was going up to Holme Farm. He knew this Italian thing was Bernie's new baby, he was expanding into Europe and into European food.

There had been plenty of publicity about the healthy Mediterranean diet for many years, and olive oil was thought to be one of the main contributing factors. Jack had read all the blurb that the company had published, it appeared on his computer regularly.

All the sales team had been asked to come up with an idea that would help to promote the Italian line of products. He was expected to take a mocked-up sales campaign with him to the monthly meeting at the end of February. The only problem was that so far, his mind was a complete blank.

Anna popped her head round the door. "Dad," she pleaded, "Can you help me with my homework, pleeease?"

For once, Jack leapt at the chance. "Of course poppet, I'll be right there."

Anna's room looked like a bombsite. Magazines, scissors, various mutilated pictures and tubes of glue were scattered all over the place.

"What are you trying to do?" Jack asked in amazement.

"It's this thing for art – a collage, but we've got to cut up a picture we like and then stick it back together, but leave spaces, as if it's been smashed and stuck back together badly, and I can't find a picture I like," she wailed.

"I'm not surprised with all this lot everywhere – right, let's get some semblance of order in here. What sort of pictures do you like?"

"I don't know, I've told you." She was now pouting and looking very much as if she was about to abandon the whole thing.

"OK, OK. Let's look through some magazines together and see if we can find something, shall we?"

They set about restoring some kind of order to the room; then Jack took one pile of magazines and gave Anna another pile.

"Now then, let's look through and if we see a picture we like for any reason at all, let's tear it out and put it here, in the middle, then we'll look at them together and decide which one to use. Does that sound OK?"

His daughter nodded solemnly, and they both began their search.

Gradually, a pile emerged between them – certainly a varied selection, there were pop stars, fashions, lakes, mountains, beautiful houses, sports stars, horses, cars, and many more. Eventually, Anna was able to choose a picture of a mountain bike, which, when cut-up and spread out, made a very interesting collage. She was delighted.

"Right, let's clear this lot up then and see if we can find your bed," Jack teased her, and they began to sort out the debris, suddenly Jack shouted, "Don't throw that away!" so forcefully that poor Anna jumped and stopped dead.

"I'm sorry, poppet, it's just that I've had an idea for *my* homework, that's all," and he started to gather up the magazines and loose pictures, then he pecked his daughter on the cheek, and carried them back into the study.

When Hilary popped her head round later, he was banging away on the keyboard for all he was worth.

Angela put the finishing touches to her make-up and surveyed herself critically in the mirror of the Ladies room. She had bought this brand-new suit for the occasion – it looked quite formal, double-breasted jacket, short-fitted skirt, an executive suit. However, now it was on her, Angela thought it wasn't quite as formal as she had imagined. The jacket was very fitted and accentuated her waist and bust, and the vest top she'd brought from home to go underneath it, was low-cut. Added to that, the only pair of shoes she could find that matched the lovely smoky pink colour was a pair of strappy grey suede sandals with high heels.

The whole effect wasn't exactly cool executive, more sexy secretary. Still, what the hell! It was too late now and the Italians were a very sexy race, so it was in keeping. She sprayed on her perfume and walked determinedly to the door. Her public was waiting.

Bernie introduced the festivities and welcomed all the employees and their families. He was in a particularly expansive mood and insisted that Angela should join him at the front of the hall so he could praise her for her efforts. He also announced that there was going to be a prize for the best sales campaign put forward by the sales team. This prize was a week's holiday in Italy for two people, paid for by the company. A cheer went up at this announcement and Bernie beamed benevolently down upon his workforce.

Angela recognised a glint in his eyes and was just wondering what else he had up his sleeve, when he reached out a hand and beckoned to a young woman standing quietly at the side of the room.

"I should also like to take this opportunity to welcome Dr Tutuola to our company. She will be replacing Dr Anderson who has accepted a post at the new factory near Turin."

Angela worked very hard not to punch the air with her fist, but she couldn't take the smile off her face and had to rush off to the loo at the first opportunity to jump up and down and shout, "Yes, yes, yes!" much to the amazement of an elderly woman who was just washing her hands. She watched Angela in the mirror with a very straight face and shook her head as she made her way out of the Ladies.

The main event of the evening was to be the fashion show, followed by the Italian buffet and wine-tasting, but there were also lots of stalls dotted about the building, selling or promoting various aspects of Italian life and culture. Angela had particularly enjoyed this aspect of her preparations, because the Italian tourist board had sent her a selection of young, Italian students to interview. She had tried hard to keep an even balance between the sexes and had succeeded until the very end, when, instead of choosing a woman, as she should have done to keep it even, she had chosen Angelo, a tall, blonde, hazel-eyed, superb example of Roman manhood. He had opted to run the opera stall and Angela managed to buy three CDs during the course of the evening. The fact that she hadn't the faintest idea what she'd bought didn't seem to bother her at all.

The other stalls were just as popular with the rest of the guests and they did a roaring trade, which resulted in most people wandering around the building with arms full of designer-label packages.

Carla and Danny were no exception and Carla's eyes were shining when she reeled off her list of purchases.

"Are you pleased with the news then?" Angela asked them.

Carla bent forward and gave her a kiss. "Thrilled to bits, aren't we, Danny?"

Danny nodded and grinned. "Thanks for everything, Angie, you've been great."

"Do you think he wanted to go?" Carla asked.

"I've no idea, you'll have to pump that friend of yours and find out. It's really Bernie we should be thanking though, I told you he was a canny old so and so."

"That's true," Carla said with emphasis, "He's certainly enjoying himself tonight."

"Yeah, well, I've put enough effort into it, he jolly well should do."

"The fashion show was great, I got loads of photos," Danny told her.

"Oh, good. Could I have some copies for the works magazine later on?"

"Sure, no problem."

"Did you have to interview all the models for the fashion show as well?" Carla asked with a cheeky grin – she had been well versed in the attributes of Angelo.

Angela grinned back. "No, you know I didn't. Florenza's did that for me."

Florenza's was the upmarket boutique in Lancaster that had staged the show.

"The clothes were beautiful, but a little bit out of my price range I'm afraid." Carla sighed, but Danny turned to her. "You never know, maybe you can find your going-away outfit there."

Angela stared at him and then clapped her hands in delight.

"You're not!" They both nodded. "Oh, that's wonderful news." She gave them both a hug. "When will it be?"

"Well, as soon as we can arrange everything really, we've got no reason to wait."

"Oh, I'm so happy for you." Angela was beaming.

"Will you be my maid of honour?" Carla asked it rather shyly, and Angela was touched.

"Of course I will. I'll be honoured." She giggled and then kissed her friend again, whispering, "You've got to tell me when he asked you and how and everything."

Carla whispered back, "I'll tell you later."

Just then, Bernie came bustling through the crowd. "Ah, there you are Angie – someone over by the buffet is looking for you, they want to know how to go about ordering a crate of wine," and he was off again.

"I'll have to go, you two, see you later at the Fellside, we'll have a drink to celebrate."

Having sorted out the potential customer, Angela was having a well-deserved rest by the buffet. She had a cheese nibble on a cocktail stick in one hand and a glass of red wine in the other, and she was thinking what a good night it had been. The evening had been a complete success – Bernie was delighted, and she had heard two lots of good news, one about Dr Anderson and another about Danny and Carla.

"Would you like a refill?" Don White was standing at her elbow, bottle at the ready.

"Yes, thanks."

"I was wondering if you knew where my old friend Jack had got to this evening."

"No, sorry, I've no idea."

Don sat down beside her and leaned closer; she realised he was very drunk.

"Oh, come now, I think you do. I think you know a lot more about Jack than you are letting on."

Angela stood up. "I have no idea where Jack is and I don't know what you're talking about. Now, if you'll excuse me, I have work to do," and she strode away as quickly as the strappy sandals would allow.

An hour later, safely ensconced in the bar at the Fellside, Angela told Danny and Carla about her run-in with Don White.

"He really is an obnoxious man, he's slimy enough when he's sober, but when he's drunk – yuck!"

"Well, it sounds as if you dealt with him pretty successfully anyhow." Danny smiled reassuringly.

Angela couldn't get over the change in him – it wasn't just the stone he'd lost, it was his hair, which was now cut in a much shorter style, and his clothes which were new and more up to date, but more than that, he just seemed more confident. It was amazing what falling in love could do.

231

While he went to get more drinks, Angela quizzed her friend about the proposal.

"It was just before we were coming out tonight, we were all dressed up and we'd got a drink to celebrate him doing so well in his assessment – another half a stone off! He turned me round to face him and said, 'You look beautiful'. I just went to kiss him but he put his fingers on my lips and said, 'Will you marry me?' Well, I was gobsmacked, but I managed to say something that meant yes, and then we were kissing and hugging and laughing and talking about it all the way to Holme Farm."

"Oh, it's so romantic, Carla, I'm really looking forward to it."

Danny came back with the drinks then and after one more, Angela felt really tired.

"I'm off, folks, I'm shattered, I'll see you on Monday."

The newly-engaged couple didn't look too upset at being left on their own. It was at times like this, that Angela felt the most lonely – it would have been nice to have someone to share the triumph of the evening with, but, as it was, she had to go home alone. She reached her car andrummaged around in her handbag for her car keys – she kept meaning to get a large key ring that would be easy to find, but somehow never got round to it.

"Lost something, have you?"

She swung round. Don White was swaying slightly and standing far too close for comfort. She took a step back, but her car was behind her.

"No, thank you. I'm fine."

She turned her back on him and carried on looking for her keys. Next thing she knew, she'd been pulled round and his foul-smelling mouth was on top of hers and she was being pressed backwards against her car. Angela wrenched her head away.

"How dare you!" She took a swipe at him but he side-stepped with surprising agility considering he was so drunk and pulled her round with him, so that he was now leaning against her car and gripping both her arms.

"Feisty little thing, aren't you? No wonder Jack took a fancy to you, he likes strong women."

There was only one thing for it – knee in the groin – trouble was, she had a tight skirt on. She jerked her knee up as hard as she possibly could and heard a satisfying grunt, then she pulled away and ran back towards the entrance.

She found Danny and Carla in the bar and managed to convey, between gasps and expletives, exactly what Don White had done.

"Where is he?" Danny's face was set.

"I left him in the car park."

"Right!"

All three of them made their way outside and met the offending person staggering towards the door. Danny grabbed him by the arm and took a swing and the next thing they all knew, he was flat out on the ground.

"Ooh, Danny, you haven't killed him, have you?"

"No, of course not, I hardly touched him, he's dead drunk, that's all. Help me get him inside, we'll put him in the breakfast room and he can sleep it off."

The three of them manoeuvred Don, who by now was groaning, and managed to sit him at one of the tables, where his head fell forward and he started to snore loudly.

"Will he be alright?" Carla wasn't really worried about Don at all, only the effect the incident might have on Danny if anything went wrong. Danny had no such worries.

"He'll have a headache in the morning."

"Serve him right. I hope he has an ache somewhere else as well," Angela remarked with feeling.

"Don't worry, I'll find him when he's sober and have a quiet word in his ear, he won't bother you again." Danny was quite confident.

"Do you want us to come home with you?" Carla asked.

"No, I'm fine, but thanks anyway." Angela turned to go.

"Oh, Angie, you've torn that nice new skirt, it's split right up the back."

Angela twisted round to look. "Damn! Ah well, it was in a good cause," and she smiled.

CHAPTER 20

"Is it alright if we go upstairs now, Mrs Baker?"
One of the council workmen popped his head round the kitchen door. Charlie was busy baking cakes ready for Simon and Anna's visit.

"Yes, that's fine." She was enjoying having someone around the house, but, she wasn't enjoying what they were doing. There seemed to be rails everywhere, up the stairs, in the cloakroom and now they were going upstairs to adapt the toilet and bathroom up there. The house suddenly seemed like an old people's home. She kept telling herself it was so that Alec could come home, but part of her didn't want him home. She stopped what she was doing, horrified at her own thought – of course she wanted him home, she loved him. Part of her realised though, that while he was in the rehab unit, he was being cared for properly and all she had to do each day was go and visit him – once he got home he would become her responsibility and she wouldn't have anywhere to escape to. She shook her head to clear her thoughts, she would get used to it and he would get better, she must concentrate on the positive. Yesterday, her driving tutor had told her she was doing very well and that she must get some practice on her own, so she was going out later. She also had the children's visit to look forward to. The sound of hammering interrupted her thoughts; she sighed and concentrated on her baking.

"You don't look very well, my dear, overdid it with the Italian evening I expect. It was a great success though, great success. Why don't you go home and put your feet up? There's nothing really urgent going on today, go on, off you go!"

Angela didn't need telling twice. She went home and crawled into bed. She didn't agree with Bernie about overdoing things because she'd done next to nothing all weekend; it was probably a virus and a good rest was all that was needed, so she drifted off to sleep and woke to the phone ringing – it was dark.

"How are you feeling?" Carla sounded concerned.

"I think I'm OK, just incredibly tired and I was very sick this morning."

"Maybe it was something you ate?"

"I hardly ate anything yesterday, I felt sick all day, I'm a bit hungry now though."

"It wasn't anything to do with the delightful Mr White was it? Do you think it upset you more than you thought?"

"No, I really don't think so, I'm tougher than that."

"So you'll be in work tomorrow?"

"Oh, yes, don't worry, I'll be there for coffee in the morning."

She put the phone down and, almost immediately, it rang again – it was Pete, phoning from China. They talked for a while, and then he told her he'd be home in April, as the contract was due to finish then. He asked her to start thinking of where she'd like to go for a holiday, maybe she'd like to fly out and meet him in Hong Kong? Now that was an idea. After his call, she got out of bed, feeling a lot better and padded downstairs to get herself something to eat. The trouble was, once she started looking around, she didn't really fancy anything, so she ended up opening a tin of tomato soup and eating it on her lap in front of the TV.

"Now, Grandma. What do you want to use the laptop for?"

Charlie stopped to think. "Well, I'd like to be able to do all the stuff I did before, only sitting down here instead of in the office."

"OK, so what did you do before?"

"Well, let me see. Banking, emails, online shopping, letters, storing photos and holidays."

"OK, that's no problem. You need to think of a password."

Charlie gave him one and then wrote it down with all her other passwords. It was impossible to remember them all.

Simon was clicking away at the keyboard. "Now, is there anything else you want it to do?"

"I don't think so – what else can it do?"

"It can do just about anything. Dad uses ours to pay bills, remind us all of appointments, remind him when the car needs servicing, all sorts of things."

"Well, let's leave it at that for now, shall we? Then when Grandpa gets home, we might think again – now, it's time for some cake."

They joined Hilary and Anna in the kitchen; they were busy putting together a dried flower arrangement.

"This is for you, Grandma," Anna told her.

"Thank you, it's lovely, just the right colours for our bedroom."

"Is everything set up for Grandma then?" Hilary asked her son.

"Yes, no problem." Simon was eyeing the cakes.

"He's been a great help to me, I think some of those functions will be very useful once Alec's home. I don't think I'll have much time then to go shopping, or fetch his medicine."

Charlie started setting the table for tea. Hilary took a deep breath. "Did you read the part in the booklet about diet, Charlie?"

"Well, I scanned it quickly, but Alec's been getting a balanced diet in the unit and he says he's looking forward to my cooking when he gets home."

"Yes, but it says that a low-fat diet is advisable for people after a stroke, so you might have to adapt your cooking slightly."

Charlie stopped laying the table and looked at her daughter-in-law.

"What are you trying to say?"

"The doctors recommend a low-cholesterol diet, like the one that Jack's been on – they think it helps to prevent further strokes, so you might want to change your way of cooking, it is pretty high in fat."

Charlie sat down heavily.

"Are you saying that the food I cook might have caused Alec's stroke?"

"No, of course not." Hilary was getting exasperated and wished desperately that she'd never started this conversation. "There are lots of different reasons why people have strokes, all I'm saying is, you should read the booklet, there are some suggested recipes in there and some of them look quite nice."

The two grandchildren were munching on their cakes and silently looking from their mother to their grandmother and back again – they both knew this was a tricky situation.

Both women were silent; Charlie sitting as if in shock, and Hilary pouring out tea and chewing her lip.

Suddenly Charlie stood up and announced, "I made some extra cakes for you to take home for your Dad, I'll put them in a container for you."

Hilary shook her head sadly, and Simon and Anna let out sighs of relief.

Jack was sitting in the dentist's waiting room; he looked round to see if anyone was watching. When it was safe, he ripped the pages out of the magazine as quickly and quietly as he could and stuffed them into his pocket, then he went on nonchalantly flicking through.

The pages in his pocket contained an article on how to put the romance back into your marriage. In his case, it meant, how to get back into your wife's bed.

He was beginning to feel quite desperate; he'd dropped a couple of large hints about having a bad back, and how hard the bed settee was, but they had fallen on deaf ears.

He'd tried hovering in the bedroom, last thing at night, with vague excuses like looking for antacid or headache pills, but Hilary had always calmly told him where they were and then put out the light, saying goodnight very dismissively. He'd tried coming into the room early in the morning, sometimes with a mug of tea and sometimes with the excuse of looking for a particular pair of socks or tie. Hilary had always been grateful for the tea and always been helpful about the lost items of clothing, but that was all, she had never encouraged him in any way to get into bed.

He couldn't wait to get his check-up over, so that he could get back to the car and read the article.

The first section was rather disappointing – it suggested the usual things, candlelit meals, flowers, little gifts and so on. Then it went on to suggest doing things that your particular woman enjoyed – it might be opera, or the theatre, or maybe the ballet. Hilary did like the ballet, but Jack couldn't face the thought of men in tights, they certainly didn't turn *him* on! He quite liked the idea of a romantic evening at home, watching a film and eating a meal together, but he thought the best bet for him was the 'weekend away' idea.

'Take your woman out of the humdrum environment of her everyday existence – take her away for the weekend and spoil her.' This was an excellent idea, because Jack could book a double room and she'd have to let him into her bed. There would only be one bed.

He grinned to himself – yes, now all he had to do was persuade Hilary to come, see if Charlie would have the kids, and find somewhere to go. Not a lot then!

Jack knew he didn't have very much time, because Alec would be home soon and he couldn't ask once that happened, Charlie would be too busy.

This next weekend would be ideal. He had to go up to see Anderson on Thursday, so Friday would be OK and Hilary was still on half-term, so she wouldn't have any matches.

Once he'd decided, he set about looking for a suitably romantic retreat and found the ideal place in the back of the paper; an old smugglers' inn on a harbour in a North Devon village. Just the thing. It had a five-star restaurant and newly renovated rooms. Right, next he must phone Charlie and then persuade Hilary. The most difficult was last – ah well, nothing ventured, nothing gained.

As it happened, Jack had picked a good day. Hilary had been curled up on the settee for most of the rainy afternoon, watching old movies and was actually feeling quite mellow.

There was a meal waiting for him when he got in, and the family sat down together for the first time in ages.

Jack cleared his throat nervously. "Um, I was wondering if you fancied going away for the weekend, this weekend actually. I thought it might do us good, and Mum has said she'll have Simon and Anna. It might be our last chance for a while, as once Dad's home, she'll have her hands full – there's a place I've found that looks perfect and ..." He stopped because he'd run out of breath and because he had to look at Hilary to see her reaction, he hadn't dared before. Hilary was smiling.

"I think it's a lovely idea," she said quietly.

The relief was amazing. Jack beamed at all three of his family. Simon and Anna had exchanged knowing glances when Jack had started speaking, but now they appeared to be concentrating on their food.

"I'll book it right away then." He got up from the table and rushed off.

Hilary finished her meal and wandered off into the lounge, in what appeared to be her own little world, and Simon and Anna took bets on how long it would be before Jack moved back into the double bed.

Jack felt perfectly confident about his visit to Dr Anderson – he felt he'd been given a second chance, in both his job and his marriage and he wasn't going to blow it in either case.

He drove up to his appointment without incident, his mind turning over the sales campaign he'd been working on – it was a good one, and for once, he was looking forward to the monthly meeting, when he would present it. He might even have a chance of winning the prize holiday, but it didn't matter, all that mattered was that his life was getting back on course.

When he was shown into the medical room, Anderson was writing something at his desk. Jack stood awkwardly for a couple of minutes and then the doctor turned round.

"Ah, Mr Baker, it seems you have been redeeming yourself, been working very hard, I hear. Well, let's have a look at you."

After the examination and the weigh-in, Jack sat in the robe and waited for the verdict. Anderson wrote some more, then turned to face him.

"Excellent. Yes, you've done very well. I shall be able to write a very positive report this time." The doctor smiled, but Jack just looked down, he didn't trust himself to look at the other man, he might give away his thoughts. Luckily for him Anderson's pager went off and saved the day. He stood up and cleared his throat.

"Yes, well if you'd care to get dressed, I shall just go and see what this is all about."

Jack sighed with relief and stood up to find his clothes; he was just slipping out of the skimpy robe when the door opened, and a Nubian princess walked in, or so it seemed to Jack. She had dark skin that shone like ebony and doe-like eyes that melted him on the spot. Her crinkly hair was long and beaded and taken back off a face that looked like a statuette of a goddess. He only noticed her magnificent figure later, partly because; it was covered by the white coat, and partly because, he was so transfixed by her eyes, that he didn't notice anything else. She was smiling at him.

241

"Good morning, Mr Baker. I'm Dr Tutuola."

Jack drew the ineffective robe around him as best he could. "Good morning."

Luckily, Anderson came in just then, otherwise Jack was sure he might have pinched himself to make sure he wasn't dreaming.

"Ah, you've met Dr Tutuola, good – she will be taking over from me in a month's time."

Jack was suddenly very much awake. "Oh, you're leaving us then?" he said as casually as he could.

"Yes. Mr Holmes has offered me a post in Italy, at his new factory there. I'm absolutely thrilled. Always wanted to spend some time abroad."

Jack could hardly contain his joy. He'd have to find Angela after all, to tell her the good news, she deserved a medal for what she'd achieved. He hadn't spoken to her for a while – she had said she'd phone him after the foodie bar night, but she hadn't. He had the feeling she wasn't very pleased with him for some reason.

At that precise moment, Angela was being sick again.

She had finally decided, by Tuesday, to go to see her doctor, convinced that she had got some dreaded disease. When he told her she was pregnant, she was stunned.

"Didn't you notice your periods had stopped?" he asked her, somewhat cryptically.

"Well, no, not really. They are always fairly erratic anyway and I've been so busy lately, I just didn't think about it."

He had shaken his head and written out a prescription for iron tablets and anti-sickness pills, but he said they'd take about a week to work.

She had driven home in a daze and tried to phone Carla three times before she realised it was only eleven o'clock in the morning. Eventually, she'd pulled herself together – she had some serious thinking to do.

Later on, Carla too, was amazed.

"How do you feel about it?"

"I'm very happy."

"Have you told Pete yet?" Angela shook her head. "How will he react? Does he want them?"

"I really don't know – he knows I want them, but we haven't talked about it much. Isn't that sad?"

The friends were sitting in their favourite place, Angela's kitchen. Carla had rushed over to give support and was drinking coffee. Angela had ginger beer which, for some obscure reason, she'd just taken a fancy to. Carla seemed deep in thought.

"Well, it is really, but then you don't see enough of each other to do much talking."

"No," Angela agreed, "all we do is have sex and talk about his next job or the next time he'll be home."

"Well, things will certainly be different in the future." Carla sighed, "Some people just aren't interested in kids," then she added, "I suppose Pete *is* the father." She said it tentatively, looking into Angela's face as she did so.

"Of course," Angela said hurriedly.

"Well, it's just that I know your periods are so erratic, that's all."

"Yes, I know, but I had one while he was home at Christmas, I'm sure I did. It's definitely Pete's baby," she finished with conviction.

Carla let out a sigh of relief. "That's alright then."

They were both silent for a while, thoughtfully sipping their drinks, then Angela said,

"Well, it doesn't matter anyway, because I want this baby and I'll have it with or without his help. You'll have to get married before I get huge though, I can't be your matron of honour looking like a beached whale."

Carla laughed, "Good job we're planning it soon then."

Pete had been stunned at first and had hardly said anything; Angela had put the phone down in tears, but he phoned about an hour later and told her he was very happy and was already making plans to wind up his contract, so he could get a job back in the UK and support her during the rest of the pregnancy and the birth. Her family had also been delighted and her mother in particular was ecstatic and already looking at prams.

All this had made Angela realise that she wasn't the only one who was happy about the pregnancy and she felt more contented than she had in years.

Now, she splashed her face with water and combed her hair, turning sideways to look in the mirror. Did she look bigger already? Maybe she should start just looking at maternity clothes, so she'd be ready to buy when the time came. She walked back to the office, trying to imagine what it must be like to be huge in the middle.

Carla was waiting. "You'll never guess who I've just seen."

"Who?"

"Jack!"

"Really. Where?"

Coming out of Anderson's office – he didn't see me. He looked very pleased with himself. Anderson must have told him he was going."

"Yes, I was supposed to phone him, but I forgot."

"He didn't tell you he was coming up here, did he? So, I shouldn't worry. You've got other things to worry about now." She glanced down at Angela's flat stomach.

"Yes, quite."

"He might have thanked you though."

"Well, maybe he'll phone me to thank me."

"He's got off lightly really," Carla muttered.

Angela laughed. "Last week you were telling me he was in trouble and needed my help. We don't know what his wife is like – she may be giving him hell."

"I s'pose so. But you didn't see that smug expression on his face when he came out of Anderson's office. When you think

244

about it though, that baby could have been his and then what would you have done?"

Angela was quiet for a moment and then she shook her head. "Well, it isn't his, so it doesn't matter does it."

Jack was feeling particularly magnanimous. His job was safe, his marriage was out of danger and he was working on a good campaign, plus, he had a new fantasy figure in the shape of Dr Tortola, or whatever her name was; but she would remain just that, nothing more. The sun was shining and it was a beautiful spring day. He decided to buy Angela some flowers and a card to say thank you, and chose a spring bouquet – the smell of the freesias drifted up to him as he made his way back to his car. He was deep in thought, trying to decide what he could write in the card that would hit just the right note, when he very nearly bumped into Danny.

Danny recognised him first because Jack wasn't sure that this smartly dressed and decidedly thinner young man was the same person, but then something about the cheeky grin and the way he walked, rang a bell.

"Hello, how's it going?"

"Fine thanks."

"Someone in hospital then?"

Jack looked down at the flowers. "Oh, no, they're for Angela, to say thank you, I've just been to see Anderson and heard the good news."

"Oh, yeah. Great isn't it. Sorry to hear about your old man, by the way."

"Oh, he's coming along now, but thanks. It will be a long haul, but he'll get there."

"Are you off to Holme Farm now then?"

"Yes, I want to drop these off before I head off home."

"They'll cheer her up, she's not been feeling too well lately."

"Oh, what's wrong with her?"

Danny suddenly realised that this was a subject he'd best keep away from, it could just get a bit too complicated, he thought quickly.

"Well, she's been busy with the Italian evening and then that business with Don White upset her quite a bit."

"What was that then?"

Danny relaxed, happy that he'd got away from the awkward area and enjoyed telling Jack the sordid details of Don's activities.

Jack was furious; he thanked Danny for all he'd done and got back in his car. When he saw Don White again, he'd give him a piece of his mind.

He drove back to Holme Farm and took the flowers and card down to Angela's office. He knocked on the door, and when she shouted, "Come in," he put the flowers round first and waved them about, before he went in.

She was sitting at her desk, looking slightly bemused. "Hello."

"Hi. These are for you, to say thank you for all you've done. I saw Anderson this morning, and he told me the good news."

"Yes, I'm sorry I didn't phone you, I ..." She stopped.

"It's alright, I met Danny in town and he told me all about it – I'll thump that Don White myself when I see him."

Angela smiled. "So, Danny's told you the news then?"

Jack looked puzzled. "Yes, he told me about the Italian evening and how Don White was a complete shit and – "

Angela shook her head. "He didn't tell you then."

"Tell me what?"

"I'm pregnant."

Jack's mouth fell open and he looked, as Angela described it to Carla later, like a drowning man.

"Oh, my God!" he said, and sat down heavily in a chair. His mind was racing; someone up there didn't like him. There he was, only this morning, thinking his life was back on track, and now this – now what was he going to do? He put his head in his hands. Angela stood up and looked at him for at least a minute before she said, "It's alright, Jack, the baby isn't yours, it's Pete's."

The change was remarkable. He leapt up again and came and kissed her on the cheek.

"Oh, congratulations! That's wonderful. I mean. Is he pleased? Are you pleased?" He stopped in confusion.

Angela smiled despite herself. "Yes, we're both very pleased, he's giving up working abroad and coming back to be with me."

"Oh, well. The flowers are doubly appropriate then," Jack beamed.

"Yes, I suppose they are. Anyway how are things with you? How are your father and your wife?"

"Well, Dad's getting better all the time, he's coming home next week, and Hilary, well, things are improving slowly, these things take time, but I think it will be alright."

"I'm glad. It's been a difficult time for you." She looked at him for a moment and then turned away.

"Well, I've got to get going. Thanks again and take care of yourself now." He was backing towards the door.

"And you," Angela said, and he was gone.

She sat down at her desk and picked up the card – it was a blank one and Jack had written.

'Thanks for everything,

Jack.'

She tore it up and put it in the bin, then she took the flowers and put them in the bin in the Ladies room – the smell was making her feel sick again. She splashed her face and combed her hair, took a deep breath, and walked slowly back to her office.

Jack sat in his car and let out a deep sigh. God! That was a near thing – that baby could so easily have been his, the pill wasn't a hundred per cent effective. Nothing was a hundred per cent effective! Well, he'd learned his lesson, no more extramarital sex for him ever again. Fantasies were much safer.

247

CHAPTER 21

It was one of those rare late February weekends, when the spring sun shone down on everything. People who had come out in winter clothes out of habit were peeling off layers.

Jack and Hilary strolled around the harbour, breathing in the salt air and basking in the sun's warmth.

"Do you fancy some lunch?" Jack asked.

"We've only just had that huge breakfast," Hilary chided.

Jack looked puzzled. "Have we? I'm starving, it must be the sea air." He looked at his watch. "How about a walk up on the moors then, to work up an appetite?"

Hilary thought that was an excellent idea, so they drove out to Simonsbath, parked, and walked for a couple of hours, not talking much at all, except to comment on the scenery and the odd tourist they came across. A chill wind whipped around them and they were glad of their fleeces. They were also glad of the pub they found later, quite close to where they'd parked the car. They sat by a log fire, and ate crab sandwiches washed down with local beer. Hilary stretched out like a cat, arms above her head. "This is just blissful," she purred, "Why don't we do this more often?"

"I don't know – we should. We could find someone to have the kids, even if Mum can't."

"I expect she will, once she gets used to having Alec home again. By the way, I had that little chat with her about her cooking."

"Did you? You're brave. What did she say?"

Hilary grimaced. "Well, she thought I was accusing her of causing Alec's stroke, but when I reassured her I wasn't, she just ignored the whole thing."

Jack was quiet for a moment. "That probably means she'll do something about it then."

"Does it?"

"Yes. When Mum goes quiet, it means she's thinking – if she didn't argue the point with you, it means she thinks you're right."

"Well, let's hope so, for Alec's sake."

They stood up and started to make their way back to the car.

"It's a pity though." Jack sighed.

"Why?"

"Because I love her cooking."

Hilary gave him a playful shove and they both laughed.

They spent the rest of the day meandering around the Devon villages, taking photos whenever they saw a scene they liked. Jack managed to hold Hilary's hand a couple of times, and once, when they stopped for an ice cream, she wiped some off his nose and gently kissed it, quite unconsciously. His hopes were rising, along with something else, and he felt that at last he was getting somewhere.

Jack had booked a room with a double bed, and when they had arrived the night before; Hilary had stopped for a moment and looked at it. Jack had held his breath, but then she'd carried on unpacking and said nothing. They'd arrived quite late in any case, and after their meal, had gone straight to bed and fallen into a deep sleep.

This morning, Jack had reached across to find that there was nobody there – Hilary was already in the shower and she'd reminded him quite sharply, on her return, that if he wanted any breakfast, he'd better get up!

His hopes now rested on tonight and tomorrow morning – the eternal optimist.

The restaurant at their hotel was an excellent one and they both made the most of it that evening. Holiday areas seemed to be exempt from the most draconian government food regulations, so the menu was extensive and far from boringly healthy. They both chose Lobster Thermidor, one of their favourites, and for once Hilary joined Jack in having all three courses, so by the time they got to the coffee they were both full to capacity.

"Let's go for a walk around the harbour," Jack suggested, in the hope that it might release the steel band around his diaphragm.

"That's a good idea. Just let me go to the loo first."

He watched his wife walk away from him and his heart ached – he had to get things back to the way they were – he loved her, and what's more, he fancied her. She was looking particularly attractive tonight, in tight-fitting, black velvet trousers and a soft, fluffy jumper thing – the whole outfit showed off her excellent figure. He knew she'd taken extra care over her hair and make-up because she'd taken ages in the bathroom – surely that meant that she wanted to please him.

They walked around the harbour hand in hand. It would have been romantic, but for the growing feeling of discomfort around Jack's middle. He had stomach ache and he felt nauseous. By the time they got back to the room, he had to rush for the loo and he was in there for quite a while. When he came out, Hilary was sitting up in bed, reading a book.

"Have we got any antacid with us?"

"I might have some in my toilet bag. I'll have a look."

She hopped out of bed, long legs flashing beneath a skimpy little silky slip and Jack flopped onto the bed, groaning out loud with both frustration and pain. There was no way he was going to be able to perform, feeling the way he was.

Hilary handed him a glass of the fizzy liquid and put her arm round him.

"You've been on that health food diet for quite a while now and your system just can't take the rich food anymore. I'm sure you'll be fine in the morning."

Jack nodded and they climbed into bed. After a couple more trips to the loo, he managed to get to sleep. He woke in the morning with a bit of a headache, but his stomach ache had gone. It was now or never!

He turned over and started kissing Hilary's neck; just where he knew she liked it, under her ear. She stirred and turned towards him, hooking her legs between his, just as she used to. He pressed her to him, hardly daring to breathe – he couldn't believe his luck. He must take it slowly. He began to stroke her thigh, firmly and gently, then her buttocks, she sighed and nuzzled into his neck, returning his hug. He could tell she was aroused and he felt incredible relief that she actually wanted him again. Then she stiffened and pulled away, turning over onto her back.

"I can't do it."

He propped himself up on one elbow and looked down at her.

"Why not?" He tried to say it as gently as he could.

"Because I keep thinking about that woman. What was she like? What did you see in her? What does she have that I don't have? Then I get angry again and I don't want to go near you."

Jack sighed and lay back down, his hands under his head.

"How many times do I have to tell you? Nothing happened. I just pecked her on the cheek. I don't see anything in her; there is nothing to compare her with you, Hilary. I love you. I don't love her. I don't know what else I can say that will make it any better. All I know is, that I wish I'd never met her and I wish we could just get back to the way we were before it all happened."

There was silence for a while. They were both lost in their own thoughts, then Hilary said, "Maybe if I met her, I'd be able to get her out of my head and then we could move on."

Jack couldn't believe his ears – this was getting worse and worse!

"I think that would be a terrible idea!" he almost screeched. He sat up again and turned away from Hilary, sitting on the side of the bed.

"Why would it be so terrible?" Hilary asked him. "She wouldn't have to know I'd seen her. I wouldn't make a scene or anything."

Jack turned back to look at Hilary. He felt trapped for some reason – he didn't like the way things were developing and he didn't trust Hilary, she was up to something.

She was lying there, looking up at him with an innocent enough look on her face, but he knew her well enough to know she was at her most dangerous when she looked like that. His mind was racing. He had to throw her off the scent – there was no way she must find out who the woman was, especially now Angela was pregnant.

He got up and went over to the window, frantically praying for inspiration.

Then – bingo! He had a brainwave.

"If I tell you a bit about her, do you think that will help?"

"It might do."

"Well, her name's Louisa and she's Italian. She's married and she works as a waitress in a foodie bar."

"What's a foodie bar?"

Jack went on to explain. "So that's why you were putting so much weight on." Hilary snorted.

"No, it's not. I've only been twice. I told you, we met on the fitness weekend. She needed to lose weight and get fitter – for her job."

Hilary could now imagine this fat, motherly Italian waitress and she was beginning to feel better.Somebody to spoil him with her cooking, just like Charlie did.

Jack was talking again; "so I've done all I can. I want us to try and start again, Hils, please. I can't sleep in the study forever, the kids are beginning to get worried about it. Besides, we've got to start somewhere, just the odd kiss and cuddle maybe?"

"Alright. You can come back into our bed again and we'll take it from there, but I'm not promising anything. You'll just have to be patient, Jack. This has been very traumatic for me and I don't want any pressure."

She hopped out of bed and made for the shower, smiling to herself at the thought of this mountainous woman in a tight overall, balancing plates of steaming steak and kidney pie and beaming at her customers as she placed the food in front of them. She probably treated all her 'boys' the same, rather like the typical extended Italian family. She would have given Jack a lift that night out of the goodness of her kind Italian heart, hidden beneath her ample bosom, and Jack had pecked her on the cheek to say thank you; after all, that was all she'd seen, just a peck on the cheek.

She hummed to herself in the shower.

Jack lay back on the bed and let out a sigh of relief. He could tell that the waitress story had worked – he was back in his bed and it would only be a matter of time now before he was back in his wife! Life was looking up.

The magazines were scattered all over the floor. Carla was looking at wedding outfits and Angela was supposed to be helping, but she kept getting distracted by pictures of mothers and babies and articles on childbirth.

"You keep getting that dreamy, motherly look on your face. Will you just concentrate! We are supposed to be looking at outfits for the wedding!" Carla tried to sound irritated but she couldn't help smiling.

"I'm sorry. I keep getting distracted."

They were sitting in Angela's lounge, bathed in early spring sunshine.

Angela put her magazine down and looked across at Carla. "Are you sure you can get everything organised in time? It's only just over a month, you know."

"I don't see why not. Early April is an ideal time for a wedding. Besides, if we leave it any later you'll start to show, and you don't want that."

"No, I don't. I want to be a sexy and glamorous matron of honour," Angela said with determination.

"Well, you'll be a matron alright." Carla giggled and then ducked, as a cushion flew towards her.

"Has Danny booked the registry office yet?" Angela asked after a few moments of pretending she was sulking.

"Yes. He did it last week. This week we've got to buy the outfits and decide where to have ' The Do'."

"It's a pity you can't have it at the foodie bar."

"Hey, the rumour is that it's moved to the Fellside until the fuss has all died down."

"Well, I knew Anderson would report it, but Bernie will have it well covered – they won't find anything. Whereabouts have they put it?"

"Apparently there's a really big cellar there."

"I told you Bernie was cunning. We'll have to go and see. Maybe you could have the reception there after all."

"No, we want it in Lancaster. We're not having many people, so it won't be a big affair."

"Is your family getting excited?"

"Oh, yeah. My mum's already got her outfit and my sister Josie, the one with twins. She's asked if they can be pageboys. They're certainly a handful but I said yes. It's not like we'll be in a church or anything."

"How old are they?"

"Coming up to four."

"Ahhhh."

"There goes that look again."

They both laughed and looked back at the magazines.

"These 'mother of the bride' outfits are gorgeous." Angela slid the page across to Carla.

"Yeah, but my mum's got hers."

"What about Danny's mum?"

"Yes, well. There's only one problem with that. She weighs about sixteen stone!"

"Oh dear," Angela giggled. "Have you met her?"

"No, not yet. She's the only one coming from Danny's side and she's a widow, so she's staying with us. He's taking me up there next weekend to meet her."

"What if you don't like her?"

"I'll just have to, won't I?"

"I'm really lucky. Pete's parents live down south so I hardly ever have to see them. They think it's totally uncivilised up here. A lot of southerners think that. They're really difficult to talk to in any case, they just sit there in silence most of the time."

"Aren't they excited about the baby?"

"I don't know. They never seem to get excited about anything. I haven't heard from them."

"Well never mind. You're excited and Pete's excited, so that's all that matters. Now, let's decide on colours. What colours suit you?"

Karen and Hilary were walking the cross-country course, checking markers. It was pouring with rain and freezing cold; typical cross-country weather, in fact.

"Are you running?" Karen asked.

"Yes. I promised Dai I'd keep pace with the back markers." Hilary grimaced; she'd far rather be up with the front runners.

"This is a bit of a shock to the system after a week off." Karen shivered. "How did your romantic weekend go, by the way?"

"It was great. Very relaxed. Jack was very attentive. I must admit he's trying really hard."

"Is everything back to normal then?"

"What do you mean?"

"You know – are you back in the same bed?"

"Well, yes and no. We are back in the same bed, but we're not having sex yet."

"Why not?"

"Because I'm punishing him, if I'm honest."

"Do you think that's a very good idea?"

"I don't really know. I suppose eventually I'll feel like sex again, but at the moment, I can't get that woman out of my mind and it puts me off. I told him I wanted to meet her."

"You must be mad!" Karen was horrified.

"Well, it worked to a certain extent. He told me a few things about her."

"What did he say?" The two women had stopped walking and Karen was overcome with curiosity.

"He said she was an Italian waitress in a foodie bar, and she's married."

"Well that doesn't tell you a lot, does it. How old is she? What does she look like?"

"I don't know how old she is, but it sounds as if she's one of these motherly types with a weight problem."

They walked on again and Karen seemed lost in thought, then she said, "I think you should have sex as soon as you can. You know yourself, if you don't do it for a while, you get out of the habit and that could be dangerous. Jack might get fed up and decide to look elsewhere. Besides, you said yourself that you only saw him kiss her on the cheek. You could be punishing him for nothing. Look at Dai. I bet he's not punishing Lynda. I bet he got her back into bed as soon as he could."

Hilary looked stunned. "Has Lynda come back then?"

"Yes, during half term. Geoff and I saw them in town. They looked so happy."

"I'm very glad for them. I just hope she stays this time."

They were almost back to the school buildings and children were starting to mill around the entrance. Karen stopped and looked at Hilary. "Think about what I've said, Hils. Don't let things go on too long, will you?"

Hilary sighed, "I know what you mean and yes, I'll think about it." She walked away towards her classroom, deep in thought.

The cross-country was going pretty much as usual. There had been the usual crop of absences and sick notes; the usual sporty types, who knew it was their turn to shine and had been taking their rightful place as stars for the day. The usual heroic and unfit types who knew they would be last, but took a perverse pleasure in it, struggling on amidst tremendous encouragement from friends and staff alike.

It was these back-runners that Hilary had said she would stay with, and she jogged slowly and steadily beside Go-Slow Joe, as he was called.

Joseph Matthews was a big lad for his age, tall and hefty for a thirteen-year-old. He could never be described as a sportsman, but he took part in everything with a stoic good humour and he was a popular eighth year. Some of the Year Sixes who had run earlier on were cheering him, and he puffed silently and relentlessly on, his beetroot face set in a determined grimace.

They had reached the top of the sports field where the spectators thinned out and something caught Hilary's eye. Over by the perimeter fence, there appeared to be a struggle going on. A man and a boy were arguing and the man was trying to pull the boy towards the fence. Hilary stopped and turned, increasing her pace. She recognized the boy as Sean and instinct told her that the man was his father.

She shouted to the nearest group of pupils, "Get Mr Evans, quickly!"

Then she ran as fast as she could towards the struggling pair.

"Sean. Are you alright?" she gasped as soon as he could hear her. It was all she could think of to say. The man scowled at her, but he let go of Sean's arm, and that was enough. The boy stepped back out of his reach and stood his ground, glowering.

"Is there a problem?" Hilary asked.

"Yes, there's a problem," he sneered, "The problem is that this little shit won't tell me where his mother is."

"Please watch your language, Mr Abbot is it? There are children listening." Hilary looked round to emphasize her words and she could see that quite a crowd had gathered, some of them calling to Sean, asking him if he was alright, asking him if that was his dad. Hilary glowered them into silence.

This was a very tricky situation. The man could just decide to grab Sean if he wanted to – she must somehow placate him until help arrived.

"Sean is still taking part in the cross-country race, Mr Abbot, perhaps you'd like to watch him finish and then we can go inside and talk about this."

His face flushed up and Hilary could tell he was very drunk. "I haven't got time to hang around and watch any races and I'm sure as hell not coming inside to talk about anything. Do you think I'm stupid?" He lunged towards Sean but the boy was too quick for him and he dodged behind Hilary. His father staggered a little after his lunge, and he and Hilary were just weighing up their next move, when a calm and commanding voice said, "Sean, please go back into the building and get changed."

Hilary swung round to look, and was highly relieved to see Dai and behind him several other staff, including the Deputy Head with his mobile phone; they were ushering children away.

"Mr Abbot wanted Sean to tell him where his mother was living," she explained to Dai.

He stepped in front of her. "I'm afraid Sean doesn't want to talk to you, Mr Abbot, and you know as well as we do that you are not supposed to know where Mrs Abbot is living, that is the whole idea, considering the circumstances."

He's squaring up to him, Hilary thought. *I bet he's longing to have an excuse to flatten him.*

The other man must have sensed it too, because his eyes went down and he muttered something that Hilary didn't hear, but obviously Dai did, because he said, "I'm afraid I'll have to ask you to leave the premises, Mr Abbot. Your language is offensive and you are trespassing on school property. Do you want to hop back over the fence and go home, or shall I ask our Deputy to phone the police and they can escort you?"

There was a moment when everyone held their breath, and then the man clambered back over the fence and ambled off, stopping now and again to make gestures and shout obscenities.

The Deputy came over. "I've phoned the police anyway and they say they'll escort Sean home and then have a word with our friend there." He nodded in the direction of Mr Abbot and then bustled off, shooing children in front of him rather like a sheepdog worrying his flock.

Hilary and Dai watched as Sean's father diminished into the distance, his gestures and shouts taking on a more comical aspect, rather like a silent film.

CHAPTER 22

*T*he rain was torrential. Jack's windscreen wipers were on overtime and, between their relentless rhythm, and the dazzling reflection of headlights bouncing off the waterfall that his windscreen had become, he could barely see the road in front of him. His head ached, his throat was sore and he kept sneezing. All he wanted was a hot lemon drink and his bed.

He arrived home with great relief, and ran from his car to the front door, but he still managed to get soaking wet, so he headed straight for the stairs, not even bothering to shout his usual 'Hello' to whoever was there. He threw wet clothes onto the bed and ran into the shower, letting the steaming flow ease his aching bones. He had always thought it strange that the same substance, water, could have such a diverse effect, according to its temperature and the circumstances in which you were immersed in it.

Ten minutes later, in dry, warm clothes, he made his way into the kitchen to find Hilary dressed in a slinky, long dress, with a cheeky pinny tied round her waist, cooking a stir-fry.

The table was set for two, the candles were lit and a bottle of red wine was 'breathing' expectantly.

"Have a drink while you're waiting. This won't take a minute," she smiled at him.

"I was just going to make myself a hot lemon drink – I've got a cold coming." As if to underline the fact, he sneezed twice in quick succession as he was filling the kettle.

"Oh dear. When did that come on?"

"As I was driving home. I don't know where I got it, probably from some client."

"Typical!" Hilary muttered.

"Why? What's the matter?"

"Well, I've gone to a lot of trouble to get rid of the kids for the evening, so we can have a romantic meal and just – well, you know, spend some time together."

"Well, we can still do that," he said nobly, sneezing again as he carried his drink over to the table.

They ate the meal, mostly in silence, interspersed by Jack's sneezing at increasing intervals, and then they retired to the lounge with their coffee.

Jack was sweating, his nose was streaming and he ached all over.

Hilary looked over at him. "Why don't you go up to bed?"

The relief showed on his face as he stood up. "I'm sorry, love. We'll do it when I'm feeling better. I'm afraid I'm fit for nothing tonight." All this was said as if he had a peg on his nose.

Hilary just nodded and smiled weakly as he staggered past her.

She took another mouthful of wine and sighed.

Charlie lay in the dark, listening to Alec's regular breathing. It was lovely to have him home again and feel his warmth next to her in their bed. They both knew that they had a lot of adjusting to do, but in one area, at least, they had proved there would be no problem.

They had always had an active and enjoyable sex life, and with a little imagination, they'd proved to their mutual satisfaction that Alec's stroke would not impair their activities. Charlie turned on her side and settled down, safe in the knowledge that one hurdle had been overcome successfully.

Hilary spent the week playing nursemaid as Jack's cold turned into flu; at least he insisted it was. He took to their bed and became rather like a fledgling in the nest, demanding drinks, food and sympathy.

At times, the thought crossed her mind that she wished he'd stayed in the study and then she wouldn't have been kept awake by his sneezing, coughing or snoring, but he looked so sorry for himself that she took the thought back as being particularly unkind.

By the weekend, both Simon and Anna had succumbed to the bug and Hilary almost wished she could get it, just so she could have a rest!

Jack emerged from his sick bed on Sunday and headed straight for the computer. Moments later, the whole household heard him swear loudly.

"What's happened?" Hilary had rushed upstairs, convinced there had been a disaster.

"Apparently I'm supposed to report to Holme Farm in the morning for two days of training on the new Italian line of products. Bill Holroyd has been taken ill and I'm next on the list."

"Well, it's inconvenient but it's not the end of the world, surely."

"Not in one way, No, but I've got to hand my campaign in on Wednesday and I've still got a lot of work to do on it."

"Would you like a coffee?"

"Yes please, love – looks like I'll be burning the midnight oil tonight."

Hilary pottered in the kitchen, telling herself not to panic, not to jump to conclusions – she must learn to trust him again. She took the coffee back upstairs and stood for a while, watching what Jack was doing.

Streamlined Italian cars were appearing on the screen, followed by seductive Italian models parading up and down the catwalk.

"What's the campaign about then?"

"Well, the idea is, that the Italians are famous for their design – so, I'm stressing their sleek, sophisticated image and going for the classy, yet sexy aspect of their food. I want the packaging to be upmarket and the advertising to stress the connection between the food and an upmarket lifestyle, aimed at the young professional."

"That's a good idea, but won't it leave out a big chunk of the market? Like us for example?"

"Well, yes, in one way, but not in another. Everybody wants to appear sophisticated and when we do buy convenience food, it's more likely to be just for the two of us, so it would still apply."

"Will you be eating at the foodie bar when you're up there?" she said quietly.

Jack turned round from the computer and looked at her.

"No, I won't. I've no desire to go to the foodie bar and I'll be very busy with the course and finishing this off." He leant forward and kissed her very gently. "Don't worry. I know it's difficult, but you're just going to have to learn to trust me again."

The room seemed very hot and stuffy and the remains of the cold meant Jack had a fuzzy head and he was having difficulty concentrating on the lecture; coffee time had never been more welcome.

"How's the campaign coming along then?" Don looked his usual dapper self.

Jack glowered, he just wasn't in the mood to confront Don, but he didn't want to talk to him either.

"It's OK," he muttered and tried to walk away, but Don followed him.

"Well, I'm particularly pleased with mine, been working on it for weeks. It's based on the main tourist attractions, the Leaning Tower of Pisa, Sistine Chapel, Pompeii, St Peter's Square etc. Each one will be used as the backdrop for a particular line in food. I'm aiming for the sophisticated traveller – not bad eh? What's yours about?"

"Italian design appealing to the upwardly mobile," Jack told him reluctantly.

"Ummm. Sounds interesting. So, do you think you've got a chance?"

"As much as anybody else I suppose."

People started drifting back towards the lecture hall, as Don said quickly, "I'll see you in the bar tonight then."

"Sorry, I'll be working on my campaign, still got a lot to do."

"Yeah, tomorrow's the deadline, then we've got a week to wait for the results. Well, I'll be in the bar. I handed mine in this morning." He strolled off confidently, and Jack had a ridiculous desire to put his tongue out behind his back, but he managed to control it.

"But I don't want to arrive at the registry office on a milk float and I don't want to leave in a delivery lorry either," Carla was protesting, "I want something romantic and classy – you'll be wanting me to dress up as a milkmaid next!"

"That's a good idea!" Danny's eyes lit up, but the lights went out rather rapidly as half a pint of lager hovered over his head.

Angela laughed, "Lighten up, you two. There's always some stress before weddings but as long as you keep your sense of humour, you'll be fine." She looked straight at Carla as she said this, but she didn't look impressed.

They had arranged to meet for lunch in the pub, so that Danny could give them a progress report. He had taken a day off to arrange the reception, order his suit and do a bit of shopping.

"Well, at least we don't have to worry about a photographer," Danny observed, "now Bernie's offered to feature us in the works magazine; that will all be taken care of for nothing. That was why I had the idea about the milk float – I thought it would make a good angle."

"Since when have you been a bloody journalist?" Carla flashed back.

"Did you sort out the reception?" Angela said quickly.

"Yes, it's all done. We're taking over 'Toni's Place' for the afternoon. They're going to put 'Private Party' on the door and he's promised not to put a sparkler in each portion of wedding cake." He smiled at Carla and she smiled back, much to Angela's relief.

"Well, you must be almost there by now," she said brightly.

"I think so." Carla rummaged in her bag for her list and ticked off a few more things. She turned to Angela. "Will you come with me to the florist and help me decide on the flowers? I said I'd go Thursday lunchtime."

"I can't make it on Thursday, I've been asked to attend the meeting to look at the Italian sales campaigns. How about Friday?"

"I'll give her a ring and ask." Carla made another note.

"Some lucky salesman's going to get a holiday in Italy out of that lot. It's a pity we couldn't all enter." Danny looked peeved.

"I think Bernie's got something in mind, but don't say anything, it's not finalized yet. It would have made a good honeymoon though. Have you sorted anything out for that yet?" Angela asked, hoping for a clue.

They looked at each other and smiled shyly. Danny nodded at Carla and she lowered her voice. "We're going up to this place in Scotland. It belongs to a friend of Danny's. It's right on the northern coast, miles from anywhere and he's said we can have it for a few days, but don't tell anyone."

"I won't say a word," Angela assured her, "Well, I'm off back to work, see you later."

She wandered back to the office reminiscing about her own wedding and honeymoon. She had had the works, big white wedding, followed by a fortnight in Mexico; it had been wonderful. What had happened then? She really couldn't say; they'd just sort of drifted apart. Ah well, he would be home soon and a whole new phase of her life would begin. She touched her stomach and smiled.

Jack finished working at about nine o'clock and realized he was very hungry and very thirsty. The bar was crowded and noisy, with the course residents being their usual rowdy selves.

Don spotted him and waved him over. Jack joined the group somewhat reluctantly.

"I'm not staying long. I'm starving. I'll have to go out and get fish and chips or something," he told Don.

"No need. Just walk out that door and through the door on your left and all your problems will be solved."

"What do you mean?"

"The foodie bar is in the cellar."

Jack was stunned. "In the cellar! What's it doing there?"

"They had to move it for a while because your favourite doctor discovered it apparently, so it's relocated, temporarily, downstairs."

"Well, would you believe it! I'll go and peruse the menu then."

The atmosphere wasn't quite the same as before, but the food was up to its usual standard. Jack decided to have steak pie and chips, followed by trifle, and, as always, he enjoyed watching Louisa as much as he enjoyed the food. She seemed to be in a particularly happy mood, smiling and joking with the customers and strutting about in a tight leather skirt, stretchy top and the usual mules.

She presented Jack's trifle with a flourish. "There you are, enjoy. You seem to have lost weight. What you need is to win that holiday in Italy and we can fatten you up a bit eh?"

She patted his stomach and then flounced away again. Jack felt quite flattered that she'd noticed his weight loss and also that she obviously knew that he was a salesman. It was only as he was finishing his trifle that he remembered he'd promised Hilary he wouldn't come here. Oh well, it didn't count really, because it wasn't in the same place anymore, and she'd only been bothered because she thought he'd been having a fling with Louisa.

The bar was even rowdier by the time Jack got back, but at least he was entering the fray with a full stomach.

"It's typical!" Hilary was complaining to Karen as they did break duty. "As soon as I make up my mind to sleep with him again, he gets the flu, then the kids get it, then he goes away. I give up!"

Karen couldn't help laughing. "It's called Sod's Law," she said. "I'm sure once he gets back, everything will be fine."

"Well I'm not. I think the Fates are punishing me. I should have done it during our weekend away. It serves me right."

"Don't be silly. It's bound to work out eventually. Oh God. Billy Carter's about to have a temper tantrum again by the looks of him." She dashed off across the field to avert a major incident and left Hilary unconvinced and feeling decidedly tetchy. She had a headache, which she put down entirely to a lack of sex.

Jack was feeling a lot better as he drove home from work on Wednesday. He'd finished his campaign and handed it in that morning and he was looking forward to cooking a meal and having a quiet evening with his wife. He was surprised to see Hilary's car there when he got back. She must have had the same idea and decided to get home early.

Simon and Anna were in the kitchen, tucking into mountainous sandwiches; they had a whole week's eating to catch up on.

"Where's Mum?"

"She's having a bath," Anna mumbled through a mouthful.

Jack almost rubbed his hands together in anticipation, but he refrained and made two cups of coffee instead. He knocked tentatively on the bathroom door and heard a muffled voice, but he couldn't hear what it said, so he went in anyway.

"I've brought you a cup of coffee."

"Thank you."

Hilary was up to her neck in steamy, foaming water and the bathroom smelt like a chemist's shop.

"What do you fancy for dinner? I'll cook for the kids now and then create something special for us, if you like."

"I don't like. I feel like death and I'm not hungry," Hilary complained.

"You haven't got the dreaded bug, have you?"

"I think so. I ache all over and I've got a splitting headache."

Now Jack recognised the smell in the bathroom – eucalyptus.

"You poor thing." Jack put his hand on her forehead. "You finish in here and then hop into bed and I'll bring you up a hot drink."

So for the next few days Jack made nourishing soups that everybody, except him, refused to eat, but he enjoyed it anyway. He moved back into the study so that he wasn't kept awake by Hilary coughing, and he generally took over the household chores.

Anna and Simon were quite indignant that they had to make their own sandwiches for school, and even more indignant when Saturday came and Jack insisted that they help with the cleaning before going to see their friends. Jack had to go downstairs and laugh out loud where Simon couldn't see him, because he'd happened to catch a glimpse of his son cleaning the toilet bowl by bending over it from about three feet away and flicking the toilet brush round once whilst holding his nose. He was only doing it because he'd lost the toss with Anna.

Sunday was Mother's Day and Hilary was still in bed. She received the usual flowers and chocolates, but Simon decided to give her an extra present to cheer her up. He designed a computerised card, which consisted of a woman rushing around the screen, being bombarded with dirty washing, muddy football boots, discarded sandwich boxes and dirty pots.

Finally, she trips over a school bag, and lies on the floor holding her ankle. The caption then reads.

'Mums are an endangered species. Preserve them for the future.'

The screen then scrolls up to reveal the woman relaxing on a lounger next to a pool, sipping an exotic-looking drink.

"That's wonderful," Hilary said proudly, "When you're a high-earning graphics designer, I'll hold you to it and you can treat me to a holiday."

Jack was impressed too, but a little disappointed that there was no toilet bowl in the sequence.

In the afternoon, he took the kids to see Charlie. He had brought her a bouquet and kissed her on the cheek.

"How are you getting on?"

She wiped her hands and took the flowers from him.

"We're doing fine really. It's different, but we're gradually getting into a routine. Mornings are the worst, because if we've got to be out of the house for a set time, I have to stop myself doing everything for him. He's so bloody independent and stubborn – we just end up getting irritable with each other," she smiled at him, "The flowers are beautiful. Thank you."

Anna and Simon were sitting with Alec in the lounge.

"Is it good to be back home, Grandpa?" Anna asked him.

"Oh yes, much better. I wish your grandma wouldn't fuss so much though. I think she's secretly enjoying bossing me about."

"How are you getting on with the laptop?" Simon wanted to know.

Alec looked enthusiastic. "You know, I'm really enjoying it, I like the fact I can work on it anywhere, especially as going upstairs is still a bit difficult."

"Simon made a really cool card for Mum this morning." Anna seemed unusually impressed by her brother's abilities.

"You must show me how you did it – unless Granma wants it for anything; she's getting a bit fed up with me using it all the time."

"What did I get fed up with?" Charlie asked as she carried in the tea things.

"You got fed up with me using the laptop all the time."

"Yes, I did. You'll have to get your own. Every time I want to use it you're playing those blessed games on the thing! "

Alec had the grace to look a bit sheepish and the children laughed.

She offered the cakes around and the children pounced on their favourites.

"Slow down you two," Jack warned.

He watched Alec holding his plate on his lap with his left hand, while he ate with his right. His arm was still at an awkward angle, but at least he was using it. He was wearing a T-shirt and cardigan, but the buttons were done up in the wrong sequence and he'd missed some patches on his face when he'd shaved. Jack felt a lump in his throat and he was relieved that the kids were chattering away, seemingly oblivious to the situation.

As soon as they'd eaten, the three of them went off with the computer and there was silence for a while. Charlie rested her head back on the chair and closed her eyes.

"It's very wearing for you, Mum. You need a break."

She opened her eyes, but didn't raise her head. "I'll be alright – it will just take time to adjust, that's all. Susan and Geoff are coming next weekend, so I expect she'll bully me into having a rest."

"We can come over and be with Dad if you want to go out any time."

"Thanks, love. I'll take you up on that when I feel I've got to get away for a while."

They could both hear laughter from the other room. Charlie closed her eyes again and Jack picked up the paper. He couldn't remember when he'd last read one.

270

Hilary was restless. She hadn't felt well enough to go into work that morning, but now, by lunchtime, she was beginning to regret it. She was feeling better, and she was bored.

She wandered into the study and logged on, just wandering around, in and out of things, until she found herself in Jack's work file. He had an urgent message it said, so she used his password and there it was.

Update on Italian Sales Campaign

We have great pleasure in informing you that you are one of the finalists of the competition. Please be prepared to make a presentation to the Judges on the afternoon of Wednesday March 24th.

This will be followed by a Formal dinner where the prizes will be presented. Partners are invited to attend.

She couldn't believe it. They actually had a chance of winning the holiday. She phoned his mobile number and left a message for him to phone her.

"Are you alright?" Jack sounded quite concerned.

"I'm fine. A lot better, in fact, I'm going back to work tomorrow."

"Oh good. Well umm, what's the problem then?"

"There's no problem. I just wanted to tell you the good news."

"What's that?'

"Your campaign has made it to the last three. They want you to take me up to Holme Farm with you on Wednesday. They're going to make the presentations."

There was silence.

"Jack. Are you still there?"

"Yes. I'm here."

"Aren't you thrilled? We could win the holiday."

"Yes, it's brilliant news. Are you sure you're well enough to come all the way up there?"

"Yes, of course. I wouldn't miss it for anything. I'll see you later."

"Yes, I might be a bit late tonight. One of my clients wants to see me and his plane's been delayed. Will you be alright?"

"Of course. I've only had a cold you know, not a major operation."

Jack switched off the phone in a daze; it was good to know that he had a chance of winning, but the problem was, with Hilary coming up to Holme Farm; what did he stand a chance of losing?

CHAPTER 23

"*I*'m sick to death of Italy," Angela said emphatically.

"You've never even been there," Carla pointed out.

"I know, but I feel as if I have – I've seen so much of it over the past few days that I might as well have been."

They'd stopped shopping to have tea and cakes. It was a rainy, miserable Saturday afternoon and they needed the break.

"Who's winning then?"

"I've no idea. Bernie won't let us know who submitted which campaign,' we're to judge the material, not the person' he said."

"Well, that seems fair."

"In theory, yes, but he knows, and so does Bob Simpkins, so it might not be as squeaky clean as they're making out, but you never know. Anyhow, we've got it down to three, then Bob and Bernie, sounds like a double act, make the final decision, after they've been presented on Wednesday."

"Does that mean you're going to the presentation dinner then?"

"Yes! I've organized it after all. That's why I've got to find something to wear today. Nothing fits me!"

"I hope your wedding outfit's OK."

"Oh that's alright. We deliberately chose the skirt with the elasticated waist if you remember, and it's only my waist that's expanded. Are you all set now then?"

"Yeah, barring last minute hitches – talking of which, the twins have got chicken pox!"

"Oh no! You're sure it is chicken pox and nothing else?"

"Yes, positive, and they should be fine in time for the wedding. Josie's just going mad at the moment trying to stop them scratching."

Angela looked relieved. "How's Danny? You're not still niggling at each other are you?"

"No." Carla sounded defensive. "I think we've done very well considering all we've had to do."

Angela smiled. "Yes, you have, but all couples get nervous before a wedding, it's only natural. They usually lose weight as well."

"I have. So has Danny, but he can still afford to. I can't."

"Never mind, you'll just have to eat fish and chips and chocolate for a week. Most women would give their eye teeth to be like you. Come on. Drink up. I've got to find a dress for that dratted presentation."

Jack realised as he switched off the engine that he didn't remember driving home. His mind had been on other things.

The house was empty, and there was a note from Hilary saying she'd taken Anna and Simon with her back to school. She had to attend an open evening, part of the Head's new campaign to encourage new pupils. Jack was glad there was nobody home; it gave him a chance to think.

He and Hilary would have to drive up separately, because he had to do his presentation in the afternoon, so Hilary would only really be up there for the night. So, what was the worst that could happen? She could confront Louisa, who wouldn't know what on earth she was talking about; there could be a fight, which Louisa would probably win, whilst babbling incoherently in Italian. That was a pretty worst case scenario!

He would have to say that his wife was paranoid, or hated Italians, or both and that would be the end of it. There was no way that Hilary could suspect Angela and Angela had far too much sense to say anything, so he should stop worrying. It would be fine. Yet somewhere, something was niggling at him and he couldn't quite put his finger on it.

He looked at his watch. Ten-thirty! They were late. He got up to go and get himself something to eat, and was just finishing a sandwich when he heard the car.

"God, I'm shattered." Hilary flopped down at the kitchen table. "There's always so much to do when you've had any time off. I could have done without that tonight as well. I could sleep for a week!"

Jack handed her a cup of coffee. "Maybe you're not fully better; you probably went back too soon."

"It's a good job I did! I've managed to get tomorrow afternoon off and Thursday. They weren't too keen, but they've had to go along with it. I have so little time off, they couldn't really refuse."

Simon and Anna were crowding round, making sandwiches and grabbing drinks.

"You two have never stopped eating since you had that flu," Jack teased them.

"Can we come to Italy if you win, Dad?" Simon managed to ask through a mouthful.

"'Fraid not," Jack told him, "There's only two tickets."

"It's not fair!" his son wailed. "We never get to go anywhere!"

"Well, you can go somewhere now young man – up to bed." Hilary proceeded to usher her offspring out of the kitchen, much to their disgust.

"We'll have to go up separately you know, 'cos I've got my presentation to do in the afternoon,"

Jack announced.

"I realise that. I've booked to have my hair done after lunch and then I'll drive up. I should get there about five-ish."

"Good. When you arrive, book into our room at the Fellside and I'll get there as soon as I can."

Hilary smiled. "It's quite exciting isn't it? I'm sure we'll get some kind of a prize, even if you come second or third. Bernie's renowned for his generosity."

"We'll see. Don't get your hopes up too much – you never know."

"Well, I'm off to have a soak in the bath, and then I'm off to bed. I'm so tired, I can hardly stand up."

Jack sighed. Ah well. Tomorrow would tell. There was nothing more he could do for the time being, so he poured himself a brandy and settled down in the armchair.

Don White was enjoying every minute of his presentation; he was milking it for all he was worth. Talking the audience through his very professional PowerPoint presentation which depicted suggested venues for adverts, set in Italy.

The current one showed the Leaning Tower of Pisa as a backdrop to a young couple, sitting facing one another across a table. They were seductively sucking up strands of spaghetti from each other's forks.

Jack felt quite sick; not just because of the advert, but because he'd suddenly realised what the nagging doubt had been. Don, of course, Don, who knew Hilary, Don, who'd been convinced all along that there was something going on between him and Angela. Don, who would be there tonight, because he was one of the three finalists!

He needed some air. He excused himself and went for a drink of water. Luckily, he'd done his own presentation earlier, whilst still in blissful ignorance. He'd made quite a good job of it too, passing around mock-ups of the sleek packaging he'd designed, and talking the audience through his sequences of Ferraris, Lamborghinis, catwalk fashion shows and designer label goods.

He took a few deep breaths and went back inside, just in time to see Don sitting down.

The last presentation was by Lesley Jones, the newest recruit to the sales team. She was a very self-assured young lady, who seemed to have impressed Bob Simpkins with her capabilities, and her campaign was certainly eye-catching and unusual.

It started off in New York, then moved to Paris, then London, each time focusing on a typical Italian family restaurant. The atmosphere seemed relaxed and the patrons were enjoying themselves. Then, it flashed to a black and white scene, and showed a clip from an old gangster movie where the Mob sat round a table, all eating together. Suddenly, a rival gang burst in, and there was a shootout, but several of the senior members just calmly went on eating.

The final scene flashed back to the present and a group of kids sitting in a kitchen. The dad put a plate of steaming pasta in front of them and the caption read,' The Mob have got it covered'.

Everyone clapped, and then they filed out for tea and cakes.

"What do you reckon then? Do you think prissy Miss Jones will win?" Don was trying to talk through a mouthful of Danish pastry, and crumbs were flying everywhere.

"I've no idea. It was certainly different."

"I think she will – it's a forgone conclusion. You and I will probably come away with a year's supply of frozen pizza or something equally obnoxious."

"Well, never mind. At least we got to the last three."

Don nodded. "Yeah, but Trish is already planning her holiday wardrobe, and the dress she's bought for tonight has cost half a week's holiday," he sighed. "Is Hilary coming?"

Jack could only nod. "Oh well, that'll be good then." Don's face brightened. "Haven't seen her for ages. Shall we all meet up in the bar for a drink before the do?"

Jack almost choked on his tea. "Um, I'm not sure what time she'll be arriving, what with her working and everything. It might be best if we just say we'll see you there." Jack took a deep breath. *Over my dead body*, he thought. Luckily, everyone was starting to move back into the hall for Bernie's final words of wisdom.

"Well, you've done it again. It never fails to amaze me just how much talent we have within this company Thank you, everyone for all your efforts. I can tell you now, that the two runners-up this evening, will be receiving tickets for two for a weekend in Rome."

A cheer went up, but Bernie held up a hand. "And, for everyone who entered a presentation, there is a voucher for an Italian meal, which can be taken to a designated restaurant in their area."

Another cheer went up, but Bernie silenced them again. "Finally, I have to tell you, that as there is so little to choose between the final three, we are going to have to keep you in suspense a little while longer, and the winner won't be announced until this evening."

This time there was a groan, but Bernie just smiled. "Off you go now and get yourselves ready for the big event."

Jack smiled to himself – Bernie was such a showman. He was loving every minute of this.

Angela pirouetted in front of the mirror. She looked passable. The black velvet dress was cleverly cut, which meant it fell from her bust line, disguising her waist and emphasizing her cleavage.

"You look stunning," Carla assured her.

"Are you sure?"

"Positive. Very classy."

"It should do, considering what I paid for it!"

"It's true what they say about pregnant women. You are positively blooming. Your skin is glowing and your hair is glossy."

"You're making me sound like a horse." Angela was quite indignant.

"You're never satisfied," Carla scolded her, and sighed, "Just think, if I ever get pregnant, I might even put on some weight. I might even get some boobs."

"You might even get some stretch marks." Angela flopped down in front of her mirror and attacked her glossy hair with a hairbrush. "I don't really want to go, you know."

"Why not? You'll be the belle of the ball. I bet Bernie will escort you. Mrs Holmes never goes to these functions, she prefers to stay at home."

"I'm just fed up of going to things on my own, I feel like a widow most of the time. I just want to lead a normal life."

"It won't be long now. It's only a week to go, and Pete will be home for good. Your life will be so normal after the baby is born, that you'll probably long for it to be different again."

Angela sighed, and put on some lipstick. "You're probably right. It's just now and again that it gets to me."

"Well, just buck up. You've so much to look forward to – the wedding – the birth." Angela pulled a face. "Well, after the birth then, and what about tonight? You'll be seeing all the other halves of the sales team, including Mrs Jack Baker. I want to know all the sordid details please. I'm relying on you to be my eyes and ears for the evening."

Angela saluted. "Yes, ma'am. Would you like me to put a camera and tape recorder in my handbag?"

"I wish you could," Carla said with feeling, "there's bound to be some scandal."

Hilary was pleased with her hair. It had been highlighted to show off the blonde, and the slightly longer, softer style suited her. She was walking back to the car when she passed a dress shop, and for once she followed an impulse, and walked in.

It was the colour that did it. It was the colour of the amethyst in the pendant that Jack had bought her for Christmas. The dress was long and cut on the bias; it went over one shoulder and was draped softly across the front, before following her slender frame to the floor. The effect was breath-taking and she had to have it.

By the time she'd been home and found appropriate underwear and shoes and thrown a few things in a bag, time was getting on – she'd better get a move on!

Jack was getting nervous; he could have done with a drink, but he didn't want to risk bumping into Don and Trish so he'd opted to stay in his room and wait for Hilary. She should have been here over an hour ago, according to his calculations; they'd have to leave soon. He paced over to the window again, just as there was a knock at the door. Hilary raced in like a whirlwind.

"Where have you been? I was getting worried."

"The traffic was terrible. I didn't think I was going to make it in time. God, I could do with a cup of tea," she said as she was throwing stuff onto the bed and stripping off, "I need a shower. Did you win?"

"Don't know yet. We'll find out tonight."

"That's so typical of Bernie," she said over her shoulder as she went into the bathroom.

Jack went in search of tea, and by the time he got back, she was sitting at the dressing table, wrapped in a towel.

Jack poured tea for them both. "The runners-up are going to get a weekend in Rome, so we won't go away empty-handed whatever happens."

"I told you, didn't I? Bernie is so generous. Well, at least I'll get some wear out of my extravagance then."

"What extravagance?"

"I've bought a new dress. It was ridiculously expensive, but it was just an impulse. I couldn't resist it," Hilary confessed.

Jack looked bemused – it was so out of character that he just didn't know what to say.

She stood up and slipped the dress over her head, twisting this way and that, to look in the mirror. She turned to look at him with a sheepish look on her face. "What do you think?"

"I think you look stunning." He wanted to carry her straight over to the bed, and judging from her expression, she wouldn't have objected too much. Instead, he kissed her gently on the forehead and held her at arm's length to admire the view.

"I think you ought to act on impulse more often. Oh, I wish we didn't have to go out," he groaned.

"So do I. How much time do we have?"

Jack looked at his watch. "None at all. I ordered a taxi for seven and it's five past now."

"Ah well, abstinence makes the heart grow fonder, or something like that." She picked up her wrap and bag, while Jack held the door open. "We might have a lot to celebrate by the time we get back."

Jack just prayed that she was right.

The dining room at Holme Farm had been transformed again, mostly due to Angela's efforts. The tables had been formed into a horseshoe, draped in white linen cloths and decked out with formal settings. Candelabra and flower arrangements added a certain formality, and the plentiful bottles of wine and small gifts for the ladies were testaments to Bernie's generosity.

A young employee, playing usher for the evening, showed Jack and Hilary to their places. Jack noticed that Angela was sitting at the top table, next to Bernie. She looked gorgeous, rather like a Botticelli painting, all cleavage and glowing cheeks, but he daren't look too long, in case she saw him.

He was right, she had seen him, the moment he walked in, and she had taken particular notice of Hilary, kidding herself it was so she could report back to Carla. She noted the blonde hair, slim figure and elegant dress, but the overall impression was of an ice maiden; she looked detached and untouchable somehow. Poor Jack, no wonder he needed affection and warmth in his life, she definitely looked as if she could give you a hard time. Now she could understand why Jack had been attracted to her. She smiled to herself and took a sip of wine.

Jack was just breathing a huge sigh of relief, because he'd noticed that Don and Trish were sitting over the other side of the room. Maybe tonight the Fates were on his side.

The meal was excellent, and efficiently served by more young employees. The wine flowed, and everyone seemed to be enjoying themselves.

Bernie, in particular, was having a good time. He had Angela on one side of him, and Bob Simpkins's wife, Brenda, on the other side. He was waxing lyrical to Brenda about the advantages of a joint venture with the Italians when, almost in sympathy with the continental habit of expansive hand movements, he swung his arm out to emphasize a point, and knocked a glassful of red wine into Angela's lap. She leapt up, and everyone flapped about ineffectually with serviettes.

"I'm so sorry, got a bit carried away I'm afraid." Bernie was mortified. "I'll pay for any dry-cleaning, of course."

"It's alright, don't worry. I'll just go and sponge it down. I'm sure it will be fine."

Angela was annoyed, but not distraught. The red wine would soon come out with dry-cleaning, and at least the dress was black; all she needed to do for now, was dry herself off a bit.

She headed for the toilets, but unfortunately, there was a queue, so she made her way into the kitchens and dabbed away at her lap with a tea towel.

When she was satisfied that she looked presentable again, Angela started to make her way back to the dining room, but she realised that the sensation of wetness in her lap, coupled with the red wine she'd been drinking, meant that she really had to go to the loo, queue or no queue.

"Is your dress alright?" Hilary looked concerned.

Angela had been staring into space, and hadn't even noticed someone come and stand beside her. "Yes thanks. Luckily, I didn't wear the white satin."

Hilary giggled. "Well, there's one thing. If you had, your husband would have had to fork out for another one."

"Oh, he's not my husband, he's my boss. I'm only here because I arranged the evening. I'm his personal assistant."

"Oh, I see, I'm sorry. I just assumed, I suppose."

"It's quite understandable. Mrs Holmes has more sense than to attend any of Bernie's 'do's'. I should think she has to listen to him enough at home."

Hilary laughed, "That's probably it." They shuffled closer to the door. Angela couldn't help smiling to herself. If Jack knew what was happening, he'd have a purple fit.

"The food was lovely anyway," Hilary was saying, "I was starving."

"Yes, the caterers are local. I always use them, they're very good."

"My husband goes to a foodie bar round here somewhere." Hilary leaned nearer, the wine had loosened her tongue. "Actually, between you and me, I think he's had a bit of a thing about the Italian waitress. I was worried about it for a while," she said as they shuffled closer, "but now I think I was being paranoid. Are you married?" Angela could only nod. "Well, you'll know what I mean. Sometimes you just go through a wobbly patch don't you?" Angela nodded again. "Anyhow, from the way he's described her, I think she must be the motherly type."

If Angela had been eating or drinking, she would have choked, but instead she put her head down and brushed away at the front of her dress. Motherly eh! Wait 'til she saw Jack.

"Actually, you're quite right. She is extremely maternal." She put her hand on her stomach and thought, *you'll never know just how maternal, darling*, and she giggled. "Your husband isn't alone, more than one man has a soft spot for Louisa. You've no worries now though, the foodie bar's been closed down. The food inspectors caught up with it."

They reached the toilets just in time, and she fell inside the door, her eyes rolling up to the ceiling. Oh, if only Carla had been here. Men!

On her way back to her place at the top table, she passed behind Jack and tapped him on the shoulder.

"Oh, hi, Angela." He was looking round anxiously, and she knew he was looking for Hilary.

283

She bent down and whispered in his ear. "Your wife and I have just had a lovely little chat in the Ladies, all about the foodie bar and your infatuation with the 'motherly Louisa'. She'll tell you all about it when she gets back." She walked on without looking back, but if she had, she'd have seen Jack with his mouth gaping like a fish out of water.

A couple of minutes later Hilary came back, and Angela took a sadistic pleasure in watching the sweat break out on his forehead.

"There was a queue of course," Hilary complained, "Has there been any announcements yet?"

Jack's mouth was dry, and it came out in a croak. "Not yet."

"Are you alright? You don't need to be nervous, you know. We're going to Italy whatever happens. Talking of which, I met ever such a nice woman in the loo – that one up there."

She smiled at Angela, who responded with a wave and an angelic smile.

"Do you know her? She's Bernie's PA. She arranged all this – must have been a lot of work. Anyhow, she told me that the foodie bar has closed – pity that, I was going to ask you to take me there. Anyhow, she said that quite a few men had a thing about Louisa. Apparently she's very maternal, just shows you doesn't it."

Jack had turned away, taking a gulp of red wine, and when he turned back Hilary was looking at him expectantly.

"I said it just shows you."

"What does it show you?" he said weakly.

"Honestly, Jack, you are acting stupidly tonight. It shows you that most men really just want mothering."

"Do they?"

"Of course they do."

Just then, Bernie stood up and said, "Ladies and gentlemen." Hilary looked away to listen to him and Jack could see Angela sitting beside him with a Mona Lisa smile on her face.

"I've kept you all in suspense long enough. As I said this afternoon, the job of deciding on a winner has been extremely difficult, but a decision has been made, and before I tell you who the winner is, I'd just like to explain why this particular campaign won.

"Over the years, the one thing that we have strived for at Holme Farm Products has been excellence. We have always gone for quality in our product, no matter what our competitors have been doing. Sometimes this has not been easy, and sometimes our profits have not been as good as they should have been, but nevertheless, we have survived.

"When I decided to merge with an Italian company, I searched for a company with the same philosophy and that is why I am sure that we will be successful. The winning campaign epitomizes this search for excellence, and so, without more ado, I'd like Jack Baker to come up and receive his prize."

Jack stood up in a dream. He could hear the applause as he walked up to the top table, but it seemed to be a long way away. There were calls of 'speech' and he started to turn away, but he caught Hilary's eye and stayed where he was. "I'd just like to say thank you. It is most unexpected. I'll bore you all with the photographs when we get back." A good-hearted groan went up and he escaped thankfully back to his seat.

Hilary kissed him on the cheek. "You see, you're cleverer than you think you are."

Don White and Lesley Jones were then called together as joint runners-up, and they received their prizes very graciously. Jack was impressed with Bernie's diplomatic skills.

The rest of the evening went in a haze of congratulations and much celebratory drinking. Jack had begun to relax and was enjoying the praise and the banter. Several of his colleagues had suggested that he might be interested in the sales manager's job. "No way!" Jack was emphatic. "This was just a one-off. It's surprising what I'll do for a free holiday."

"Are you ready to go yet?" Hilary whispered.

"What? On holiday?"

"No, of course not," she hissed, "Back to the hotel."

"Yes. Are you?"

"Definitely!"

"OK. I'll just pay a visit to the loo and order the taxi, and we'll be off."

Hilary wandered into the entrance hall to wait. She felt weary, yet happy. The only cloud on the horizon was her feet, which were killing her – she wasn't used to wearing high heels these days. She bent down to ease the straps off her heels, and as she stood up again, she wobbled a bit, and a hand came out to steady her.

"Take it easy there, you don't want to fall over and break an ankle."

"Don! Thank you. My feet are killing me. Where's Trish?"

"Powdering her nose, as she would so delicately put it. Well, I bet you're very proud of him, aren't you?"

"Yes, of course, but you've done very well too, haven't you?"

"Oh, can't complain you know. It will keep Trish quiet anyhow."

At that moment, Don staggered forward slightly, and Hilary, not wanting him to stumble into her, stepped back. Unfortunately, she forgot that she'd taken her feet out of the straps, and consequently, she fell off her shoes, and grabbed out at Don as she stumbled sideways. The result of all this was that Hilary and Don ended up in a dishevelled heap on a very conveniently placed sofa, just as Jack emerged from the toilets.

The next thing Hilary knew, Jack had bounded across the reception hall, grabbed Don in a headlock, and proceeded to march him towards the door. She struggled to her feet just in time to see Trish emerging from the Ladies, looking somewhat bemused.

"I've had it with you, Don. You just can't take your drink, can you? Well, that's it. Don't come near me or my wife again, because if you do, I might just be tempted to persuade a young lady we both know to sue you for assault!"

Don tried to reply, but it was extremely difficult to talk when you were bent double and someone had his arm round your throat, so all that came out was a squawk.

Jack bundled Don into a taxi, closely followed by Trish, still looking bemused.

Hilary was putting her shoes back on and generally attempting to regain her equilibrium, when Jack stalked back in through the door.

"Are you alright?"

"Yes, I'm fine. What was all that about?"

"What?"

"All that grabbing Don round the neck and marching him out. He didn't do anything wrong, you know. We just fell over."

Jack looked shocked. "Oh! Well, he just gets on my nerves. He can't hold his drink and he gets all stupid. I thought he was trying to get too friendly, that's all."

"I suppose you put him in our taxi." Hilary was starting to look very amused.

"Yes, I think I did." Jack ran his fingers through his hair. "I'll phone for another one."

"Better hurry up then, or else my mood might go."

"What mood is that?" He was already punching numbers on the phone.

"The mood that makes me want to lock you in our room for twenty-four hours and have my evil way with you."

Jack looked slightly surprised, yet decidedly cheerful at the prospect.

Bernie and Angela walked by a few moments later. "Can we offer you a lift anywhere?" Bernie was nothing if not chivalrous.

"No thanks, we're fine," Jack called out and then quietly to Hilary, "What do you think I am? Stupid? My wife is in the mood!"

THE END

ACKNOWLEDGEMENTS

First of all I'd like to thank Sally, who all those years ago in the Philippines, encouraged me to keep going with this. I suspect she gave up hope years ago that I would ever publish.

To Marie and Julia, Gemma, Lisa and all at Archway who gave me the recent encouragement and courage to 'Put it out there.' Sorry it took so long!

To Dave, who calms and supports me when technology bites!

To all my friends who have given me so much support and wonderful shared moments over the years.

Finally, to Simon, who sorted out the technology and introduced me to Sarah, without whom this definitely would never have happened.

Thank you all.

Cherry.

ABOUT THE AUTHOR

Cherry spent many years as a teacher, both in the UK and abroad, brought up four children and when the last one left home, she got the chance to travel once again.

Her husband was working on a contract in the Philippines so she joined him for a couple of years.

What a fascinating country! They both had many adventures out there, but on a day to day basis when her husband was at work, Cherry was bored out of her mind and missed her family dreadfully.

She had always wanted to write a book so she made a start and discovered that she really enjoyed it and it helped to keep her sane.

Cherry wrote it by hand and the words just flew onto the page, but when she tried to use a computer everything became very slow and very frustrating. Typing wasn't her thing! However, she persevered and managed to get it all onto a disc.

Yes. This was all twenty years ago and since then, having been back in the UK for fifteen years, lost both her parents to Dementia, gained six wonderful grandchildren and enjoyed retirement, she got a bit bored again!

She was persuaded to publish her book, which amazingly, since set in the future, was still very relevant.

So here she is, still struggling to type, but managing; because, as she says, there are so many clever people around out there to help her.

Cherry actually didn't need to change very much from the original script, but as her mother used to say, "Times change, but people don't."